Tomorrow There Will Be Sun

Tomorrow

Tomorrow There Will Be Sun

A Hope Prize Anthology

SIMON &
SCHUSTER

London · New York · Sydney · Toronto · New Delhi

TOMORROW THERE WILL BE SUN: A HOPE PRIZE ANTHOLOGY
First published in Australia in 2024 by
Simon & Schuster (Australia) Pty Limited
Level 4, 32 York St, Sydney NSW 2000

10 9 8 7 6 5 4 3 2 1

Simon & Schuster: Celebrating 100 Years of Publishing in 2024.
Sydney New York London Toronto New Delhi
Visit our website at www.simonandschuster.com.au

A catalogue record for this
book is available from the
National Library of Australia

NATIONAL
LIBRARY
OF AUSTRALIA

ISBN: 9781761428715

Cover design: Alissa Dinallo
Typeset by Midland Typesetters, Australia
Printed and bound in Australia by Griffin Press

MIX
Paper | Supporting
responsible forestry
FSC® C018684
www.fsc.org

The paper this book is printed on is certified against the
Forest Stewardship Council® Standards. Griffin Press holds
chain of custody certification SCS-COC-001185. FSC®
promotes environmentally responsible, socially beneficial
and economically viable management of the world's forests.

Contents

CONTENTS

Foreword

Dame Quentin Bryce

As you get older you think about things more deeply, you care more deeply, love more deeply. People assume you have more time but you don't, you have less, so you distil those things that really matter — family, friends, and the beauty of the arts, the glory of nature, and the values we hold dear that we respect and admire in others.

Across my life, hope has been a guiding light. Its glimmer illuminated the path of my early career, a time when opportunities for girls were limited. Hope gave me the courage to move forward with purpose. It enabled me to translate dreams into reality, to discover my own strengths, and to work with others to create a more just and compassionate world.

In its smallest, most personal form, hope is the gentle force that encourages us to rise each morning. It reveals itself in simple joys – a kind word, a good book, the smile of a stranger. At its most profound hope emboldens us to face our fears, to walk onto stages we find daunting, to step into shoes we never imagined we could fill, and to break through barriers that once seemed impossible. Hope moves us forward.

As I read the stories in this anthology, I was struck by the talent of each writer and the beauty of their words.

Gathered from around the world they reflect diverse cultures united by common truths. The message of hope woven through each narrative and the roles of companionship, neighbourhood and kindness in shaping a hopeful outlook transcend place, race and gender.

In these stories, we witness the way our shared humanity truly matters – how reaching out when we sense need, becoming involved, and taking care of one another can make the difference between life and death, hope and despair. Over and again, the power of giving, of connection, generosity and friendship beams through, offering a path through life's most challenging times.

I hope, that as I do, you will savour these stories and in them find the inspiration we need for a life filled with joy and contentment.

Introduction

Georgie Harman, CEO of Beyond Blue

Hope.

It's a word we hear often but what does it really mean? What is its purpose? What is its essence? And how do we find it?

At a time of significant global upheaval, answering these questions feels urgent.

Because in times of uncertainty, hope can anchor and guide us. Not by providing certainty, but by inspiring possibility. Not by solving our problems, but by giving us the motivation to try. Not by denying our struggles, but by helping us persist and believe that we can bounce back.

Hope cultivates optimism in the face of change and adversity. Hope allows us to see the potential in ourselves and others. It shapes our outlook on life and influences our mental health and wellbeing in fundamental ways.

Typically, we think of 'mental health' as an individual phenomenon – a uniquely private and solitary experience that reflects how we think, feel and behave. This is true, yet there's more to the story.

Our mental health and wellbeing is defined as much by the world around us as what's happening inside us. We're influenced by our environment in profound ways.

So it makes sense that our mental health is under pressure right now.

Globally, we're at what feels like an inflection point for humanity.

We're living through a time of rapid technological change, irreversible climate change and growing social and economic division and inequality. The world and our collective future seem more volatile, complex and uncertain than they've ever been.

For many of us, this reality – and the way it plays out in our daily lives – provokes feelings ranging from discomfort to despair. It might be undermining our sense of safety and belonging, confusing our search for meaning and identity or inciting fear and negativity which, though evolved to protect us, too often do us harm in our modern lives.

Hope. Recovery. Resilience. These were Beyond Blue's founding principles as Australia's national anxiety and depression initiative, and they continue to guide us today.

Since 2000, we have provided millions of people in Australia with information and support for anxiety, depression and suicidality, wherever they live, work and play. Beyond Blue is one of Australia's most trusted and recognised names in mental health.

Our work has never been more important.

Research tells us that 1 in 5 people in Australia live with a mental health condition. At some point in our lives, one third of us will experience anxiety and 1 in 7 will, like me, experience depression. Almost half of all mental health conditions have emerged by age 14, and over 75% occur by the age 25. Preventing adverse childhood experiences could avert up to one third of all mental health conditions. And reaching a place without hope can put us in a precarious position. Nine people in Australia take their own lives each day. Seven of them are men. Suicide disproportionately affects our First Nations communities at tragic levels. And more than 65,000 people attempt suicide each year. It often surprises people to learn that suicides can happen in the absence of mental ill-health – employment and relationship circumstances can contribute too.

Yet most people experiencing poor mental health don't seek professional support and the average delay for seeking support after symptoms first emerge is about 11 years. Many people simply can't afford to get help. Others won't reach out, or might delay doing so, because they think their problems aren't serious enough or they're fearful or feel shame. Perhaps they're not sure where to start or what to say, or maybe they don't feel ready for other reasons.

Once they do, though, the outcome can be transformative. Because support is there and effective.

Our experience shows that just one phone call with Beyond Blue reduces distress, helps people feel heard and understood and motivates further action.

Every day Beyond Blue offers hope by guiding people to understand what's going on for them, to feel heard and understood, and find their path to better mental health.

We're perhaps best known for our national support service. This free service supports more than 300,000 people in Australia each year with immediate counselling, advice and referrals via phone, webchat and email, 24 hours a day, 7 days a week, right around Australia. Right now, the most common reasons people contact us are anxiety and worry; relationships; depression; adjustment and loss; and isolation and loneliness. Understandably, given the complexity of the world today, people are grappling with more than one issue at a time and their needs are getting more complex too.

It surprises people to learn that the Beyond Blue Support Service is funded entirely by donations and partnerships, like The Hope Prize. It's a service for the community, made possible by the community.

That means over 800 people a day find connection, comfort and hope thanks to the generosity of others.

We're saturated with news and feeds about what's wrong in the world but reflections like these remind us of humanity, of our capacity for caring, and give me hope every day.

Every day we see the community at its best, too, in our online peer forums, which attract tens of thousands of visits each month. Here, people discuss their mental health struggles in a safe, moderated online community. Discussion is guided by people who draw on their own lived experience of mental ill-health and suicidality.

Similarly, our communities use social media to learn, share and support one another; Beyond Blue's social media channels reach up to 8 million people a year. For all its ills, social media can do a lot of good, too.

A perhaps lesser known – though no less important – part of Beyond Blue's contribution has been designing services that fill gaps in Australia's mental health system. We believe that not-for-profits, governments and philanthropy can achieve great things by working together, which is what we did to expand suicide aftercare in Australia.

Before 2014, if a person presented to hospital after a suicide attempt, they would be treated for their physical injuries then sent home, back to the life circumstances that very likely contributed to their attempt. So Beyond Blue, in partnership with the community, researchers, philanthropy, and then governments, developed The Way Back Support Service, providing people with a safety plan and one-on-one practical support in the community after a suicide attempt.

We wanted to give people hope after a suicide attempt, to help them find their way back to living.

We joined with philanthropists to fund and pilot the model at a small number of sites around the country, subjecting it to rigorous evaluation. We were free to test and evolve the service in bold ways that governments alone could not.

We built an evidence base that led the Australian Government to fund the national expansion of the service, in partnership with state and territory governments.

Ten years after we started setting up The Way Back, free, government-funded aftercare services were baked into the National Mental Health and Suicide Prevention Agreement between Australian governments.

Today, Beyond Blue is sharpening its focus to prevention and a type of mental health support we call 'earlier intervention'.

In the face of heightened community distress and stubborn rates of depression and anxiety, workforce shortages and a stretched mental health system, it makes sense to stop small problems from becoming big ones, so people don't reach their crisis point. Because for too long, Australia's mental health system has been crisis driven. Beyond Blue is working to support people to get well, stay well and feel better sooner, before things get beyond them.

We commence early in life. Beyond Blue delivers the national mental health in schools initiative with our friends at Early Childhood Australia and headspace.

In workplaces, we offer structured, one-on-one mental health coaching that improves both mental health and productivity. This matters because 15% of depression is related to job strain and mental health problems cost the Australian economy up to $17 billion a year.

We've been delivering this innovative, tailored coaching model in the community and to small business owners for several years, giving people tools and practical strategies to change their perspectives so they can problem solve and overcome the obstacles in their way.

Beyond Blue funds applied research that's designed to find solutions to real-world issues. We advocate for changes to the systems and structures that shape our lives.

Day-to-day, we're working to make it as easy as possible – for as many people as possible – to access mental health support. We're using digital channels and technology to make it smooth and simple for people to find the resources they need to support themselves and others. We encourage action by acknowledging our basic emotional needs – for empathy and trust, for example. This gives me hope.

The Hope Prize promotes 'hope, courage and resilience' which mirrors Beyond Blue's commitment to 'hope, recovery and resilience'. These shared values are brought to life here, in these pages, through the power of storytelling.

Stories educate, motivate and inspire. They evoke and provoke. They promote empathy and drive connection. For 65,000 years, Australia's First Peoples – Aboriginal and Torres Strait Islander peoples – have used stories to pass knowledge through generations.

When it comes to our mental health, literature and the arts are powerful forces. Research shows creativity can protect our mental health. Arts-based interventions have some of the highest quality evidence for improving mental wellbeing. Australian research has demonstrated that dancing is one of the best ways to beat depression. Reading can reduce stress and journaling has been shown to promote emotional exploration and support coping. As well, we know that music therapy, art therapy, and even narrative therapy – essentially storytelling – have proven healing power. Creativity brings hope to life.

Sharing stories about our mental health can help break down stigma by deepening our understanding of what it means to live with anxiety or depression.

While our stories are always unique to us, reading and listening to others' experiences remind us that we're not alone and there is a way through. Beyond Blue has a Speakers Program, where community members share their personal stories about the lows and highs of their mental health experiences at community events, in workplaces and in education settings.

One of those speakers is Georgie Mollison, whose depression emerged at the age of 10 in the form of thoughts that told her she was at fault and not good enough. These are Georgie's words:

I grew up in what was seemingly the definition of the 'normal' Australian family, and perhaps it was from the outside looking in. I, like hundreds of thousands of children, grew up in a household dominated by extreme domestic violence. Now in hindsight I have the unfortunate but profound knowledge of how common domestic violence is in Australia and the realisation perhaps I shouldn't have worked so hard to hide it . . . If there is one thing I have learnt through dealing with my depression is that I am strong. Incredibly strong and I have an inbuilt instinct to survive. It's not like that every day, some days are wobbly and others feel like the world is shaking, but the difference is I like myself now and I refuse to bow to shame or stigma surrounding so many of the issues I have dealt with in my life.

Stories like Georgie's offer hope. They make us feel less alone in the messiness and scariness of life. They show us recovery is possible.

Hope helps us navigate uncertainty and believe in the possibility of transformation.

I hope you enjoy this book, an anthology of hope.

The Sorrow and the Pity

Ani Kayode Somtochukwu

Shortlisted

L et's say a boy is lying beneath a tall, shady tree. And that another boy is sitting next to him in a shared and serene solitude. Let's say Boy B's legs are stretched out so his lap can cradle Boy A's head. Let's say these boys have Igbo names and miraculous origin stories, bow ties and cowsheds, classrooms and sports fields, church gardens and village farms. Let's imagine that a herd of sheep is grazing nonchalantly in the distance, under the gentle morning light.

Boy A should maybe be tall and fair in complexion so that his scars find easy contrast on his threadbare skin. Maybe the breeze sings as Boy B helps Boy A scratch and count all the blemishes they can find. Maybe his fingers tenderly caress the taut remnants of Boy A's wounds as he tries at consolation.

'I'm so sorry this happened to you,' he says. 'So so sorry. This world is so cruel.'

There are probably broken electric lines and barbed wire fences where these boys live. After all, that is how it is in all places but a few. Newly hatched chicks follow wise hens through littered gutters and dust paths; and a little girl takes her brother's old bicycle for a spin and almost falls, near a barber's shop. Children sent on errands by their mothers stop for pleasantries, allowing the time to fly. They live a few bus stops apart, but it's nothing Igbo boys have not trekked before for love.

Let's assume without conceding that these boys have mothers that still want something to do with them. That both their fathers died in the Biafran War. And that all their sisters have louder voices they never use in public.

Boy A doesn't have brothers, but let's imagine that Boy B has two. The brothers have Igbo names as well.

So, to demarcate these boys' stories with names: Boy A was named Chidiebere the day he was born, but people called him Ebere while he was young and then called him Chidi when he grew older and they saw that he was funny, sensitive and beautiful in a way that was idolatrous and difficult to tolerate.

Boy B was named something more divine and cruel, like Otito, so that he would search so long for that praise, refusing to be disheartened by what he continued to find: an emptiness that frightened and baffled, a resistance that disappointed and shattered the heart.

Otito's brothers have less ironic names like Ndubuisi and Azubike and they really don't like sheep. Or Igbo boys that don't know how to be Igbo boys.

Otito and Chidi take a bus together. The bus moves before they can take their seats. One falls back on the other and they laugh like the world does not exist around them. The day is probably bright, brilliant even, the sunshine rushing through the bus windows creating ethereal halos. The bus may be barely empty or half full but at that time of day they easily find two empty seats next to each other. They sit and Otito looks out the window, at the rows of shops as they speed by, the children with trays of boiled groundnuts balanced on their heads, the wheelbarrows filled with watermelons and other April fruits, or phone accessories, or tubers of yam and potatoes.

The conductor shouts *Garriki! Garriki!* banging the side of the bus to the syllables of his chant, in threes. On the radio, Nnamdi Kanu's angry voice is raging. The grass is especially green today, and the sheep munch on without concern.

'God, I hate this man so much,' Otito says, rolling his eyes, taking Chidi's left hand in his right. Perhaps he fiddles distractedly with it, forgetting that they are not alone. Or he tries to crack Chidi's knuckles just to hear the pops. Chidi turns around slowly to look at the rows of empty seats behind them.

'If his fans tell you to get off the bus, I'm not with you o,' Chidi says.

'Ọ dị egwu,' Otito quips back, hissing with annoyance, and it makes Chidi laugh. 'As in even with my uniform they'll chase me down? And then me I'll come down? Let me see it.'

'When they come now, it's still you that'll be the first to say, "Sorry sir,"' Chidi says. He looks out the window and tries to gauge how much more time they have left with their sheep.

'That's if I'm alone nau. Thank God you're here, anybody that talks to me anyhow, ọgụ immediately.'

'Thank God who is here?' He asks, scoffs, his gaze holds Otito's with mock seriousness, their fingers still twiddling about.

'Are you going to allow me fight alone before?'

Chidi laughs, so ardently. 'Please I don't know you o, ka m gwa gị now,' he says.

The conductor swings by, holding a huge wad of naira notes in his left hand. Their hands separate as fast as they can manage. If the conductor saw them holding each other, he's probably too tired, too distracted, too over-worked, to make it his concern.

'Ebee?' the conductor asks, and Chidi says, 'Amokwe

Bus stop na Meniru,' reaching for his breast pocket to fetch the 100 naira note he kept there.

He finds his breast pocket empty. He looks up at the conductor, feeling his trouser pockets with his open palms.

'Did I drop it somewhere?' He asks no one in particular.

The conductor registers his impatience with the tap of his foot on the rusting metal floor of the bus. He shouts for the upcoming stops before looking back down at Chidi.

'Bia this boy or girl, whichever, don't waste my time.'

'Do you remember where exactly you put it?' Otito steps in, handing the conductor two 50 naira notes. Chidi finds the money in a trouser pocket he'd searched before.

'Found it,' he says, holding the note up between his fingers. 'Ego Nigeria,' he mutters, this time more to himself. 'Rubbish money. Zoo money. Useless.' He is rushing the words like they're hot to his lips, the way Nnamdi Kanu always does.

Say they agree without deliberation to not acknowledge the conductor's remark, to not let it dampen their day. Maybe their fingers even unite once again, as soon as the conductor walks off.

They start saying their goodbyes three bus stops before Amokwe. Before the bus halts at Amokwe, Otito slides past Chidi, brushing against his crotch with a mischievous chuckle. A smile remains on Chidi's lips even after the bus continues its journey. His street is still a few stops away, past the congestion at the bustling Mayor Market, past the old walls of the Awkunanaw Boys' Secondary School with *Biafra Forever!!!* still graffitied on it in white paint that dripped down the concrete wall before drying.

'Meniru,' the conductor shouts, looking at Chidi, holding his gaze.

'Ọ ga-apụ,' Chidi shouts back, growling his voice as deep as he could. Maybe it works. The bus stops, and the conductor says nothing else as Chidi alights onto the sun-baked tarmac.

Chidi's family has an old faulty freezer that sits empty until there is meat or soup to freeze and keep frozen; a celebration or an expected guest, in which case bottled drinks would be bought from the store up the street where students converge after school to buy biscuits or sweets.

The fridge can only hold drinks briefly. Imagine that now is one of those times, and that Chidi's sister who left a yoghurt drink in the fridge for days wants to know who drank it. Picture her standing arms akimbo, looking from face to face searching for signs of guilt. Everyone looks at everyone else, and then at the fridge standing inches from the wall. For Chidi's sake, and because it is the most likely scenario, let's make it one of those nights when the electricity is out, so that faces are not so visible in the dull yellow light of the kerosene lantern standing on a single sheet of newspaper on the wooden centre table.

'Mee mee, was it you?' Chinaza asks.

'No,' Mmesoma replies, 'I swear. With all my truth.'

Chinaza turns to Adaku. 'Tell me the truth, I'm not going to do anything,' she pleads. 'I just want to know.'

'Why would I drink your yoghurt?' Adaku asks, 'I even thought it was brother Chidi's yoghurt.'

Chinaza, still undeterred, turns to the only other younger person in the room she was yet to ask. 'Mercy, was it you?'

Mercy looks her up and down and lets out a drawn-out hiss.

'Mercy please if you took my yoghurt better return it. I'll not let this one go o. Mummy,' she turns to their mother, who cradles her head in her hands and lets out a sigh.

'Mercy did you drink Chi Chi's yoghurts?' Chidi asks, resisting the smile threatening to form on his lips. He reaches for his phone, turns on its flashlight and points it at Mercy.

'No,' she says, shielding her face from the harsh light.

'Liar,' Chinaza shouts. 'Brother warn her o, I'm older than her, I will beat her o. Nobody should say I'm wicked.'

Chidi turns his flashlight to Chinaza. Maybe he heard the beginnings of tears in her voice. 'Is it cry that you want to cry?' He asks, his Igbo tender and sympathetic.

'No, I'm not crying but anything that misses from that fridge, nobody should ask me about it.'

'Biko how much is this yoghurt from heaven? Can't you leave it for them as an older sister?' He says, puts his hand in his breast pocket and retrieves his remaining hundred naira note.

'Five hundred,' Chinaza sniffs. Chidi's hand pauses mid-air, his eyes widen theatrically but maybe the room is too dark for Chinaza to see even that. The wick of their lamp probably burns low on the last few drops of kerosene left.

'Mary, mother of God!' their mother shouts. 'You took five hundred naira and used it to buy yoghurt? Is yoghurt food? Whoever drank it did well. Serves you right.'

Imagine that she nods for emphasis, that she unties and reties her wrapper around her armpits, snaps her fingers to make sure her disapproval is heard if not seen. Chidi contemplates owning up to drinking the yoghurt and decides that it is already too late.

'It's okay,' he says instead, stretching out his closed fist towards her. 'I'll complete it for you when next I get money.'

'Brother, me I don't know when next you'll get money o,' she retorts, shaking her shoulders from side to side instead of her head.

'Okay, next week when Mummy gives me my transport fare, I'll give you two hundred, then another two hundred upper week.'

She sniffs again, and reluctantly collects the crumpled note, opens it in her palm and wipes her face with her palm. 'And tell whoever is the thief in this house to know that God will judge her.'

'Whoever took Chi Chi's yoghurt, please, you knew it was not your own so I don't know what you thought would happen. That she'll forget that she kept yoghurt there or what? Please, this type of thing is embarrassing. But it's Mummy you people are embarrassing, not me.' He looks at the battery life on his phone. Then up at Chinaza who is still standing there.

'And please brother, tell Mercy that I'm not her mate.'

'Mercy, Chi Chi is not your mate,' Chidi says, and a giggle rises from somewhere in the room.

'Warn her seriously o,' Chinaza says.

Chidi hisses in exaggerated annoyance and his younger sisters laugh.

Adaku asks their mother what's for dinner, slowly, timidly. And the room falls silent with her older siblings' gratitude and apprehension.

Their mother raises her left hand in the air, cups the fat of her underarm, and gestures to Adaku. 'Come and cut. No nau, go and bring knife. Mtchew.'

'You don't see we don't have kerosene?' Chinaza muttered.

The light bulbs buzz with static, and bright yellow light follows. The freezer hums on, and excited shouts of *Ha e weta ọkụ! Up NEPA! Thank God!* thunders across the neighbourhood, even from Chidi's sisters.

Like all other evenings like this, four sets of hands immediately scramble to find the TV remote first. Their mother smiles to herself. 'Look at what big girls like you are doing. Shame.'

Chinaza squeals, jumping in the air, the remote pressed close to her chest. 'God, thank youuuuu,' she cooed. 'God has compensated me.'

Now the boys are back out with their herd of sheep. Real sheep, in real grass, with real jackets of white wool and real flies hovering above in an idyllic swarm. Or we could say the sheep are a metaphor for beautiful but ultimately sorrowful ideals. Boy loves boy. Boy wants to be sheep with boy. Content, without worry, without haste. But of course, quite tragically, God rarely ever allows things to play out that simply.

They can only be with sheep on some days, for a few hours at a time, somewhere quiet and unoccupied. Maybe one of them really likes the story of the lonely sheep that wandered from the flock. And its kind shepherd who abandoned the remaining 99 to seek out the one that was all alone in the cold and empty wilderness. Maybe it reminds them of their love.

In another telling, the stray sheep does not exactly wander off. It runs away while its shepherd is asleep, torn apart from within by the boredom and routine. Then, lost and alone, finding there were many things worse than an uneventful life, it regrets and submits itself to its fate. Still, in all versions of the story, the shepherd finds the sheep long before it is too late.

On an indecisively rainy day, Otito sits on the sofa of the living room on a call with Chidi. His guard is down at home, as is standard practice among Igbo boys. Ndubuisi enters, hears the happiness in his voice and snatches the phone from his ear. A tussle immediately ensues.

The boys tumble through the chairs, pull down the curtain rods, and the television falls off its stand and cracks. It would remain cracked for a very, very long time. Many years, till everyone in the house forgets the type of joy it used to bring.

The fight stops, somehow. Perhaps another sibling walks in and intervenes, or a parent hears things breaking. Ndubuisi gets the bulk of their father's punishment, for being younger and for having started the quarrel. Let's assume he takes all the strokes of cane in agonising silence, to protect his brother's secret, because it is the sort of thing Igbo brothers do for one another. Wouldn't that be so kind?

So, maybe Otito's father did not die in the Biafran War. The boys are too young to have been fathered by men that died that long ago anyway. Maybe Otito's father isn't dead at all. Maybe he's a long-distance bus driver who stays out most nights on the roads between Enugu and Lagos, Enugu and Abuja, Enugu and Onitsha, Enugu and somewhere else.

Let's make him a stern man who talks ceaselessly about respect, humiliation, and the undying dream of Biafran independence. A man who has an English name but has lived long enough to feel like he would never be at home in this country. Otito feels the same way, for different reasons, but father and son rarely talk to each other. He is not exactly cruel to Otito. He drives so many bus routes to put Otito through school.

'Don't worry,' he sometimes says to Otito. 'At least you're a little smart. If God has his way, maybe you might even go to university.' He says university in Igbo, not knowing how much it scares Otito. *Mahadum*, as if anyone could ever know it all.

*

But Chidi's father remains very dead, leaving his son only a few memories to hold on to. Shadows, lurking in the corners of their flat. A figment he sees just before he closes a door. A voice, an image, a disapproval he shouldn't have to worry about but still does. There is a collection of lesson notes too. *Introductory Technology. JS1–JS3.*

However, it is more likely than not that Chidi is unable to picture his father teaching a class of rowdy secondary school students. Perhaps he can barely picture his father at all. Maybe all he has are photographs from times he cannot remember. Clothes and shoes that are almost his size but have long gone out of fashion. And a bloodline only he can keep alive. Being the only son of a dead Igbo man is probably quite difficult and tasking. But what choice does he have?

Otito and Chidi are both Catholic, and like many Catholic Igbo boys before them, they are trained in the ritual of serving mass. Floating in robes, nodding solemnly, swinging incense in a blessed way. They volunteer to serve the same mass and maybe God watches over them as they waltz to the altar, holding up crosses, swaying to Igbo hymns that sound too Latin, and marching out of the church in a procession while the rest of the flock stands and sings. Such beautiful synchrony. Maybe God looks at their sacrifice and sees that it is from a pure heart.

Even if their parish chaplain figures out what they are doing, he is probably not the type of man to make such an allegation against anyone, particularly not against boys so devoted to God. Let's assume the chaplain holds his peace. And that Chidi and Otito share so many sacramental blessings that they begin to think of their love as hymns.

Ndubuisi holds a grudge against Otito. But more importantly, he sees it as a duty to do something to push his older brother back to his senses. He decides to tell Azubike, that way Otito's secret would at least remain protected. They lock the boys' room and ask him to explain himself. The room is small and cluttered with rumpled clothes, books, slippers, sandals, and anything else someone might have dropped carelessly on that day.

Otito is younger than Azubike so he cannot possibly fight them both. He lunges for the door, but Azubike kicks his legs clean off the floor. Maybe if the room was a bit larger, Otito would not have been so within striking distance. He begins to scream at the top of his lungs. His brothers try to shut him up. They stuff his mouth with a brown woolly shirt that has been pilling for quite some time. But each time they take it off, he screams and screams. Nobody comes, and screaming that loudly takes a lot of effort. His throat grows tired, and he sits on the floor, looking up at the two of them, so broken-hearted that they would do something like this to him.

Maybe there is another version of this story where they don't go that far. Where they let him go when he starts shouting. Or when a sister knocks on the door. A version where they don't hold him bound and gagged until he begins to fade, falling forward on his face. Where there is no need for their frantic scrambling to untie him, to take the shirt from his mouth and fan him with an old oil company brochure. No need to carry him to the toilet and pour buckets and buckets of water on him till he jolts awake. A version where something is left intact. Badly damaged and weathered, but not completely destroyed. Something that could still be nurtured to health. Ordinarily, because these are Igbo boys, it's safe to say brotherhood is already such a complicated endeavour, even if we assume all other things to be equal.

Chidi's WAEC results are okay, but nowhere near extraordinary. His mother takes him to an uncle, with all his school documents tucked neatly into a white office file. The uncle gives them his audience, because that much is an obligation every Igbo man owes his dead brother's son. He offers them drinks and showers Chidi with compliments.

'Such a handsome man you've turned out to be,' he says. 'Be very careful o. I know girls must have started disturbing you. If you enter any university now, you'll cause wahala o.'

Everyone in the room laughs. It is a Sunday afternoon. There is a sizzling sound coming from what must be the kitchen. The smell of thyme, garlic and curry leaves tugs something in Chidi's stomach. His uncle's wife steps out into the living room, fanning herself with the palm of her hand.

'I'm around o,' she says. 'My sister,' she turns to Chidi's mother, 'I hope there is peace?'

'There is peace, my sister. Good news even. Your son has cleared his WAEC in one sitting.'

Chidi lets his mother do all the talking, all the suggesting, all the begging.

'You know how things have been for us. My husband, may his soul rest in peace, would have liked his only son to go to university. But this problem is bigger than me.'

She gets on her knees, and his uncle's wife jumps from her seat. 'No, no. Why would you be kneeling down in this house? Is this not your house as well?' she shouts.

Chidi's uncle clears his throat and then agrees. 'No need for kneeling,' he says. 'We're one family, anything we can do, we will. What was his JAMB score?' He looks at Chidi when he asks this.

'He did not sit it with his set,' his mother answers.

'Hmmmm,' the man replies, 'Okay. Let's be seeing. When the next one comes around, we'll know how to manage. But before then, nwoke m, I'm sure you're not just sitting on your hands? You're a man now o, so you should act like it, be agile. You know even this university, who's to say you'll get a job afterwards? You can see the sort of zoo Nigeria is? Even the education sef is rubbish. So, you have to have your own something doing at all times.'

Chidi nods, his stomach grumbles, and he prays for the meeting to end.

Otito's WAEC results are similar, but he sits the JAMB exams and gets a surprisingly high score. The news shocks his entire family. Azubike had already failed it twice and though Otito had never failed an exam before, he had also never gotten such a high grade. His mother prepares chicken stew, and his father buys a carton of Viju milk on his way home. There is still a screening exam between Otito and an admission letter, but this is the closest anyone in their family has ever gotten.

Their living room cushions lack the space to seat the whole family so assume that the youngest two sit on the floor, with their plates of rice cradled in their lap.

Otito eats his fill, trying not to overthink what this would mean, in practical terms, for he and Chidi. At university he would at least have more freedom to call. Having four siblings does not offer a lot of privacy for things like this.

After dinner, the whole family prays together, asking God to watch over Otito on the campus of the university he would soon surely get into. In the boys' room, he lies in the darkness and listens as his brothers' breathing relaxes into a familiar sound. He clicks his phone on and reduces the screen brightness to zero before typing: *Can't talk atm but I wanted to tell you I finally got my JAMB today. 342. Don't call this night though. I'll call tomorrow. I love you.*

Chidi holds Otito's hand in the Keke Napep as it snakes its way through Zik's Avenue. They stop at a popular Abacha joint on Ogui Road and sit on one of the wooden benches. Their fingers are no longer interlocked, perhaps forced apart all the way back on Independence Layout when another passenger joined them in the back seat of the tricycle.

They sit next to each other now, shoulder to shoulder. No one pays them mind, two boys eating Abacha from blue Styrofoam plates. Their dishes are almost identical: Abacha, ukpaka, and some chopped garden egg leaves. Otito pushes the piece of dried fish around with his plastic fork to scoop up every last morsel of Abacha. They save the fish till both their plates are empty. Chidi picks it up with his bare hand, divides it into two and drops one half back onto Otito's plate.

Ntachi-Osa is one of the most expensive Abacha spots around but given the occasion they relish every second.

'You should have let me pay,' Otito says as they walk back to the curb to wait for a bus to take them to the main market.

'Rich man,' Chidi teases him, 'Odogwu wey dey clear bill.'

Otito laughs and pushes him with a forced and theatrical annoyance.

'Don't worry, this one is just Abacha. What if I now took you to Shoprite like other boyfriends?'

A yellow Danfo bus stops and they haggle for a cheaper fare before they board. They talk about other, less private things while on the bus. Popular rumours about Benin City, and Benin boys, and university lecturers, and many other things in-between.

Chidi listens and makes a mental note of all the trivia Otito reels out with excitement. He tries to look happy and full of joy. And maybe he is. Maybe he prayed, fasted, started so many novenas he never saw through to the ninth day, said decades and decades of the rosary till his fingers began to ache where they pressed into the beads. Maybe this is his blessing as much as it is Otito's. But he hears a distance already in the way Otito says *Elect-Elect*, and in Otito's giddiness and ironclad plans, which for the first time in so long do not include Chidi.

'I knew you would clear your screening. I said it since,' Chidi said, pushing his thoughts away. 'How can someone that scored 342 in JAMB fail screening?'

'If I start counting all the people that scored high that didn't get admission, you'll know that these people really do not always send you,' Otito says, only realising after the words left his mouth that it might hit a sore spot.

Chidi is about to say something else but catches himself mid-sentence. He looks around, meeting a few uninterested sets of eyes. The bus will soon get to the main market. He reaches for his pocket, lifting off the seat a little to ease his access.

'What?' Otito asks.

'Don't worry, I'll just text it to you.'

Otito's phone buzzes as the bus comes to a stop, joining a queue of buses parked on the side of the road. They get off the bus and make their way into the crowded market. Otito retrieves his phone from his pocket and a smile forms on his lips when he reads the message: *You know you're not others. You are so smart. You're such a doubting Thomas but I'll be here to keep reminding you.*

Otito feels the same nagging in his stomach, chest, ears, maybe even the back of his head. It is nothing in particular, at least not something either of them have the words to describe. Otito tries many times. He tussles in his bed, turning this way and that while his brothers snore gently.

'Be careful when you get there,' Azubike had told him the day he printed out his admission letter with UNIVERSITY OF BENIN written boldly, in a colour so bright it looked like a warning, a sign.

Now, in the darkness of his room, he picks up his phone and begins so many sentences he never completes:

I feel so bad about leaving . . .

I feel so bad about leaving alone. We were supposed to go together . . . . .

What if you don't get into UNIBEN next year . . .

He sends none of them, deciding they all sounded overly dramatic and immature. UNIBEN is not that far and, though this is yet another rumour he heard about universities in general, not just UNIBEN, the four years fly by quickly. And many lovers walk in and walk out, stronger than ever. There are so many stories of diehard love that survive the fire of distance and school, but none of them have ever featured two Igbo boys. Before he succumbs to troubled sleep, Otito decides that anything is possible, anything.

They are back at the main market. This time they stop at the Old Park entrance where they find buses heading to Benin. Otito pays for his fare, feeling a tingling in his nose.

The tears feel like they are about to come, but crying is not the sort of thing you find Igbo boys his age doing in a market. There are a myriad of reasons why, but for him, on this day, the tears near and near without arriving.

Chidi helps Otito load his bags onto the back of the bus, which fills with passengers in minutes. They have too little time for proper farewells, but they make an attempt still, reminding each other to call and text daily, a bit jarred by the very real possibility of not keeping their promises.

Above, the early morning sun is a soft circle without outline. The sheep are gone now, there's only loud buses and cars that blow dark exhaust smoke into the air. But maybe they don't talk of sheep at all. Maybe they are both strong boys who know how to hold on at all costs, or at least are very determined to learn how, for each other. We all know sheep don't live forever. Ten to twelve years if they're really nurtured and doted on. But for the sake of this story, let's say these ones are made of something special and adamant, something beautiful and impossible to ever subdue.

About the author
Ani Kayode Somtochukwu is an award-winning writer and queer liberation activist from Enugu, Nigeria. He is the author of *And Then He Sang a Lullaby*, which won the Edmund White Award for Debut Fiction and was Gold Winner for the 2023 *Foreword* INDIES Book of the Year Award in Literary Fiction.

Leaving

Alison Batten

Shortlisted

Smoke had blurred the horizon since midday, looking like a scratchy old blanket pushing into the sky. Not a good day to be travelling, Hayley knew that. She glanced at Joe in the rear vision mirror. He was still asleep, curled up in his booster seat like an empty gunnysack, his thumb planted in his mouth. She saw the tear stains on his cheeks, and there'd be bruises flowering under his shirt, she knew that without seeing them. Her guts took another dive.

Any other time she would have enjoyed driving along this road, with the big open sky and wildflowers everywhere. She'd have stopped once or twice to let Joe have a run around, but not today. She needed to keep going, clear the wheatbelt by sundown, find somewhere safe to sleep. Where exactly was the bushfire that was making all that smoke? West of her, down towards the coast, she could tell that much. Some burn-off that's gone wrong, she supposed, or some tourist's furtive campfire that got away unattended. But how far away was it?

If she kept going north, she'd put the smoke behind her. Like her town, put it behind her. And Brad. She imagined Brad coming home after work later on – he'd notice her car not there, then see her few belongings gone, and he'd realise she'd left. Really left, this time. Then what? He'd take it out on the furniture, rage around kicking things, swing the fridge door open and grab a beer, sit out on the back steps with his anger, try to phone her.

She cringed. Couldn't believe herself, day after day waiting for the next outburst, taking the backhanders along with any decency he offered. She touched the fresh bruises on her ribs. She just hadn't known where to go. Still didn't. But once she was even further north, well past the smoke, she'd have a look round the bigger towns, see what might be there. There could even be some adventure in it, the idea of starting again, once she was far enough away. Once she felt safe, got used to what she was doing. And she would start again – she had to.

He would assume she'd fled to Perth, or down to the south coast, places she knew. He always said if she went he'd come after her, track her down, but he wouldn't think to go north, wouldn't even think she'd have the guts to just head somewhere completely new. They knew no one north, either of them.

And besides, he might not even bother to come after her now, after what happened. After what he did this time.

She was gripping the steering wheel too tightly. Every time she remembered the ultimatum she'd bargained on Joe's behalf, it hit her like another smack in the belly. Vowing that if he ever laid a hand on Joe it was the end . . . What was wrong with her, to wait for that to happen?

Poor little devil. She glanced at him in the mirror again. She'd get things better for him, she had to. She'd make this into a road trip; something good. The worst of it was already over, when she thought about it, getting this far away. It would be alright. Because they were going into new country, and when you looked around, things seemed good already.

The wildflowers, like jewels on the bare earth.

Those black cockatoos, the slow way they fly, with their wings scything the air.

Little mallees, full of blossoms and muttering corellas.

And those gentle low hills covered in pastel-coloured bushes. It was lovely, really lovely.

Noongar country, her Nan Juney used to call it. You'd wonder what it must have looked like once upon a time, her grandmother would say.

She still missed Nan Juney. She would have loved Joe. She would have helped.

*

Hayley had been determined to clear a few towns before she stopped this morning. Drove straight through the closest ones, saw them slip away in the rear vision mirror. Wheatbelt towns, flat and dusty, main streets blotted with flimsy leaf shade and hard-edged verandah shade. Shops for lease, pubs doing counter lunches. A memorial park with big old gum trees. Stone houses from a more prosperous era, and fibro houses plonked in fenced-off rectangles of dry grass.

Pretty towns though, and not unfriendly, not at all. She knew southern wheatbelt towns, had spent some of her childhood in them. And she'd quickly grown fond of the one where she and Joe, only a baby, had arrived with nowhere left to go. The townsfolk had made her feel welcome. No one had pried, no one judged her, at least not openly, even when she took up with Brad. They'd encouraged her to join things, bring Joe to playgroup, invited her to go on wildflower walks.

She grew to appreciate how people here still valued wildflowers. They still kept that love for them, stitched in-between the hard work and the practical – sometimes awful – decisions it took to live here. Their worn out old part of the country could still land a surprise on them, astound them with its beauty the way it brought its extraordinary gift year after year, laid it out to quilt the armour, soften the edgy drought. It had surprised her too, when she'd never especially thought about wildflowers before.

Hayley had given it a real go in town, she really had, but she had been worn down by the fact that no one said anything; they must have known what was going on with her and Brad. Even the other mothers at playgroup. Or when she went to social things. That complicit happiness, jollity, with the cakes or the barbeque and the chatty or bitchy conversations, as if that was all it took to ignore whatever else was happening in your life. Never allowing her the opening to say anything.

Or maybe she never allowed the opening — it was hard to tell. There was always that silence around it, as though it was just an unspoken fact of life. Some men are bashers; that's just how it is. You mind your own business. She'd thought about what would happen if she'd said it, just blurted it out, but she didn't know where the mine-fields lay in a close-knit town. And strictly speaking, she was still an outsider . . .

Brad's family had lived in the district for three gener-ations. They'd once owned great tracts of land there and no longer did. He had some angry blaming story about it. Everyone knew the family, and they all seemed to have some connection with Brad — they'd gone to school with him and his brothers, or their husbands worked with him, or drank with him at the Wheat Sheaf or the Imperial. Some were related, cousins or second cousins. They'd have known what he was like. Good old Brad. Bit of a rough bastard but turned out alright, eh? Making a go of it with that Hayley girl who turned up out of nowhere with her kid.

No one other than his mates visited. His house, his rules; that was fair.

It had felt strange driving out of town. Leaving. She'd felt so detached. Just had to block out Joe's deeply drawn sobs which she knew weren't going to stop for a while whatever she did or said. Just kept driving.

South at first. Unsure of where to go, she'd taken the road to the south coast, the one she knew. Then a safe distance out of town, she'd turned off, swung around and followed the minor roads which skirted her town until she came to the inland highway and turned north. It had suddenly felt right, doing that.

She'd kept driving north, into the morning and into unfamiliar country, and then she'd stopped in a big town, one where no one would recognise her. It was early for lunch but they hadn't even finished breakfast, and Joe needed to eat something.

She remembered his breakfast, all over the floor where Brad had hurled it, and she felt a wave of nausea again. She'd felt so nervous, stopping in that town. But she'd needed the break, needed to help Joe. She'd bought a map, and some food, and she'd taken Joe to a park, tried to help him feel better, though she was too depressed to feel anything much, even towards him.

'Teddy. Where teddy?' he'd asked.

His tears had started again. She'd found his bear among the hurriedly-packed box of clothes, hugged them both, held him and felt him wince then relax against her.

'It's okay, baby. Let's give Teddy a biscuit, eh?'

She'd disabled her phone, then she'd studied the map, and thought she knew where they might go. Where it was that looked big enough to start again, and far enough north to feel safe.

Next, she'd found one of those big camping shops you see on telly. She'd tried to engage Joe in the adventure of it, looking at two-person tents, choosing a colour. There'd be enough money if she was careful.

He hadn't controlled her money; that was something. She was to keep her pension going, pretend she wasn't living with anyone, that way she could pay her share, he'd decided.

In the early afternoon she'd set off north again, and Joe had finally fallen asleep. She'd been so glad for that. It was then that she'd started noticing the sky, the creeping stain of smoke rising from the west. It travelled along with her for ages, kept her going, set a mood.

It had been a shit of a day so far, and she'd been so scared, but she didn't feel so scared anymore, that was one thing.

*

By mid-afternoon the smoke had either dispersed or she'd outdriven it. Big golden-edged clouds replaced it, stacked on the horizon like hay bales, and when they finally rolled away she was a long way north, with Joe still soundly sleeping, a full tank of petrol and a clear run ahead. She could see the sun now that it was freed from smoke and clouds, and it was getting low to the horizon, but she could still make it to a big town and find a campground for the night. Things were working out; it would be alright.

Just up ahead she saw a cluster of buildings. It would be that little town she'd seen on her map, which meant the bigger towns weren't too far along now. As she approached she slowed, and felt the car become unsteady. Not much, just a slight wobble, barely discernible. It was nothing; she probably imagined it. Or it was just the uneven road. She pulled over, checked all the tyres, and allowed herself a flooding of dismay and anger at the unfairness of it. A puncture. A fucking puncture.

Well, at least it hadn't happened where it was dangerous to pull over, she could be thankful for that much. And there was even a petrol station, just along there, so she could get some help, get it done quickly. She'd make it over there if she went carefully.

She carefully drove over to the petrol station driveway, turned the motor off. A man was just closing up, but he'd been watching her drive in, so it was alright, she was just in time.

Joe was whimpering. He was struggling out of sleep, starting to cry again. She went around to his door, opened it and leaned in. His eyes were swollen and snot crusted his nose.

'Hey there sweetheart, you dozed off, didn't you? Look, Teddy's still sound asleep.' She unbuckled his seat belt. 'I know what, let's see if the man sells ice cream. And he might help me fix our tyre, because wait till you see what's happened to it, silly old tyre!'

She scooped him out of the car, held him awkwardly against her own bruises, and showed him the tyre. He didn't care; she knew he wouldn't, poor little boy. It was going to take more than a tyre, or even an ice cream, to shift how he was feeling today. She carried him over to the door the man was just closing. Why did he do that? She knocked and called out. The man was still in there; she could see him through the glass. He'd been watching her. She knocked and called out again. Knocked again, looked through the glass. He'd disappeared from sight. Why?

She heard a car starting up somewhere to the side of the garage, then there was the man driving past her, looking straight ahead, onto the road and away.

'Oh seriously?' she said, astounded, and she could feel herself slumping.

No, what's it matter, she thought, when she'd recovered a little. She could change a tyre, it's just easier with help when you're tired and you've got a little kid to watch. And Joe could have done with an ice cream, too. She straightened up, wiped Joe's nose and stroked his forehead. Worse things have happened than a flat tyre. Or some arsehole ignoring you. She'd get it done – just needed to collect herself for a minute.

Across the road the sun blazed through the canopy of a gum tree. It was late, and she'd need to get a move on before darkness fell. But she kept watching the sun through the gum tree for a moment, just to have a breather, make herself completely calm.

There was a woman over there. Hayley hadn't even noticed her before. She was watering the garden at the front of an old weatherboard house, standing there holding the hose, and as she was watering, she was turning, oscillating like an electric fan. She completed a turn and looked over the road at Hayley. Waved to her. Then she turned the hose off and walked across the road.

'Saw what happened just then. Don't worry about that bastard, he wouldn't help his own grandmother unless she paid double,' the woman said. 'You out of petrol? I've got some you can have. Ah, no, I see, got a flat.'

'Yep.'

'Let's fix it, then eh? Easier with two people.'

'No it's okay. We can't bother you like that.'

'Hardly a bother.'

She was only young, maybe early 30s, not much more than a decade on Hayley, but there was something wise about her though, and impressive. Angular and tall, frizzy hair pulled into a ponytail and wearing a plain cotton dress, feet in sandals.

'Spare tyre good?' she asked.

Hayley nodded. 'I got it checked not long ago.'

'Rightio good, won't take long, but this close to sunset better let someone know you'll be late, eh?'

'It's okay. My phone's not working anyway.'

'Welcome to use mine.'

'There's no one needs to know,' Hayley said, pulling her sleeves down over bruises.

'You got somewhere you're heading to?' the woman asked.

Why's she want to know all this stuff? Why doesn't she mind her own bloody business?

'Nuh. Just north.'

The woman thought about that.

'Well,' she said, 'what if we get the tyre done then have a cup of tea at my place?'

It was too close to sundown to matter now. Hayley wasn't going to get to any big town before dark, regardless. The woman just probably wanted to do more stickybeaking, but what the heck? And Joe could do with a break. So could she, if it came to that.

'Thanks, that'd be nice.'

'I'm Sarah, by the way.'

'I'm Hayley, and this is Joe.'

'Howdy, Joe. You know what? We've got chooks, speckly ones. And they're going to sleep soon, so you can say goodnight to them eh? You like chooks?'

Joe gave a little nod.

'Thought you might,' she smiled.

She's kind, Hayley thought. She put Joe down where he could watch the tyre being changed, and they got to work.

'Better get the car off dickhead's property, eh,' the woman said when the job was done. 'What if you drive over and park in my yard and we'll get the kettle on. I'll carry Joe over so you don't have to buckle him in again.'

Hayley parked in Sarah's yard just as the sun tipped the horizon. They went around to the back of the house where there was a wide verandah, and there was a girl there, sitting on an ancient couch which spilled blooms of kapok from its arms. The girl was playing on a mobile phone, and she looked up and smiled, looked like Sarah. Hair like the couch stuffing, soft and unruly.

'This is my girl, Emily. Nine last week,' Sarah said to Hayley. 'Emily, this is Hayley, and this little bloke's Joe. You could show him the chooks eh? He could see them going to sleep.'

'Yeah good,' said Emily. 'Come on, I'll show you me favourite.'

'Come through to the kitchen,' Sarah said to Hayley.

The kitchen was an old-fashioned one that didn't seem to have been changed since the house was built, which Hayley thought could've been a hundred years ago. Olden days, anyway. There was a wood-burning stove, a dresser with old canisters and plates, a big wooden table, and a cupboard with coloured glass set into its doors. It was lovely. The sort of kitchen, she thought, that the city bric-a-brac people would love to get wind of so they could offer nothing much for taking the old stuff off the owners' hands, that old furniture and kitchen-ware the owners hadn't realised was actually valuable. The people in Hayley's town – her old town, that is – had said how that happens, how the vintage dealers come out on their weekend excursions, poking around to see if anyone might have old things they might like to get rid of for a bit of cash. Offer them peanuts for it. Brad once said there were places in the town he wouldn't mind ripping off, the people were that dumb. He'd flown into a rage and given her a thump across her back when she'd said what a shit thing to do that was.

Why did she have to remember that? She was so close to crying that she had to swipe at the tears to stop them spilling over, and she glanced over at Sarah, who was making a pot of tea and not saying much. She'd probably seen the bruises.

'I was just thinking,' Sarah said when the tea was poured, 'what about if I make us some sandwiches for dinner? What do you reckon? Does Joe like cheese and tomato?'

She made a stack of sandwiches and they all sat out on the verandah eating them. The sky had closed for the day, and big stars were everywhere, with a sliver of new moon sitting among them like a little lopsided canoe. Sarah and Hayley sat and watched the sky, and Emily took Joe inside to play.

'You know, Hayley, it'll be alright when you get clear of whatever you need to,' Sarah said quietly.

'Yeah, I know.'

'Do you know where you're going to?'

'Thought I'd just go and look round the towns north of here.'

'That sounds good – there's some nice places. Not many though – north gets fairly sparse pretty quickly from here on.'

'Yeah.'

'Got enough money?'

'I've got some savings. Enough to get started.'

'Probably do with extra to set up, though, just so you can feel secure? Because I was thinking that Emily's father Bill, he works in the mines and he sends me more money than Emily or me ever need, and he'd want me to make sure you were alright. Might as well stuff that old couch with what he sends, for all we spend. You're welcome to share some.'

'Thanks, I couldn't take money, though. What I've got should do.'

'Good to have an emergency fund though, especially now. Think of it as a loan if you won't take it otherwise. Just say the word. Hey, weren't the flowers good this year?'

'God yeah. Still lots of them too, all along the way.'

'Imagine what they must've looked like in the olden days.'

'Would have been so beautiful. Still is – the whole place.'

Sarah nodded.

'Hayley, this stuff that's been happening to you, with the bruises, it's been going on a while, eh?'

Tears stung at her eyelids again.

'Yep.'

'Are you safe from him now?'

'I'd say so.'

'You know you can get support.'

Hayley shrugged.

'There'll be a refuge or counselling or something when you get into a bigger place; you could maybe ask.'

She hadn't thought of that. It hadn't even occurred to her.

'He needs stopping,' Sarah said.

'I know.' She hesitated. 'You know, I think I'll be okay to get help now I've left. Did that much at least.'

'Huge step to take,' Sarah said. 'Listen, not trying to be bossy, but I reckon you should get the flat tyre fixed here, so you've still got a spare. We could do that in the morning if you and Joe wanted to stay the night.'

Christ. Gee some people are good.

'Would that be alright? We could pitch our tent in the yard, Joe'd love that. First time he's smiled today, here.'

'That works out then, eh? He can help Emily feed the chooks in the morning before she goes to school.'

In the morning Sarah took the flat tyre in her ute and got it fixed at someone's place nearby. A friend's place, she said.

'I never go near dickhead's joint across the road,' she sniggered. 'Rather pay a tow truck to get me to the next town if I had to.'

They both laughed, and after Hayley buckled Joe into his seat Sarah tucked a boiled egg and some speckly feathers into his hand.

'Here's a present from the chooks,' she said.

Then she put a wad of money into Hayley's hand – a roll of notes that looked like they'd just been dug out of the old couch.

'Might be handy for rent or something,' she said. 'It can be a loan if you like.'

'Okay, thank you,' Hayley replied.

'Hey, it worked out good, getting that puncture right here, eh?' They laughed. 'You'll be alright now, I reckon.'

'Sarah, thank you for everything,' Hayley said quietly.

She drove out of Sarah's yard, cleared the little town and headed off into the new morning. Not far, just a bit further north, have a look around. It was true, what Sarah said – they'd be alright now.

About the author

Alison Batten is a writer and visual artist who lives in the south-west of Western Australia. Much of her work reflects the need for a more just and compassionate world, and her belief that women's and children's rights are integral to this.

She is Gone

Julia James Burns

Shortlisted

As you drove to her house, you were nervous; there was still a lurch in the pit of your stomach. She can inflict pain so effortlessly. This morning, you weren't even sure you would go, but you made yourself get in the car and even picked up a poinsettia plant as a gift on the way. You still have manners, despite the circumstances.

The whole way there, you're anticipating the reception you'll get, especially given you're coming unannounced. You didn't let her know because you weren't sure you would go, but you need an answer. Ironically, you can't remember how to get there. The navigation app eventually announces that you've arrived at your destination.

She's probably heard the car, so no turning back now. Well, you can. Of course you can; she hasn't seen you yet. But you summon the courage to walk to her front door. There's a small desiccated shell of a long-gone snail attached to the security screen. Perhaps the door doesn't get much use anymore. You look around. The garden is immaculate: freshly clipped hedges and perfectly round topiary trees. Who does that for her now — makes life perfect for her?

You press the doorbell, but you can't hear it chime. Maybe it's ringing further inside the house. No answer. You try again but still no response. Has she already gone out for the day? Bother. You don't know if you can summon up the emotional energy to try again tomorrow and it's just so far to drive, with so many opportunities to turn around and go home. You tap your knuckles tentatively against the security door and then, just when you're thinking it's better that she isn't there, you hear someone coming. It must be her. Your stomach pitches again and you close your eyes for an instant. When you open them, the door is edged open tentatively, and a face appears.

After all these years, she's here in front of you. You're shocked to see how old she's become. A face that is not so much lined as shrunken across her high cheekbones and, despite an eyelid drooping a little more on one side than the other, her eyes are still so blue. There's a sparkle in them you've never seen before. In fact, there's something about her that isn't her. She's scanning your face in return, looking you over, no doubt summing you up for something cutting to say.

She opens the door to let you in and laughs gently. The whole time, she has a look of expectation on her face, almost as if she's waiting for you to deliver the punch line. You tell her it's good to see her because those manners are still pushing you along, and she says the same. *That*, you can't believe, given the last communication you had from her, even if it was some years ago. Those letters, those poisoned words hurled from her hand like darts, with the same piercing intention. *Is* she pleased to see you? She hated you so much, she wrote you out of her will – her only daughter. Her intention, you discovered, was that you were not to know until after her death. It was meant as her final punishment – a hard slap across your face from beyond the grave.

You stand in the entryway, taking her in. She's painfully thin, her skin-and-bone arms crossed loosely across a linen-draped frame. Long fingers tuck her shoulder-length white hair behind her ears. She is still gazing at your face, smiling earnestly. You ask her how she is; if she is well. She answers that she has never felt so well, then pauses, still carefully assessing you. You feel the imminent attack, a familiar tensing for the hurt you know is coming. Then she asks you a question that's beyond even her cruelty.

'I'm sorry, but who are you?'

There it is. The sarcasm; her usual way of making a point . . . except she's still searching your face. Then suddenly your worlds, the one in which she was always present and the world surrounding both of you now as you face each other, just fall away, so fast your head is spinning. She's serious. She doesn't know who you are. Then just as suddenly, everything stops, everything – and you understand that she's not going to be able to answer the question you've come to ask, or to hear what you've come across all these years to say.

You tell her you're her daughter. It's innocence – the thing in those blue eyes that you couldn't name when you first saw her. Those eyes that held malice for you, that always looked you over for something to requisition as a barb, are somehow new. It is as if all the venom swirling in the inky, malicious pigment of her irises has been washed away, and all that remains are clear blue pools of naivety.

She really doesn't know who you are. She isn't trying to be smart; to make the point that you never came to see her; to criticise you as she did for all your years together. She really doesn't know. Still, she looks at you expectantly. You unfasten your hair clip and allow your long hair to unfurl and hang loosely around your shoulders so she might see you as she remembers you. There's a spark of recognition.

'You look like me,' she says. 'I feel like I'm looking at myself in the mirror.'

This narcissism is familiar: everything has always existed only in relation to her. There it is again, even now. Your skin prickles. You tell her again that you're her daughter but she simply looks confused. As if to find a diversion while she tries to remember, she ushers you into the lounge and offers you a seat. The room is immaculate; soft furnishings in muted tones; the pristine fawn carpet and a dark wood sideboard filled with photograph frames. There are even some of you.

You look at her face; her eyes. The loss of memory, the failure of recognition, the lack of malice. She is still incredulous. She tells you she can't believe you're her daughter and keeps repeating that you look like her. You nod and tell her you know.

To find out just how much she's forgotten, you ask her about your father. He was more important to her than her own life. Incredibly, she pauses for a moment and says no, it was too long ago. You tell her his name and she says it sounds familiar but it was just too many years ago. It's as if you've asked about a passing acquaintance.

For you, the memories are still fresh. The nights of sitting with your little brother by your father's hospital bed. He had the strong, youthful body of a man in his thirties, covered by a crisp white sheet and his fresh young face serene in a coma.

You ask her if she remembers what she said after he died. She says again no, it was too long ago. You tell her, because you have to. You tell her how she informed you, a traumatised teenage girl, that she wished you and your brother were dead instead. That she could always have more children but she would never have him back.

She asks you if she really said that. Yes, you tell her, yes. She says, 'That's sad,' but there's no change in the tone of her voice; no remorse, not even for the things she accepts she said.

You tell her she won't remember that you've been there to see her. She nods in agreement. You realise it doesn't matter what you say to her now. That all the things you wanted to say to her and the question you came to ask, about why she wanted to hurt you, will land on ears that are not deaf but empty, neutral. Anything you say will blow away and disappear almost as quickly as it's spoken into the space between the two of you.

She asks when she last saw you and you tell her it was years ago. She wants to know why it's taken you so long to come back. You tell her, although you know it will have no impact, that she hurt you beyond measure. You tell her it's complicated and it would take another lifetime to explain the abuse, the pain, the vain efforts of a daughter who just wanted a mother. This woman who didn't know how to be a mother made you an orphan — no, worse, because an orphan can still believe her mother loved her.

She tells you yet again that you look like her and you tell her again, with a sigh, that you know. She asks if you have children and the question makes you sad for your two sons; that they have lost their grandmother — even if they never really knew her. They'd always recognised her ambivalence towards them, on the few occasions that she made the effort to see them. They're young adults now and so much time has passed. She tells you again that she can't believe you're here.

She asks why you are sad, for slow tears have begun rolling down your cheeks. You tell her again how much she hurt you, but her face, as always, is impassive, inscrutable. Then you see a hint of tears welling in her eyes and she leans forward slightly to ask:

'Did you feel like I was jealous of you?'

You gasp internally. Did she really just say that? You never accused her of that, but it's the very word used by your friends and your counsellors over all those years. You tell her no because for you no is the truth. It's far more complex than that.

Then she asks:

'Do you think I was a bad mother?'

You pause, taken aback again that she's asking this of you. All she's ever said is that you're a bad daughter. Despite her loss of memory, she's summoned this question from the depths of her conscience and brought it to the surface. You look at her and say yes, because she was. You tell her she never loved you and you hope in that moment for her to disagree and say the words you want to hear. She doesn't. Instead, she asks you why.

You have no answer. You've never had an answer. It's a question you've asked for all those years without an answer.

53

You get up to go. She can't give you what you've come for. But instead of leaving, you walk to the sideboard to point out the photographs she has of you. She joins you and immediately touches one and says it's her daughter. You remind her you are her daughter. She looks at you and at the photos again and quietly agrees. What narrative has she woven around those photos of you? Are you causing her confusion by being here?

She approaches you slowly and touches your hair, telling you how beautiful it is. Your heart aches. She's never before given you even a glimmer of hope that she thought you were acceptable, beautiful – loved for who you were. It's the gentle touch you've longed for all your life. Why didn't she ever do that before? You so needed her touch, her comfort, her embrace – but it was never, ever given.

She says she's glad you kept your hair long. She steps forward and places her hands on your arms and you melt, even though not even an hour ago, when you arrived, you might have flinched. The tears flow freely for both of you as you embrace. You say you've always loved her and she says she knows. *The words you seek will never come from her.* She says you should have come earlier because she can't remember now. It's as if she understands why you came; that the time for getting answers from her is gone. But then, as she holds the embrace, she smooths the back of your long hair and says:

'You are a lovely girl.'

This will be enough. You say it silently: *This will be enough*. You will take this moment and hold it like a delicate bird.

You turn to leave but go back to embrace her one last time. The fear you had when you arrived is gone. She asks if you will return and you tell her perhaps. You walk to your car and in the brief time that takes, she's already closed the door.

She is gone.

About the author

Julia James Burns is a writer from Fremantle, Western Australia where she lives with her husband and two sons. She is immersed in her current project – a hybrid-memoir of her thirteen years living on Rottnest Island off the coast of Western Australia.

The Black Hole

Carol Byrne

Equal Third Place

The mouse was a quiet woman. They called her Brigid because she was born on the first of February, but also because Saint Brigid was the patron saint of her home county. Although she couldn't remember when she was last there. Dublin had been her home for well over fifty years. Her accent rounded out decades ago without her even noticing. Darragh, her brother, pointed it out as if it were another offence in the litany of things she did wrong. He was like their father. But she didn't challenge them on anything, it was best to stay small and say nothing.

Brigid stayed quiet when she and her husband couldn't conceive, naturally assuming blame for their childless state. He died fifteen years ago just as the small hole in the centre of her vision turned into a gaping one. Like her mother before her, Brigid ignored the signs at first. She remembered her mum complained of floaters innocently drifting in her eyes. Odd flashes of light and occasional black spots from the sun burning an empty circle into her vision. Brigid never dreamed the same genetic quirk would creep its way into her own retinae years later. She too ignored the floaters and the small hole that appeared and disappeared like a magician's trick. Every year the cavity at the centre of her sight got bigger like a fierce and hungry black hole. Devouring and destroying everything that came into its orbit.

As the world around her faded, Brigid receded into the territory behind her eyes, and into the greasy tangle of memory. Dreaming of odd things that she had long put away into the deepest caverns of herself. She often dreamed of the baby she gave away. She even dreamed that the young man with the auburn hair and chestnut eyes finally returned for her. That he took her and their infant boy back to London with him. Over the years, quiet attempts at finding her lost child proved fruitless. So, she resigned herself to the shame and the constant ache in her heart.

Brigid's days comprised of very little now. At age 75, she felt like an old woman. Besides her eyes, the pain in her shoulders was growing month by month. Probably the result of a lifetime spent hunched over; of not standing up straight and claiming all the space allotted to her. Her home help took her to see a physical therapist every Thursday, and this quickly became her favourite day of the week. She liked the brightness of the therapy room and the delicate touch of the winter sun on her tired skin. But she liked the physical therapist, Paudie, most of all. There was something comforting about his manner and the amiable way he chatted as he worked on her. Maybe he wanted to distract her from the pain or simply put her at ease. Either way, he treated her with the kind of dignity that she could never quite muster for herself. They talked about the news, the weather, the state of the country; anything at all. She liked to talk as well, she even told him about being named after a saint.

'Although, I don't possess any saintly virtues!' she laughed, but then thought of her father. The memory of him stung as it often did. At random times, he would enter her mind and tower over her. Her father was known locally as the Bull. It was common knowledge that he married up and into land. That probably drove his behaviour – she saw that now. Her parents expected her to maintain respectability and status by marrying a professional, which she eventually did. That was the point of her education, they said. It promoted the opportunity for a 'good' marriage, and *this* was her inheritance. Their way of securing her future. The physical assets flowed to the boys. Even though she was the eldest, they groomed her brother Darragh to inherit the vast farm, while they sent her away to boarding school. She did a commercial course in Dublin after she finished and stayed when she got a job in the bank. Looking back now, she also saw how young and naive she was.

Paudie chatted openly about himself. He had three children and even though Brigid's eyes were bad, she felt the pride radiate off him when he said he recently became a grandfather for the first time.

'My son's girlfriend had a baby two weeks ago,' Paudie said as he deftly manoeuvred around her rotator cuff muscles.

'What did she have?' Brigid asked, trying not to let the throb in her shoulder creep into her voice.

'A boy, a bruiser of a fella.'

A genial silence stretched out between them. As Brigid basked in his happy news, she realised why she was so comfortable with Paudie. His easy manner and the way he talked reminded her of John.

Brigid met John, a hotel barman, at a dance in Rathmines in 1969. Growing up, Brigid was of little value as the eldest daughter of a clatter of children. She was merely an extension of her mother, there to help with the house and the younger ones. This changed suddenly when John saw her. It was as if she became *somebody* for the first time, and she was smitten with the idea. Of being somebody.

'I'd die without you, Breege,' he'd say as he traced his fingers along her spine and down the curve of her back until he reached inside her underwear.

'I love you too,' she'd whisper, savouring the taste of the words in her mouth, and the warm feelings they evoked in her. They had sex that summer in her flat on Claude Road, in Drumcondra, as the transistor played 'The Ballad of John and Yoko' by The Beatles. Her father wouldn't approve of the match, but she didn't care. All she cared about was how good being together felt – like nothing bad could ever happen.

By late September she couldn't ignore that she was pregnant.

'I can't support you working in the hotel,' John said slowly when she told him the news. 'I'll go to London and get a job in construction. You can follow me over, and then we'll get married,' he said after a painfully long pause. But then he beamed at her with his usual confidence.

'Why don't we get married first? I'll be showing in a few months,' she rubbed her stomach.

'You'd have to leave your job if we got married. That's the rules . . . and we need the money Breege.'

Brigid opened her mouth to say something more, but he interjected. 'Trust me . . . what's a few more weeks? You won't even be showing on the day, I promise. It's just till I get established.' She smiled to herself, images of her wedding day floating before her eyes, but John turned his face away, impassive.

Soon her flatmate couldn't look her in the eye when Brigid asked if there was any post, or calls on the shared phone downstairs. 'No,' was always the answer. Her flatmate stared at her growing belly, 'Brigid, what'll you do if—'

'He'll call, don't worry,' she said, waving her flatmate's words away with her hand.

'Do you have an address or a number or any way to contact—'

'Don't worry, it'll be fine. You'll see.'

But the weeks kept passing. Brigid wore loose-fitting clothes when she returned home for Christmas. She and her mother served the rest of the family Christmas dinner. The younger children were making noise at the end of the table until their father silenced them with one sharp turn of his head.

Darragh glanced at Brigid sideways as she finally sat down to eat. 'I see you're feeding yourself up in Dublin then.'

'Could you not just leave her alone for one day Darragh, why are you always at her?' their mother said.

'I'm not, she looks good. I'm just saying. Dublin suits you . . . That fancy school really paid off. It's good of you to come back and visit us little folk.'

'Don't mind him Brigid, he's only jealous—'

'No, I'm not! What would I be jealous of?' he said, food spraying from his mouth.

'Although you *could* come back more,' their mother continued, ignoring his comment. 'I could do with the help.' She furrowed her brow and looked at the youngest. 'But Darragh's right. Dublin suits you. Your father's always telling the neighbours how well you're doing.'

The Bull nodded, chewing Brussels sprouts with his mouth open. 'You should marry a doctor, then I'd really have something to tell them.'

Everyone laughed. But Brigid swallowed and pulled her cardigan around her growing frame.

In February, the bank quietly asked her to resign from her position. Which she obediently did, and then seldom left the flat, hoping that each day would bring news from London. Her desperation grew as her savings evaporated.

'Have you any kids yourself, Brigid?' Paudie asked as his fist slid back and forth on her scapular muscles. Working hard to get all the tension out.

'Sorry, what?' Brigid said, surprised by the question. No one had asked her that in years.

'Do you have any children?'

The knot in her stomach tightened, and the familiar old, hot flush of shame crept up her body. She was about to answer when the clinic bell rang and gave her a mild jolt. Paudie stopped working on her, mumbled to himself and pressed a buzzer on the wall.

'Are we finished?'

'No,' he said. 'My twelve o'clock always comes too early.'

The ring of the door in her flat had the same resonance. She recalled being startled that Saint Patrick's Day when, at over eight months pregnant, she waddled slowly down the stairs to answer it; wondering who it could be. Her flatmate was in the city at the parade.

All the energy left her body when she opened it and saw Darragh's face behind the glass, smirking at her swollen belly. 'Well done, Brigid. Dad won't be telling the neighbours about *this*.' He looked delighted, like he just won a prize at the fair.

'Don't tell him, please. It's just that—'

'. . . and all that money on a fancy school. I always pegged you for a halfwit.'

She slammed the door and rushed back up the stairs. She fled to the safety of her bed, clutching her belly and twirling the fake wedding band she wore on her ring finger. John would call, there was still time. He was still getting settled, that's all. They would be married, just like he said and then everything would be alright. She tried hard to control her breathing, but her heart was in high gear. Darragh rang the bell a few more times and then left. Brigid tried to relax but, to her horror, the sharp and continued pains in her abdomen let her know that her baby was on its way. She was out of time. All she could do was ring a taxi and leave her flatmate a note.

Later that evening she gave birth alone to a healthy boy in the Rotunda. Brigid told the nurses that her husband was working in London and would be travelling across the water soon. They nodded sympathetically and she was relieved when they took her to the public maternity ward, where on every bedside locker lay a glass ashtray. With shaking hands, she lit a cigarette and inhaled it as deeply as she could. Her nerves were still on fire as she imagined the scene of her parents calling to the door on Claude Road and her flatmate having to tell them where she was. She had a day, two at most, before she had to face her father. She exhaled and watched her rusty-haired baby asleep in his crib, oblivious and peaceful. The smoke hung innocently in the air like pretty ribbons floating underwater.

Dana's 'All Kinds of Everything' played softly at the nurses' station the following day when there was an almighty clatter and then a set of heavy footsteps. This was it. In her mind's eye Brigid could see her father advancing up the corridor like a bull, heaving his bulk forward, towards her maternity bed.

'You thundering bloody idiot,' he said as soon as he clapped eyes on her. The shock of his words ripped through her sore and bloated body. Instinctively, she put her hand out for her baby. 'What kind of a girl goes out and does this?' he continued, as he charged at her, her mother scurrying behind him. Brigid knew not to answer, instead she crouched down and made herself small.

'I didn't believe it; I had to come here and see it for myself, and here you are like a fucking Jezebel, grinning ear to ear.' Brigid wasn't smiling, her eyes were wide as she fumbled for her son. Searching for the touch of his skin as her cheeks grew redder by the second.

'I'm going to get married soon,' she spluttered, 'I'm just waiting for John to call . . .' But the words trailed off and turned to stone in her throat as she watched her father's nostrils flare.

'Look at what you have done,' he said through clenched teeth, pointing to the sleeping infant as if it were a rodent. 'Look what you've done to your mother and me.'

The deep crimson flush in Brigid's cheeks spread down her neck and body. The maternity ward was silent, save for the mewling of a newborn. In the cold light of day, all the stories she soothed herself with over the previous months looked pitiful. It was obvious now that John had deserted her. He wasn't coming back. The look on her parents' faces told her there was no soft place to land from his betrayal. She begged to keep the baby – she hadn't considered an alternative.

'With your help I could—'

'You're not keeping it.'

'But—'

'I don't want to hear it.'

'Please . . . he's my—'

'Stop it. And I don't want to see those tears either, it's too late for that now.'

Brigid's mother remained quiet. Brigid stayed quiet too.

'You'll get no sympathy from me, you . . . you bloody . . .' he swallowed hard, looking around, barely containing the words he wasn't saying.

Simpleton.

Reprobate.

Whore.

They polluted the air over her bed and sifted deep into her psyche. In years to come she was sure they hung around her body like invisible stains and shot outwards on the fibres of her voice as she spoke, so that everyone would intuitively know there was something horribly wrong with her.

He decreed that the baby would be adopted because 'No child of mine will be involved in this kind of scandal.' The Bull left just as he arrived – in a blaze of fury with his wife scuttling behind, trying to keep pace.

Brigid could see the other women on the ward exchange glances with each other. No one came near. She laid awake most of the night with the baby in her arms. In the early hours of the morning, she tried to commit every detail of him to her memory. Every contour of his small body and the heft of him on her chest. He slept peacefully while she breathed in his scent over and over. He smelled like a mixture of innocence and potential, mingled with sour milk. As day crept slowly into the ward and wrapped itself around the edges of every object in the room, Brigid reluctantly put her boy back in his crib and closed her eyes. But as she drifted into a light sleep, he was already slipping away from her. His outline was blurred – the memory of him fading before it was fully formed.

Her parents returned in the same clothes they wore the day before. This time two expressionless social workers accompanied them. Her father dropped some documents on her bed. The baby was asleep in the crib beside her.

'Sign here,' he said, thrusting a pen into her hand.

'I was hoping——'

'Not that again.' He said, shaking his head. 'I thought I made myself clear yesterday. Sign, here.'

Brigid looked to her mother, desperate for a last intervention, especially now that she'd seen the boy a second time.

'Why don't you hold him?' she asked, but her mother averted her eyes again and said nothing, while the other women clutched their babies and tried not to listen.

'Your mother doesn't want to hold it and neither do I. Just sign the papers and be done with it. I can't bear the sight of you anymore.'

Her transformation was now complete. She could never go back to the person she was before. She was forever marked by this. What she had done was not only mortifying to her parents' sense of morality and order, it was much more than that. It was practically criminal to a man, three generations from a famine cottage and obsessed with the idea and appearance of respectability. She was an intrinsic part of that.

'You're no daughter of mine.'

An alien hand she recognised as her own grasped the pen and signed. She moved to pick up her baby, but one of the social workers dislodged him from the crib and carried him away without ceremony. The newborn remained asleep and left her life without so much as a whimper.

Although she tried, she never did find out what became of the baby or his father.

'Brigid, are you okay?' Paudie asked.

The therapy room came back into focus.

'Sorry . . . no . . . I've no children,' but the words whipped at her flesh in protest. Why did she stay quiet after all these years? It was as if her denial of the child now was another form of abandonment. Of surrendering him once more, but the opposite was true. She would give anything to see him and hold him again. She would exchange what blurry sight she had left for some knowledge of him. Being quiet and meek paid no real dividends. Why shouldn't she tell someone? Her parents were dead, and she wasn't in regular contact with her siblings. Brigid was the only keeper of the prison she was in.

The session finished, and Brigid stood upright.

'I'll put you in for the same time next Thursday.'

'Do.'

She buttoned her blouse slowly and resolved not to be quiet anymore. She decided she would tell Paudie about the baby next week, or tell someone, anyone. If she did, then it wouldn't be a shameful black hole of a secret; sucking in all the air and light and tainting everything it touched. She would try to find him again, too. There must be organisations and experts who could help. It wasn't too late. She just had to use her voice. Her eyes had faded, but she still had her voice.

Brigid said goodbye and closed the therapy room door. Paudie wiped the massage oil off his hands and stared at the spot where she had just been. He liked Brigid a lot, and was sure he touched on something odd when he asked if she had children. He should have been more thoughtful. She really was a little mouse of a woman with all that nervous energy. Paudie would love to just lay his hand on hers and reassure her. She had been coming out of her shell bit by bit every week, and he was glad that she seemed to enjoy their chats. He should tell her he was born on a saint's day as well, and that's why his name is Patrick. She'd get a kick out of that. He would tell her next week. Although, he didn't think she would come back for much longer after that. He had already seen a big change in her from today's session alone. When she got off the table, she stood up straighter than ever before. And the way she walked out the door! Upright and strong; shoulders raised to their full height and her head tilted upwards at an angle that suggested she was ready to meet the world. She normally scurried out.

Paudie hung the towel up but grimaced, squinting in the harsh light invading the room. He walked towards the large window that dominated the space and twisted the blinds until the sun filtered in at a gentler angle. Closing his chestnut eyes, he turned his back to the light, but when he opened them, a small black hole remained at the centre of his vision. It would go in a minute. He cursed the low-lying winter sun, but he was used to this hole by now. It appeared and disappeared, like a magician's trick. He would tell Brigid about his saint's name next week. She would like that.

About the author

Carol Byrne is a writer of fiction from Dublin, Ireland. She has been published in the *Irish Times* and graduated with an MA in Creative Writing from Dublin City University. Books are her lifelong passion so she is fortunate to earn her living by transcribing books into Braille for Vision Ireland's library for the blind.

The Chicken Thief

Sam Cecins

Shortlisted

That morning we found out a hen was missing from the coop.

Her sisters scratched about the dirt and straw while Ma and I made a sweep of the yard. Clucking to each other nervously. Anxiety lingering in the cold air.

It was early and the sun had not yet broken over the hills. Everything tinged blue by the nascent light. The soil had become brittle with ice overnight and our footsteps crunched while we searched.

There were no holes in the fence. No prints or scuff marks or feathers. No blood trail.

We stood there with our arms folded in our thick coats. Our breath steaming in the wan light. Not a clue as to what happened. One chicken raptured from this earth. Pecking seed in the kingdom of heaven. Amen.

'Fox took her,' Ma said eventually. 'Must've been a fox. Damn near invisible if they want to be.'

Lulu was panting and padding up and down the chicken wire fence. She swung her nose low over the ground, pausing to snuffle at the posts. She raised her head to look at us. Her jaws snapping shut with a wet slap. Ears perked up. Knew she'd messed up somehow.

'It's alright girl,' I said, scratching along her hackles. She tensed under my hand but her ears flopped back down and she gazed up at me with her big brown eyes.

'No it isn't,' Ma said. 'What are you good for, if not this? You dopey animal.'

'Should we set traps?' I asked her.

'Maybe,' Ma replied. 'Hopefully it's just moved on.'

'Should we tell Pa?'

'Let's not cause him any worry over a chook,' she said.

It was nearly as cold inside the house as out. Some crack or gap in the clapboard letting the night's chill seep in. I lit the stovetop with a long match and warmed my hands over the flames.

Everything quiet but the guttering whisper of those old gas burners.

Through the window I could see the sun had finally crested the hills. The first rays of daylight piercing through the cloud cover. There was a spiderweb hanging in the corner of the patio rafters, beads of water glittering along its threads like the diamond settings of a necklace.

I set two pans over the burners and fixed his usual breakfast of bacon, scrambled eggs and baked beans. The sizzle and the smell brought Lulu scurrying to my side. She sat there and watched me cook, sniffing at the air hopefully. When it was done, I laid the meal out on a tray and ran the basin full and left the pans to soak in the steaming water.

His bedroom curtains were still drawn. I trod carefully through the murk with the tray balanced in both hands. I thought he might still have been sleeping, but the bedside lamp clicked on and I saw he was sitting up, watching me.

Hard to think of this haggard man as my father.

He smiled, pale and gaunt, as I set his breakfast out on his lap. The skin of his cheeks and nose translucent like wax paper. I could see the blue web of veins beneath. The faint bruises where capillaries had burst. His moustache ashen and drooping.

In my memories he still stood tall with his hairy chest and forearms and his beefy hands held to his hips. Red cheeked and red nosed. Hot blood boiling in him and laughter booming in his throat. All that life and vitality turned inward and spent fighting his own organs.

'Ah yes, excellent,' he all but whispered as he looked over the meal.

'No problem if you can't eat it all,' I said.

'Oh I'll give it my best shot.'

'Okay, Pa,' I said and turned to leave.

'How are the animals?' He rasped. 'Are they all keeping out of trouble?'

When I turned back he was holding up a spoonful of beans. His bony hand trembling.

'They're fine, Pa,' I said.

'Good. That's good,' he breathed.

I could see him thinking of another question to ask, but I made my exit before he could summon the strength.

Ma had stayed outside to feed the animals. She didn't need my help, but I fetched my gloves and coat and wandered outside anyway.

As I passed the stables, the horses stirred and whined to me. I stopped to rub down their muzzles, but they would not be soothed. Flaring their nostrils and snorting. Their breath like puffs of smoke in the cold.

There was a rustle behind us and I turned to see a red-furred fox peering back from the tall grass. It regarded the horses and I with more curiosity than fear. Head cocked to the side. From the fox's jaws the limp body of our missing chicken hung by its neck. A slimy strand of drool and blood dripped from the fox's chin into the dirt.

The fox glanced left and right and then back to me. Sensing no danger, it loped forward from the cover of the grass onto the path and dropped the chicken onto the ground. The horses snorted again and the fox gave us one last wary look before lowering its head and taking a nip at the bird's stomach.

I stamped my foot at it.

'Get out of here,' I cried.

The fox looked up at me, snout glistening red. It bared its teeth soundlessly then resumed eating.

'Go on,' I said, shooing at it. 'Get out of here, mutt.' I stomped my foot a little closer.

Begrudgingly, the fox dipped its head and picked up its meal and loped across the clearing. The carcass of the chicken jostling lifelessly up and down with each bound. It disappeared into the grass on the far side.

'And don't come back,' I called after it.

At sundown Pa came downstairs for dinner. He took each step one by one, clutching the rail with his slender fingers. His breathing already ragged by the time he slumped into his chair.

We ate in silence. Pa managed only a few mouthfuls of stew before he was done. Ma went to the medicine cabinet and fetched a syringe and drew it full from the painkiller vial. She held the needle up to her eye and flicked it twice and then gave Pa his injection while he sat there at the table.

He winced at first, but he slowly sagged lower into his chair. The lines held taut in the corner of his eyes loosened. When he looked at me he might not have even seen that I was there. Like staring through a candle flame to whatever was on the other side.

'Goodnight,' I said to both of them.

'We might stay up and watch a movie or something on the telly,' Ma said. 'Do you want to stay and join us?' She was sitting by Pa's side holding his hand in her lap.

He blinked sluggishly. A labour to simply reopen his eyes.

'I'm a bit tired, Ma,' I said. 'Goodnight.'

'Okay, goodnight.'

I lay restless in bed. Staring at the timber beams. Counting dusty, old cobwebs.

The wind had picked up, spurned by the gathering of some faraway storm. I could hear it moaning over the hills. Whistling through the tree branches.

Somewhere out there I knew the fox was waiting. It had not moved on like Ma had hoped. Crouched among the tall, swaying grass, glint-eyed in the dark and watching the clutch of hens as they slept. Waiting for Lulu to do the same.

After Ma and Pa went to bed, I rose in my bedclothes and crept down the stairs and out to the toolshed. Gusts of leaves and straw chased me down the track. It was probably below freezing. The wind held a sharp edge that made me turn my face away. Cold enough to sting.

I wrestled the metal shed door open and fastened the barrel bolt. Fighting against the pull of the breeze. Lulu had trailed along behind me and she sat at the door opening, peering in anxiously.

I looked over the tools hanging from their hooks or mounted on the pegboard. The old globe buzzing and blinking like Morse code. I settled on the pitchfork. Running a finger over the pointed tips of its prongs.

'Come on,' I said to Lulu.

We patrolled the perimeter of the chicken coop together. Nearly impossible to hear anything over the drone of the wind. After a few laps, I speared the pitchfork into the ground and settled against a fencepost. Folding my arms against the gale. Hair tousling over my face and the hem of my robe flapping like a cape.

The moon hung full in the night sky above. Its silvery light lingering over the passing clouds. I had not realised how tired I was. I closed my eyes and when I opened them I found my head had lolled down onto my shoulder. I stood up a little straighter. Unsure if I had actually drifted off.

A strange sound rose with the wind. Something between a howl and a scream.

It was hard to pinpoint exactly where it had come from. The noise snatched away by the wind. The cry came again. Closer this time. I followed it to the edge of the overgrown field and waded in with the pitchfork raised like a spear. The tall grass rippling in the breeze all around me. Caressing my knees.

I realised that Lulu was not with me. I wasn't sure if I had left her behind or if she had rushed ahead. I looked back at the chicken coop. No dog there.

Perhaps this was a bad idea.

When I turned back, the wind died. Silence and stillness over the field. As if a switch had been flicked somewhere. A circular clearing appeared in the grass before me. I was certain it had not been there before. The light of the full moon now a dusky pink. Diffusing over the field like a bloody haze.

There at the centre of the circle stood the fox. Beneath its clawed paws lay the corpse of a chicken splayed open down the sternum, like it had been vivisected. The fox lifted its face from the guts of the bird and smiled at me. Its teeth somehow square like a human's and shining with gore.

Lying beside the hen was Lulu. Spreadeagled on her back. Ma was there too. Dressed in her nightgown. Eyes fixed in an open stare and lips murmuring an endless soliloquy.

The fox stepped over Lulu and sniffed at Ma's face. It bared its wrong-shaped teeth. I lunged forward with the pitchfork, but the fox did not flee. Instead it looked up at me and opened its strange maw to laugh.

A familiar sound. The booming mirth of my father.

Stolen. Debased.

I woke with a gasp. Shivering. My throat raw from the frigid air.

It was still dark and I was sitting in the dirt with my back resting against the fencepost. Something stirred in my lap and I glanced down to see Lulu's big head resting there. Her eyes were closed and her whiskers twitched while she dreamed.

The wind had mostly abated and it was very quiet. The occasional whine of the gate's rusty hinge. I stood and shook out the cramps in my calves. Everything aching and numb at the same time. The chickens were up and bobbing about the coop. I set about counting them, but I already knew what I would find. I could tell from a glance.

Another hen missing.

Somewhere deep in the stringybark bushland beyond the fields an animal cry rose and fell. A few birds shot startled from the canopy. The sound came again. High pitched and chattering.

You might have mistaken it for a dog's yapping. But I knew no dog barked like that.

No dog ever made a noise so close to laughter.

*

After sunrise, Ma came out from the house and we spent most of the morning working in the crop field.

The last batch of pumpkins had all been killed by frost. An omen of things to come perhaps. The remains of the vines were thawing brown and rotten under the morning sun and as we tilled the soil we tore up the dead vegetation and tossed it into a wheelbarrow.

'I think we should bait some traps tonight,' I said to Ma as we worked. 'Or even head into town and check the noticeboards. See if there's a hunter looking for work.'

'Or a doctor,' Ma said. She bent to pick up some loose stones and toss them clanking into the wheelbarrow tray.

'What?'

'For your head.'

'I'm fine, Ma,' I said, genuinely confused.

'I don't know,' she said. 'You just told me you spent all of last night outside. Middle of winter. Wind blowing a gale. Just so you could spear a fox with a pitchfork.'

'It keeps taking the hens doesn't it?'

'Two hens.'

'Be a whole lot more if we don't put a stop to it now.'

'Well,' she said. 'Since you know so much better than me, why don't you go and ask your pa?'

'I thought you said not to bother him with the chooks?'

'Doesn't seem like you care much about what I say.'

'I'm just trying to help, Ma.'

'You go ask your pa about traps and hunters,' she said. 'And don't forget to tell him about your little hunting expedition, you might actually make him smile.'

She wasn't wrong. When I retold the story to Pa he hacked and coughed for a full two minutes. Laying there in his bed with a fist to his mouth. A pained approximation of laughter.

'The pitchfork?' He wheezed out when he was done. 'What were you going to do with that, beat the poor animal to death?'

'I was just going to chase it off,' I said, feeling a little defensive. 'Stab it, if I could.'

'It's a blunt instrument, my boy. Just because something has a spike, doesn't make it a weapon.'

'Well you don't let me use the shotgun,' I said, looking to the corner of the room where the gun safe stands beside his desk.

My last resort inside, locked behind a hundred-point combination dial.

'That's right,' Pa said flatly. 'I don't.'

'Somebody's got to kill the vermin while you're up here.'

'I suppose so,' Pa said. 'But that person isn't you. You're twelve.'

'I just want to help.'

'Listen,' he said. 'Your mother can handle a measly fox. You just be a good lad and do as she asks, okay?'

'Yes, Pa.'

'And maybe you could spend a bit of your spare time up with me instead of hunting vermin with yard tools? I've been hankering for a good game of chess. Your mother, well, she has other strengths.'

'Okay, Pa,' I said.

'Glad to hear it.'

I laid out the board on his bedside table so we could play. At first he tried to sit on the edge of the bed, but after a while he lay back down and just told me where to move his pieces.

He did not last long. Drifting off to sleep well before the game was over.

I packed up the chess set and returned it to his desk. I paused there. The iron key was poking out of the drawer lock. I pinched the bow of the key between my fingers and looked back over my shoulder. His breath was rattling as he dozed. I turned the key slowly, feeling the bolt slide and click. I pulled open the drawer and slipped out the leatherbound journal. The one where he kept all of his notes.

The serial numbers of the machinery.

The code to the gun safe.

That afternoon, I hiked out into the stringybark woods to lay my trap.

A marbling of storm clouds above. Grey slowly bruising black and swollen.

I settled in behind a thicket of needle bush. Crouched there with the shotgun slung over my shoulder.

About ten metres upwind I had laid a rabbit carcass on the bushland floor. Its hindquarters skinned and intestines exposed. A trail of ants had already discovered the body and begun their slow work on its eyes and tongue.

Nothing to do but wait.

The air was damp and it carried the foreboding smell of coming rain. The faint rumble of thunder rolling down from the hills every now and then.

I had not thought to bring a poncho and my thermos of hot tea was long empty. I was starting to think about returning home to restock when the faintest rustle of leaves caught my attention.

There it was.

The fox's head poked out from the underbrush. Nose twitching as it savoured the smell of my bait. It padded out from the foliage and dipped its snout down to the carcass. It lifted its head up and looked about. Almost birdlike in its movement.

It had not seen me. I raised the gun slowly and eased the pump-action back to check the chamber. Saw the red of the slug and eased the action forward again. I took aim down the barrel, drawing the fox into the iron sight, and exhaled.

I squeezed the trigger.

The shotgun boomed and the barrel kicked up so hard I nearly lost my grip on the forestock. The fox was caught in the cone of the buckshot and went tumbling backwards through the leaves. Limp like a ragdoll.

I reshouldered the shotgun and stalked forward.

It was lying there. Still but alive. Its eyes open and its chest rising and falling slowly. Dozens of small wounds pocked its front leg and shoulder and side. Blood slicking its fur. Some of the pellets protruded through its skin, gleaming red like jewels.

It was whining softly, the way a dog cries. I levelled the barrel at its chest and it looked at me sideways and bared its teeth. A lather of foam seething between them. The effort seemed to exhaust the animal. Its breathing laboured and gurgling.

I took my finger off the trigger.

This was not the square-toothed demon of my nightmare.

A mewling sound came from the undergrowth. When I looked, there was a tiny cub poking its head out from the bushes and whimpering. The fox strained to turn its neck and look at its young. A whinny attempt at a warning bark.

What had I done? Why had I done it?

I reached down towards the fox's fur, intending to examine its wounds. But as soon as I was in reach, the fox struck. Snake quick as its jaws latched onto my forearm.

I hissed as its teeth sunk through skin. Blood welling and then running down to drip from my fingers.

We stared at each other. The fox was growling through its clamped teeth, but its eyes shifted back to its cub. It released its grip and shambled backwards, the front leg that had caught the buckshot bowing as it tried to walk.

I let the gun fall to the ground and raised my palms.

The fox gave me one last look and then it turned and limped away into the bush, the cub trailing alongside, rubbing its face against its parent's blood-wet fur.

I knelt in the dirt and put a hand over the bite and squeezed. It was only shallow and the bleeding soon stopped.

If only all wounds could be healed so easily.

It was dusk by the time I returned to the house. The rain had finally broken, rattling against the roof as I trudged inside.

Ma was waiting at the front door. Arms folded. Mouth pursed into a flat line.

I surrendered the shotgun but marched passed her wordlessly, went to the bathroom and closed the door behind me. There would surely be hell to pay, but I would pay it later.

There was dried blood streaking my shirt. Maybe the fox's. Maybe my own. I stripped it off and left it to soak in the basin. The stains leaching pink whorls into the water.

I looked at myself in the mirror. More blood. Dried flecks and smears of it on my nose and cheeks. Partially melted by the rain. I ran the tap and laved the warm water up and over my hair and let it run down my face and the back of my neck. My hair plastered down over my forehead.

Had it been a fatal shot?

Would I ever know?

I was thankful that the only witness to my tears was my own reflection.

I never saw the fox again.

Perhaps it had just moved on. Away from the danger. Perhaps not.

Not long after the shooting, Pa was moved into a palliative care ward up in the city.

It was a busy and noisy place. Tyres hissing on wet asphalt. Music and chatter and sirens. Everything alight, even at night. The glare of streetlamps and neon signs and car tail-lights. Multiplied by their reflections in the blocky office windows.

His room was stark and white, but there were indoor plants and a television. When I came for my first visit, I brought a chess set too.

He was standing by the window, holding the pole of the drip stand like a walking staff. The tube drooping down from the bag and feeding a needle taped against his wrist. He smiled when he saw me and we sat together at the little visitor's table and set up the chessboard.

'You know, you can do whatever you want with your life,' he said.

'I know, Pa.'

'If you want to go to university or move up here or whatever. You don't have to stay at the farm. Your mother will manage or she can sell the place.'

I said nothing.

'But you are great with the animals and I'm sure your mother would love to have you stay around if that's what you want. I'm just saying, we both want you to live your life the way you want. Wherever that takes you.'

I took his hand in mine. His fingers were cold, but there was a faint warmth in his palm. His eyes tired, but a wry gleam in their centre. A glimpse of his old self, unwithered by drug or disease.

'I'm not going anywhere, Pa.'

About the author

Sam Cecins is an author and communications professional from Perth, Western Australia. His creative work has been shortlisted for the Rockingham Short Story Competition and placed at the Armadale Writers' Award. In 2023 he was named the runner-up in the Best Australian Yarn competition.

Tramlines

Will Cordner

Equal Third Place

His mother believed in symbols. A band of light through the ward blinds at the precise moment of his birth. She named him Ray. No father to discuss it.

She died when he was nine. First stabbed, then poisoned. A pen and its black tar ink. He recognised the plum bruises blooming down her arms. A familiar death, even then.

Roving, miscreant digressions. One failed week of school, unfairly expelled, and later the typical untangling. Eviction from shared houses, stints in jail, long winters of near-death. His first tattoo covered his heart.

He had not yet killed a man but he had failed to save one. He couldn't forget it if he wanted. His hands still trapped the echoes of his labour, the fissures and folds and splits, the colour like honey on toast. They might have been the hands of a musician or a builder, but they were not.

It was the smoke and not the flames. He'd never have guessed it to see them. Giant capering tiger fire blazing feverish in impossible shapes. The heat full on his face. The hiss and the sizzle, the whoosh like a rush of water.

In the morning it began to rain. The house lay in ruins. It was like nothing he'd ever seen. The things it called to mind were scarcely things at all. A pile of old newspapers. A crumpled shoebox. Pieces of a jigsaw puzzle, tipped on the floor.

The constable approached him. Coffee?

No thank you.

You sure?

He took it, but only to hold.

They stood in silence. The low black clouds were lifting. A sudden eruption of light like the spreading wings of some mythical beast.

You did a very brave thing.

He said nothing. The rain had been hiding his tears.

He'd overheard the medics on the phone. The man was dead before he'd even got there. No use trying to revive him or dragging him through the dirt or ever going in in the first place.

The constable turned to leave.

He called after him, dropped his gaze to the mud gathered at his feet. How did it start?

A shake of the head. Hard to say, exactly. Maybe just bloody bad luck.

By sixteen he was completely alone. Jerry the pit bull sheltered. The streets were no safe place for a dog. He began to seek friends in stub ends and green glass, shared morsels in small circles, and while he enjoyed the conversations – the shallow lamplight and the wafting smoke – always he wished for something more.

It still hasn't come.

Now he's thirty and already shrinking. None but the aims of a day, and fewer means. He treads the soft planks by the docks, planks covered in black mould that spreads like fire on the wood and casts invisible smoke to abrade him from the inside. His red eyes are the eyes of a viper. He has to rub them constantly or else keep them shut. The muddy slip-water he gulps from those mottled gloves only leaves him needing more, and the pain grows so severe that there are days when he can scarcely abandon his rumpled brown lawn for even a minute or two. But it's the spores that are killing him – that dense, farinaceous rot – and the longer he stays the worse he becomes. If only he could bring himself to leave, to drag his wrecked hull inland, following the tramlines to where his old friends still live, to where visit nightly the smiling orange angels of his youth.

Oh how he longs to return. At night-time the slick heaving tar cradles the pregnant moon. In those airy hours his mind is cool and clear and he treads the trail of his memory to those corners he's worn out most.

His mother's name was Katherine. Blooming hair the colour of cream and the feel of folded tussah. It used to spill across his face like soft snow. Some nights he can nearly taste it. Those are the nights he forgets his hunger and sleeps.

Waking gasping in the heat he kneels like a beggar on the slats. He craves it, that turbid milkshake, but he cannot keep it down. Always it returns, hot and gushing like lava, and he's doubling over, hocking chunks that catch on the fur of his teeth or his beard. Vagrant.

What they say aloud is: Come here, children. Come away. Stay with me.

He can hardly blame them. He isn't a fool. He knows just how he looks. In the water his buckling reflection conjures impressions that refuse to shallow. Gap-toothed-half-smiling-pale-as-a-ghost in the deadest black of an alleyway. She used to send him alone, trembling with the bills in his pocket. She'd say to him: Keep a coin for yourself my love. But he never did.

If his appearance is the caution, his stench is the blame. A loathsome bogging fetor that draws hands to latching throats and cuts suited men at the waist, like proud capitals reduced to minuscule. These are the men who wander in from the station, who glisten and tint in the sunlight and then fade through blue glass. Each day he sees them and they learn to keep their distance.

Now and then a stroke of luck. A dropped chip, an apple core, a thick crust. Once a bottle of Coke, practically untouched. And sometimes, when the day is warm and the lunch hour melts away on the stove of too much good cheer, a dollar or two, and a nod. He can smell the wine on their breath and he knows it must be the end of the week.

Today is a Monday, and cold. The skeleton trees have spilled their bloody leaves. The wind whips up in the laneways and flees to a streaky sky. He knows he needs to move but he can't find the energy. Instead he puts his hands in his pockets and his knees to his chest. He peers through half-closed eyes but holds out little hope. Perhaps he will die soon.

Once, as a boy, he spent a whole morning following a class of schoolchildren through the city. He kept a safe distance, lurking tree by tree. The only one to notice was a small girl with a purple band in her hair and a bright spotty rash on her cheek. She appeared to have no friends and seemed always to be falling behind. Paying close attention he discovered that her name was Molly.

They stopped for lunch in the museum gardens. The teacher was speaking about ancient Greece but he was the only one really listening. Aeschylus, the father of tragedy, killed by a falling turtle.

His eyes wandered over the children. Molly by herself beneath a tree. She was eating a sandwich and had fruit and biscuits and a small carton of juice. He caught her eye and she gave him what might have been a smile.

Later, much later, he takes to pacing the square. It's night-time and the crowd has long since dispersed. They did a good job cleaning the blood. Plenty more there was than last time. Not quite so much as the time before. Still, it's almost impossible to get all of it, and even in this darkness he can see a few droplets here and there. He stoops like a sleuth to examine them. Well-congealed and looking like egg yolks. He sniffs. No scent. On hands and knees he gazes up to where the man must have fallen from. The stars swirl in a clear sky and it's hard to get a sense of the distance.

What he really wants is to understand, but he suspects he never will. He's spent a good twenty years on it after all. When his mother died he was fostered for a time. He recalls an evening sitting with the father – Ian he thinks — on the front porch. It was his first taste of hot chocolate.

Ian said: It's not your fault son. You know that don't you?

He didn't respond. He'd gulped too eagerly and burned his tongue.

Ian repeated himself.

He began to cry. The truth was he'd never considered it till then.

It's Katherine he thinks of first when he discovers the envelope. No doubt she'd have had some story to tell. *You were meant to find it darling. Of course you were.*

He nearly collapses with the shock. He sits for a moment to gain his breathing. Then he looks out across the square and the water beyond. A boat. Voices. The hum of distant music. The city lights shimmer and twinkle and seem impossibly far away.

He turns his back against the wind. His head is aching. The envelope falls from his hands and he scrabbles like a rat to collect it. At a feeling of being watched he glances around but sees nothing. Suddenly he can smell rain on the way. He staggers round a small corner to a high wall he's slept at before. Then he opens it again.

Money like board-game money, like movie money. Money like the money he used to glimpse in stacks under pillows and lining mattresses and passed from the hands of small men to the hands of large men, the men he used to visit for his mother. Money the colours of ripe fruit. Money you're not meant to see. A dead man's money. Blood money.

Another glance. Still nothing. He begins to count it like dealing out a pack of cards, only no pack is this big and his counting doesn't go nearly high enough. He fumbles a note that catches in a gust and when he reaches for it he nearly drops the lot. *Let it go*, he thinks. *Plenty more*. But still he's annoyed with himself.

He needs to lie down. He slips the money in his underpants and finds the smallest place he can and rests on his back. He can't sleep for worrying so he thinks instead. He thinks about what he might have done for this to come his way and what he might do now it has. He doesn't know where to start. He thinks himself in circles, a delirious spiral, out from the perimeter with its wild ideas and fantasies to the nub end in the middle with its single bare truth. That he is suddenly a rich man.

He knows, somehow, that despite what his mother might have said, despite what he might like to believe, this is not meant to be happening. He takes another moment to consider his options. All of them seem ridiculous, or perhaps there are simply too many for him to properly review. In the end he stays put.

*

He's dizzy now. The rain is here and its smell calls attention to the dryness in his mouth. He thinks about a hotel or a whorehouse or anywhere. He's so wound up that he's frightened. His fear begins to drain him. Time comes when he's grown so tired that he almost wonders if he's dreaming. That's when he pulls out the money again, just to hold it. He feels his nerves calming and his breath slowing, and some time in the pink pre-dawn he falls asleep.

He wakes with a full bladder and when he faces the wall he's surprised by the weight between his thighs and he almost wets himself. He wants to see it again but he resists. Too late in the day, too busy. No longer can he afford to be rash. In his good fortune he has attained the burden of caution. In any case he has already made his decision. It must have occurred to him some time in his sleep. Tomorrow he will go into town.

He sets off at sunrise. Piercing filaments of amber through the fingers of the trees. His shadow strides the road and the hydrants and the doors of passing cars whose passengers gawk unabashed at this gypsy man. But these are rare. It's too early and the streets are too dead.

He has in mind the gardens. He thinks of poor Molly and her terrible rash. He remembers his guilt, the days and nights of it, the way he exploited her loneliness. He's never since eaten so well.

Midday. The money in his pants is making it difficult to walk. It doesn't occur to him to spend it. He goes into a public toilet to wash his face. He takes out the envelope and allows himself a brief look. Then he looks at his reflection. A near illusion. A phantom of no earthly realm. He puts the money in his pocket and goes outside.

He's beginning to realise that he's lost. The hill he was climbing has flattened out to reveal a street he doesn't recognise. He's never made plans before and now he sees he can't. He doesn't know how.

Later. There is the hunger of course, but it's the thirst that is making him sick. He's collapsing, caving in like a house of cards or a kite in too little wind.

What the people say is: Drunkard. Filth. Disgusting.

He knows he can't stay here. He's drawing too much attention. Faces, lines of them, expressions slowly shifting. A timelessness of clocks. He stands beneath them, transfixed – a daisy leaning lonely under a sky of a thousand suns. He hears the sound of trains rattling underground.

Next, a pigeon. Flecked purple and green. Standing stubborn on a bridge rail, buffeted by a high wind. He could touch it if he wanted. He reaches out with his free hand but it's trembling like a candle flame.

Beneath the bridge he spots a rocking johnboat and

a father with his son. The boy's laughter is almost like fright and the boat seems close to keeling over. He passes across the bridge to wait for it to emerge on the other side. The pigeon watches him. The wind gathers. The boat never comes.

Then suddenly a shout. No hint of joy this time. He leans out over the rail and if it looks like he's going to fall nobody tries to stop him. The envelope slides to the edge of his pocket.

Another cry for help. He can't see the boat but he can see movement in the water, an awful seething. The cries grow louder, frenzied, and it's the terror of a sudden silence that propels him to act. Climbing-stepping-falling in a single movement, the water like a gathered carpet rising to meet him.

These are the things he remembers. A pleasant day in sunshine by a body of water. Maybe the beach. Katherine, fair-faced and strong. She carries him into the shallows. He's only young, four or five, and even a little chubby. Still afraid of the ocean. He turns his face from the spray as she wades to her knees and lowers him to the surface.

It's okay, she says. I'm not going anywhere. And then she drops him in.

An hour later she can scarcely convince him to leave. He runs along the shoreline, teasing the tide in sheer delight. There is no sound like his shrieking as he goes to her with his arms outstretched, and when she scoops him up and he turns to face the water it's receding from him, crawling back into itself like a fading thought.

What else? The crowd as he emerged from the river. All those people on the promenade, a whole flock of them like long-necked birds, ten deep with their phones held aloft. They were close to silent at first, or so it had seemed as he clambered out on his hands and knees. He stood for a moment. Nobody quite knew what to do. And then they parted before him. Standing there uncertainly were the father and the son. When they hugged him he smelled the river. He didn't know what they were saying but he could guess close enough and so he told them it was nothing, and they seemed to understand him just as well. He felt the crowd jostling as word spread, bodies pressing inwards. He closed his eyes, breathed deeply, opened them. Another breath, a breath for the collective, an awakening to exactly what had happened. He felt the surge of it, the great mass, so like the swell of the water but for this – no drowning, no clasping, no flailing-choking-tipping the boat and dragging them aboard. Instead the feeling of being held, borne, lifted, and the noise of applause clearer and louder than the old pounding of his heart in his weary head. It filled him up and filled too the space around him, so that he had to lean all the way backwards, as if he were being baptised, just to see clearly the sweet celestial blue of the sky.

*

Other things too that visit him from time to time. The days afterwards, the busyness he'd never known. Questions on a loop and his first time in the front seat of a car. Meals, soap, fresh sheets and new shoes. So many people whose names he couldn't hope to remember. Most of it a blur. And then, finally, a slowing down and the chance to properly rest.

Now he has time to himself again and the freedom to spend it in precisely the ways he would like. So he ventures every evening to the city that had once seemed so far away. He likes the tram and travelling backwards, keeping an eye on the small spaces that pass by on his winding route, growing smaller still until they're gone.

He's on his way there now, sitting in his favourite seat. Suddenly gruff voices behind him. Young men.

You'll never believe what I found the other day.

What?

Two fucking grand. Cash.

No fucking way.

Yep. Just fell down in front of me.

Christ.

He puts on his orange vest and sets up the table at the back of the van. Then he instructs the younger volunteers to begin handing out the hot food while he visits with some of his old friends. So many familiar faces. Some new ones too. A woman of 60 he's never seen before. Black-eyed and slumped.

He walks over to her. Holds out a coffee.

She shakes her head.

Take it, he says. Even just to hold.

The woman doesn't respond and so he leaves it next to her and gives her a moment alone. When next he looks back she's warming her hands on the cup.

Later that night Ray lowers himself into bed. It's the first real bed he's ever had. He plumps his pillow and lets out a sigh. The last thing he thinks of before he falls asleep is this: *If I can save my own life, and the lives of two others, who's to say I can't save them all.*

About the author

Will Cordner is a schoolteacher from Melbourne, Australia, who likes to spend his spare time reading, writing, and following his favourite sporting teams.

The Cat at No 4

Jake Cullen

Shortlisted

For our late brother, Tom Turner

short –

Frank sat on the floor beside the bench, embracing his friend's lifeless body. He gently rocked her, half hoping that she might jump from his arms, shake off her ailments and walk away. Alas, she did not. One lonesome tear fell from his face and landed gently on her fur, the first time he had shown an iota of sadness since his mother's death.

short – a room with no windows or doors. the man searches for an escape.

This past year, Frank had been visiting the bench most days. He would sit on the bench and pour himself some tea from a flask. He would take out his A6 notebook and place it by his side until an idea for a short story, film or novel came to mind. Plots and characters that he thought to be trite and contrived flitted about his brain, yet he was still sure to write them down.

film – EXT NATURE RESERVE, DAY
a tired-looking man sits at a bench and sips his tea.

The ginger cat would poke her head out from a nearby bush each day and join Frank at the bench. He tried to tell himself that it wasn't only because of the ham sandwiches he often shared with her, but also because she felt the same way that he did in her presence – comforted and calm. For Frank, his time at the bench, among nature, with his tea, his sandwiches and his cat friend, was a welcome respite from his home life. The weather changed frequently; a calm air could quickly become riotous and clouds could jostle for blue space before drifting away – never sure where to call home. Frank enjoyed watching the weather do as it wished; he considered it something of a blessing to witness its fickle ways.

Up until last year, he had been living and working in Japan for ten years, teaching film studies, before he returned to England at the news of his mother's sudden passing. A few years before her death, his parents separated and his father seemingly disappeared from the planet entirely. Ever since, his mother's capacity for self-care had declined rapidly. Growing up, Frank could easily recognise when his mother was stressed or feeling down, as she would sit at the kitchen table chain-smoking cigarettes. The kitchen walls had yellowed along with her teeth. Then, with her son in another country and a vanished husband, she was perpetually down and forever smoking. All was blue, all was yellow. *Not the healthiest behaviour for anybody, never mind an overweight asthmatic*, Frank had thought. Of course, he was concerned for his mother, but not so much as to throw away the life he had built in Japan. When he received the news of her death, he felt overwhelming feelings of both sadness and guilt. Sad to know that he would have to leave the life he loved in Japan. Guilty for not mourning the loss of his mother.

novel – a woman's battle with loneliness and depression following the departure of all that she loves.

Frank knew that his return home would not be so brief as attending the funeral and then flying immediately back to Osaka. His mother had no family and, to his knowledge, no friends. He would need to take care of all her possessions, any unpaid debts connected to her name and the matter of selling the family home. Painting the walls and replacing the carpets would be a necessity, since the house reeked of smoke and misery.

Returning to England, Frank noticed how quiet it was where he grew up, how everywhere seemed grey and how it felt like there was nothing to do. He thought then that it might be a good opportunity, what with all the silence and boredom, to try and pursue his dream of writing something worthwhile, like a novel or a film.

film – INT IZAKAYA, NIGHT
a caucasian male slurps udon noodles in a cramped izakaya while reading a translated work of japanese literature. he closes the book and puts it down, on the front cover is a drawing of a cat. through the restaurant window, he sees a man and a woman arguing in the bustling street. the woman falls to her knees. the man disappears through a crowd. the caucasion male stares into his bowl of udon.

He was finding the task of writing difficult. When living in Osaka, he often felt compelled to write, but rarely did, on account of being busy with his job and having a social life. Even if he did find himself with time to write, he was so captivated by his surroundings that he was content to just observe them and to be present in those moments, something he tried to replicate at the bench. These days, sitting at home with no job, no friends, very few opportunities to stimulate his mind and all the free time in the world – though he felt guilty about not working on the house more – he could hardly muster more than a tired plot line.

short – 30-something man relives the same day over
and over again.
fuck off, that's just groundhog day.

As not to let the brief daylight slip by so quickly, and
perhaps to find some inspiration, Frank started to make
use of the small nature reserve atop a hill near his family
house. In Osaka, he only had to walk out the door to
be met by a barrage of sensory stimulants; the smells
spilling from izakaya restaurants, the jingling of bicycle
bells, a clatter of conversations he only half-understood,
dim lights from hanging lanterns and the blinding illu-
mination of protruding street signs. In England, in the
city he once loved, where all the cafes have been turned
into food banks, all the bars now betting shops, all the
libraries shut and all the museums defunded, the bench
became his spot for inspiration, a space for mindfulness,
for stillness.

haiku – dew becomes white mist
best mates with a ginger cat
it will be clear soon

He didn't know if clear was one syllable or two. He
figured nobody would ever see it anyway, so who cares.
Frank wouldn't necessarily call it enjoyable, sitting there
at the bench, but it was an activity that gave his day a

slither of purpose. Here he needn't be concerned with the past or what was yet to come, it was sitting for the sake of sitting — it was for now. There were things he could experience at the bench that he couldn't do so easily in Osaka, too, like greeting dog walkers in his native language, watching squirrels chase each other up and down trees and breathing the fresh scent of the local flora after a night of rain. The one thing that Frank did take pleasure in was having this cat for company. When she came out of the bushes, she slalomed between his legs, rubbed her head against his feet and raised her tail. She would purr like crazy when he reached for his ham sandwiches.

novel – a man and a cat form a strong friendship and work together in a quest to develop a sense of purpose in their unremarkable lives.
*   *who is the man?*
*   *where does their adventure take them? shanghai? asunción? osaka? the past?*
*   *does the cat have an owner? can she speak?*
*   *what are their stories?*
    * note: steer clear of this being an autobiography *

The morning he found her dead was like any other. The only thing out of the ordinary was that when approaching the bench he could see she was lying on the ground, not hiding in the bushes. A burst of sunshine had escaped through the treetops and he assumed that she was soaking it up, the way that cats like to. Except that she was stone dead.

When his mother had died, Frank felt sad about all the ways in which the death would affect him, but this time, he felt different. When he held the cat in his arms he felt a deep sadness, because somebody he cared for had lost their life. He checked her body for any clear signs of physical harm, but he couldn't find any. He had only seen her the day before, she seemed spritely and youthful. *Do cats just drop dead like this?* he wondered. Regardless, he couldn't just leave her body there on the ground to rot. He carried her home, and once there, padded out a cardboard box with spare sheets before laying her in it. He sat on the sofa, tears streaming down his cheeks. Something in the room had changed, but he couldn't put his finger precisely on what. He sensed death in the air; it reminded him of being around his mother. Frank closed his eyes.

film – INT LIVING ROOM, DAY
a man wakes from a nap on the sofa. the living room
walls are covered in maggots and flies fill the air.
a cat's rotting corpse lies in a box beside him. its crusted
eyes open.

Frank was startled awake by knocking at the front door. With sleepy eyes, he hurried to the door and opened it. Standing there was a woman with thick, brown hair tied up in a loose bun, worried-looking eyes and a round face. He vaguely recognised her. She held car keys in her right hand and jangled them nervously.

'Hey, sorry to bother you. I'm Joy, I live at the bottom of our street.'

Frank strained his tired eyes, 'Yeah, I think maybe I've seen you before.'

'Yeah, probably.' She tried to smile, 'I don't suppose you've seen my cat anywhere?'

Frank, half-dreaming, thought about the flies and the rotting corpse in the living room.

'I don't think so, what does she look like?'

'She's ginger,' Joy said. 'If you see her, just call her name. She's called Cyndi.'

'Cyndi, that's nice.' Frank said sincerely.

'Yeah,' Joy began to walk back out towards her white car. 'Listen, I need to head off. Just call her name, she will probably think you've got food or something and come running over. If you don't mind cats, just pick her up and bring her to my place. I live at number four.'

The number four and the word death darted about Frank's drowsy brain.

It sure sounded like the deceased cat in Frank's living room was the one she was searching for.

'Sure, no problem. I hope you find her,' Frank said, knowing very well that she wouldn't.

Joy smiled, said thank you and got into her car.

short – a man finds the corpse of a cat and, inexplicably, lies to the cat's owner about having done so. the man must fix the mess he has made.

For the next few days, Frank didn't dare leave his mother's home in case he bumped into Joy and had to lie again. In the living room, things started to smell. The air had become thick with death, clinging to the walls and burrowing into the carpet. Frank kicked himself for lying in the first place, but what was he supposed to do? Was he supposed to tell the woman that yes, in fact, he had seen her cat and that she was dead and in his living room? Having spent a year in pretty solitary conditions, Frank had no idea how he would build the confidence to head down to number four and tell Joy the truth. He told himself he was just out of practise in social situations, yet in truth he had never been particularly confident or assertive.

More days passed and the stench in the living room spread throughout the entire house. Cyndi's fur had started to brown and flies began to gather. Frank knew what cats were like, his family had them growing up, and if one ever went missing for longer than a week, the chances of seeing it again were slim. Maybe Joy would realise that soon enough. Besides, at this point, with the cat's body deteriorating, he couldn't possibly imagine knocking at Joy's door with a rotting corpse in his arms. She might even think he had been responsible. However, Cyndi was Frank's friend, someone whose company he valued and he would miss her dearly. He could not simply let her rot in such an undignified manner. Frank decided that he would bury her somewhere special, a place with sentimental value.

film – EXT NATURE RESERVE, NIGHT
a man takes a trowel from a backpack and begins
to dig a hole in the ground next to a bench. on top
of the bench sits a box padded with bedsheets.
inside the box is the body of a decaying cat. the
man lifts the cat from the box and wraps the sheets
around her.

MAN
i'm sorry, cyndi.

he places the cat in the hole and fills it with dirt. using
his hands, he flattens the mound of dirt. a few tears
drop from his eyes and hit the ground. the man sits
on the bench and looks up at the clear night sky. an
expanse of stars hang there like a million cat's eyes.

MAN

*why did we never come here at night? osaka could
never offer me this.*

Having said a proper goodbye to his friend, Frank felt
a sense of closure, like the curtain to this part of his life
had closed. He did feel guilty, however, that Joy never got
to say goodbye to Cyndi. The morning after the burial,
Frank took his absent father's toolbox and began to rip
up all the carpet with the claw end of a hammer. After a
while, the smell of dust kicked up from the floorboards
beneath began to overpower the other stenches that had
lingered for too long. The house was finally shedding its
dead skin and Frank felt happy for it. Once all the carpet
had been torn up and put outside, he went under the
stairs and found all the half-pots of paint his mother had
left from her attempts at redecorating, before she lost
motivation. The walls would be his next job, but first,
there was something else he needed to take care of.

Frank mustered the nerve to walk down the road
and knock at number four. He was going to ask her if
she would like to go on a walk to the nature reserve at
the top of the estate. He found her house, with the brass
'four' next to her red door, and was reminded that in
Japan, the number four was rarely seen in such a way.
It was seen as an unlucky number. When said aloud,
the Japanese word for four sounded like the word for

death, and as a result, the number was seldom used for houses, plane seats or elevator levels. He knocked at her door and she answered. She didn't look as sad as before. She greeted Frank with a wide smile.

'Hey, Joy. How are you?' Frank said, the words coming out heavy and jumbled like they were nuts and bolts in his mouth. 'I was wondering—'

'About Cyndi? Oh, don't worry about her.'

Frank narrowed his eyebrows, confused.

Joy smiled at her feet, 'Hey, baby.'

At her feet, a ginger cat, with the same youthfulness as the one recently deceased, slalomed between Joy's legs.

'She came back this morning. Didn't you, baby?' she said excitedly, crouching down and tickling under the cat's chin.

'I see, so this is Cyndi?' Frank replied, confused.

'She certainly is, isn't she adorable?'

Frank smiled, 'Yeah, she is.' Frank paused for a moment. 'I just wanted to check if you had found her. I'm glad she's alright.'

Joy thanked him for his concern.

The cat paused between Joy's legs and her eyes met with Frank's. Frank couldn't be sure, and neither could Cyndi, but they stared at each other with a vague sense of recollection.

'I think she likes you,' she said, looking from Frank and back to Cyndi. 'Do you like our new friend, baby?'

At home, he made some tea, some ham sandwiches and packed them in his backpack alongside his notebook. He left the house and walked up to the nature reserve. He could see the area of dirt where he had buried his ginger friend the night before, the same as he left it. *What was I expecting, an empty hole and a note?* he asked himself. He sat at the bench and poured some tea. Clouds rolled across the sky like a delicate tide and treetops billowed in the breeze. Frank held the tea near his mouth and felt the heat rising and kissing his cold nose. *It's good to be here*, the voice in his head spoke. He thought back to his time in Japan, and all those Japanese novels he used to read. He remembered how in a lot of those novels, there were cats, cats just hanging out in the background, cats who could speak, cats that could walk on their hind legs and cats whose significance almost always had an impact on the narrative.

He thought about the cat who he had befriended and he thought about the cat that belonged to Joy. He couldn't decipher what had happened, whether there were simply two cats that looked alike or whether something unimaginable had taken place. Frank wondered whether he was in some kind of realm that allowed for reincarnation, or maybe where time, physical bodies and consciousness were not linear, where they were abstract concepts that could overlap, bend, be manipulated and influenced – just like thoughts. Where yesterday and tomorrow needn't be haunting us in the shadows. Our stories, time, maybe they're cyclical, perhaps whatever happened yesterday or what will happen tomorrow doesn't matter, we may just find ourselves back in the same place; purring between our owner's legs, slurping noodles in Osaka, seeing our mothers again, sitting on our favourite bench. So much uncertainty sat with Frank, uncertainty about the nature of all things, yet one thing was clear – he felt like he had a worthwhile story to write.

short – i sat on the floor beside the bench, embracing my friend's motionless body. i gently rocked her, half hoping that she might jump from my arms, shake off her ailments and walk away.

About the author

Jake Cullen is a writer of fiction from Stoke-on-Trent, England. His writing draws from experiences growing up in an underprivileged, working-class environment and his time spent living in China. He has an MA in Creative Writing and his short fiction has been included in various anthologies.

Wetlands

Kristen Dagg

Shortlisted

The staccato helicopter blades slice through the night. Police sirens get closer and come from several directions.

Usually these sounds barely register. We live in the city.

Not tonight.

I know exactly what they're here for. To find my daughter.

A slip of a thing, willowy and long haired. Angry and scared.

The wild disbelief that helicopters and police cars are looking for my baby is overshadowed by sharp, full body throbs of panic. They tell me to wait by the car in case she comes back. I don't want to do this. I want to run into the wetlands and scream her name over and over.

But I'd already done that, before I'd shakily typed in three numbers: 000.

It's dark in there, and from my vantage point I can see flashes of torchlight like fireflies, hear her name being called by voices I don't recognise. The name I'd chosen for her and that she'd grown into so beautifully in her tender thirteen years.

Hazel.

My delicate girl, of body so new, mind so tormented.

'Can you tell us what she was wearing?' The female officer coaxes me, gently. She is young, her hair scraped back into a bun. A gun sitting comfortably on her hip. Constable Blake is her name. She is calm because she wants me to be calm too.

'Green cargo pants and a black hoodie.' The words come out with a stutter.

The oversized hoodie to hide the cuts, to swallow herself, which she'd started wearing all the time.

'And how tall is she? What colour is her hair?'

'She's tall. Her hair is long and blonde, or light brown.' It needs a trim. It's unwashed and unbrushed, hanging over her angry, sad and sometimes vacant eyes.

'Does she have a phone?'

'No.'

I'd taken it, which is why we're here. Huddled over it at late night, or locked in the bathroom, always typing furiously and angling her body so I couldn't see.

I was scared.

I hear her father's truck before I see it. I expect he'll think I've gone too far calling help.

But his face mirrors mine.

The kids are all we share now. The only thing that binds us together in our very separate lives.

Earlier in the day we'd disagreed about the phone and the computer. Isolation wasn't working, I'd said. *We have to stay strong,* was his response. Maybe *strong* wasn't what we needed to be.

'Is she a danger to herself?' Constable Blake asks.

I nod.

'She said she was going to run into traffic. That's what she said.'

My stomach squeezes in the spot that always hurts lately. A small and painful hole where I keep all my worry.

She'd opened the door of the car on the highway, despite my arm over her thumping chest. I'd sensed it, her body tense and ready, her eyes wild and darting side to side, planning, calculating.

We'd been heading to my mum's place. I thought she could help us, or just provide distraction. She always had a cup of tea ready. How stupid I was to think a cup of tea would help.

I'd lost my hold on her jumper, and she was gone, and I screamed her name.

I'd pulled into a side street and leapt out, leaving the door open. My fly was undone from trying to seek some relief from the poison in my belly. I ran along the busy road, pants falling down, calling her name over and over. It would have been funny under other circumstances. Maybe it will be one day.

She is fast, my girl. A runner. She has grace and stamina. A cliché, sure, but she *is* a gazelle. I was slow, clumsy, out of breath. But the panic made me fight my lack of fitness. And I caught her, briefly.

I grabbed her arm, too hard.

'Don't touch me,' she cried.

'Please don't leave me,' I begged her over and over, hands circling her fragile wrists, trying to pull her closer to me. We both understood this meant *please don't die*.

The cars whizzed by, drivers perhaps curious at the strange scene by the tyre shop in the fading light, or maybe not noticing at all, caught up in their own thoughts and lives.

'Leave me alone.'

But she was still, breathing hard but not fighting.

It was a trick, though, and as soon as I loosened my grip she was gone. I marvelled at her speed and was crippled by it.

She ran the opposite direction into bushland, not traffic. But the wetlands are a maze of deep water and winding paths. Night comes too fast.

*

How did we get here? How did I miss it getting this bad?

It was the sleepless nights, at first. And not getting out of bed in the morning, not wanting to go to school. But, at thirteen, that's pretty normal, isn't it? There were mean girls and getting in trouble with teachers and a boy online.

And then, silence. It was as though her head was heavy and she didn't have the strength to lift it. To speak. There was no contact with friends, only hushed whisperings behind closed doors that stopped when she sensed me there, hovering.

When she ran, I tried to follow, so pathetically far behind.

I called my mum. What else could I do?

'She ran,' I cried, desperate for her to understand and not able to get the words out.

'What do you mean?'

I didn't have time for this.

'She's run into the bush near your place. Please help me, Mum.'

I hung up.

And, mercifully, she understood.

Dark loomed, night-time sounds and smells coming with it, and I'm crashing through narrow trails, which were normally charming in daylight but now terror-inspiring.

I was trying, unsuccessfully, to push away the image of her face down in the shallow water. The bush is safer than the road, yes, but it has its own dangers. And the highway still isn't far. More horrific pictures flash in my mind; hard metal hitting her soft body. The sound of screeching tyres.

'Hazel!' I'd called. And then I heard my mum's voice too. We were night birds, calling to each other in the dim light.

Mere minutes had passed. But I knew it was time to call the police. To call her father. He was harder to call than 000. He would think I had failed her.

'We'll find her,' the constable says. And I don't think she's allowed to say that, is she? To give false hope. She's trying to comfort me, and it works.

But what if she's wrong?

I'm angry that I have to wait, and her father gets to look for her.

'I knew this would happen,' was all he said.

I ignore him.

It's only minutes and I watch them click slowly up on the car dash. 6:24. 6:25.

'Has she done this before?' The officer asks.

'No. Sort of. She tried to get out of the car at the lights yesterday.'

She nods. It feels like she is judging me. How does a child become so desperate as to want to jump out of a car?

But she's not, of course. She's only young herself. She must remember the feeling of being trapped and no one able to understand you.

A call on the radio.

'They've found her,' she says, touching my arm. I wish she would hold on tighter because my legs are weak. They are jellyfish tendrils. I make a strangled sound and the tears are hot.

The police have her at the edge of the park and I try not to hit the car on anything as I navigate the narrow street. My hands are too shaky for the wheel.

A little figure in the dark, lit up by the blue and red lights. She's bent over like an old woman. She doesn't want to exist.

I hold her as tight as I can and we cry. Then her father hugs her. We are careful not to touch each other.

She's cold and she's hurting and nothing is solved except she knows she is loved.

It's not enough.

The hospital needs to check her out and an ambulance arrives.

'I just want to go home, Mum,' she cries, exhausted.

The ER we end up in seems to be for people with mental health issues. Behind curtains we hear cries of anguish and sounds of struggle and panic. Hazel and I are silent, hands white from holding on so tight. A young man goes by on a stretcher nursing a bloodied arm followed by a worried looking woman. His sister, perhaps. She chews her nails and watches him. He is talking fast about things I can't understand, to people I can't see.

Police and paramedics stand around, chatting and making jokes. This is just another night for them.

Hazel eats a packaged cheese sandwich, leaves the tuna one. She hates tuna. We both do.

She tells lies to the psychiatrist in the dull, fluoro lit room with no air. She's fine. She doesn't need help. I know she wants to get out as soon as possible so she can run again. But there is no plan after that, no logic.

He gives her something to sleep. He refers us to a place that helps with teens in trouble. We ask if she can stay there. But it's the weekend and there are no beds, and he says that she really shouldn't go into one of those places to stay, anyway. Sometimes kids come out worse than when they went in.

I'm frightened to go home with her, the car trip especially. I don't know if I can keep her safe. At home, my partner, Alex, hugs us both. She lets him, but her arms dangle at her sides. She won't look at me.

She yells that I don't understand, and she doesn't love

me, never has. Her sleeping meds are thrown at the wall, along with the things she loves, or used to.

I try not to, but I cry.

'She doesn't mean it,' Alex says as I wipe my snotty nose on his shoulder. He doesn't mind.

We begin to guard the front and back door as she stalks around the house, looking for an escape. I sleep on a mattress outside her room. We hide anything sharp in the house, but she still finds things to harm her soft, baby skin.

She says she'll stab us in our sleep. I prefer her angry, because when she cries for hours without letting me in, it's worse.

The counsellor on the crisis line says we need to do anything we can to keep her alive.

So, I return her phone, just a couple of hours a day.

Her father is angry at me. We're both scared all the time. Our fragile peace, only possible through this, is over.

She is calmer. But we're back to where we were, and it feels like nothing will ever be okay again. I've made mistakes and will keep making them. Trying to help her feels like a big experiment with too many variables. The stakes are too high.

Her little brother doesn't want to be around her. She is awful to him. He's frightened. He doesn't want to stay here anymore.

I miss his smell. I miss knowing which socks he wears each day.

We find a good psychologist and, slowly, Hazel finds her voice. The counsellor is kind and softly spoken, but she's firm, too. She asks the questions I can't bear to.

'Mum, did you ever want to die?' Hazel asks me.

I pretend to think, but I know the answer.

'Yes. When I was fifteen. When Kurt Cobain died, I thought maybe I shouldn't live anymore.'

'That's stupid.'

'I know. But it was real at the time.'

One morning, I hear her singing in the shower. I sit outside on the floor with my ear to the door.

There are meds and appointments and family counselling and a school change.

There are relapses and not eating and tears and night cuddles.

But we carry on, day by day.

Hazel loves makeup and music and eating chips in our bed, which drives us mad. She likes to make biscuits. The black hoodie, I notice, is scrunched up in the corner of her room. I don't mention it.

The angry red lines on her skin fade to white.

She finds new friends who op shop and want to explore railway tunnels and abandoned houses. I worry about this, but they're real people, not online strangers. They're not the rich girls from her last school. They're not the boy who tried to destroy her.

Her little brother comes for a visit and they lock themselves in her room. They laugh hysterically at TikTok videos I will never understand. When I open the door they're silent, but it's different. They're good secrets.

We're in the car. I no longer hold my breath with a sideways glance when we're stopped at a red light.

'You know how you said I'd find my people, Mum? I've found them.'

My heart shatters into a million tiny butterflies. It hurts because it's so full.

I squeeze her hand and she squeezes back.

We are not perfect and we never will be.

But we are okay.

She is okay.

About the author

Kristen Dagg is a television writer, director and producer living in Sydney, Australia with her teenagers, rescue mutts and a boyfriend who, quite frankly, rescued her. She has been writing for many years for various online publications, has had several short stories published and is currently working on her third novel.

Jam It

Bronwyn Hall

Shortlisted

W hen I answered the doorbell, it was to discover everyone had arrived at once. Of course they had — if someone wanted to hide, Fate knew to send a crowd.

The two women standing on my front porch were unknown to each other. One had steel grey hair, sensible clothing and a purposeful energy that spread steadily like mist from a diffuser. She held a birdcage with a fledgling magpie squatting sleepily in a towel nest on the bottom.

The other woman was much younger, her straight, brown hair healthy and shiny, her clothes neat. In one hand, she held a suitcase, the other rested on the shoulder of a twelve-year-old girl. I knew the girl's age because I'd been told on the phone by the agency. Her energy was evident in the dart of her gaze, the tension on her face — it leaked out despair.

'Here you go, Cath,' said the woman with the birdcage. She held it out to me. 'This one's quite straightforward and he should heal up in no time.'

'Thanks, Sharon.' I took the cage. The bird opened his eyes to stare at me with a black, glittery gaze for a few seconds, then he faded back to sleep.

'Right,' said Sharon, wiping her hands on her shirt. She sent a curious glance at my other visitors and offered them a polite smile before her gaze came back to me. 'I can see you're busy, so I'll get out of your hair.' She gestured to the cage. 'Ring me if anything crops up, otherwise I'll be back in four weeks to pick him up.'

'No worries. I have everything I need.'

'Great. Bye then.'

She sent another smile towards the younger woman and the girl, but without me offering an introduction she didn't try to engage before she marched off my porch and out the driveway, taking the crowd factor with her.

I switched focus to my other visitors.

'Hi,' said the younger woman. 'I'm Zoe. And this is Kira.' Her voice was carefully calm with exactly the right amount of this-is-all-going-to-be-fine, to reassure Kira she was in a safe place.

Kira's gaze fell to her shoes. It made me realise this wasn't her first time being fostered. She'd already learned the Zoes sprinkled through her life might or might not know how this would really pan out for her; they had to hope for the best as much as she did.

I had hope too, but I didn't rely on it. As a foster carer, I'd been vetted via police and working with children checks; my home assessed as safe. In the beginning, passing all the checks had reassured me I was adequate, but now, about to start my sixth foster relationship, I knew that when going toe-to-toe with the kinds of trauma the children brought with them, to be *adequate* was only a hair's breadth ahead of failure.

'Hi Kira,' I said. 'My name's Catherine, but everyone calls me Cath.'

She barely glanced at me.

'Do you want to come in?' I stepped back with the birdcage so they could enter.

Zoe only came in as far as the entry hall, where she parked the suitcase against a wall. 'I'd better get going,' she said. She turned to Kira. 'Okay, hon, I'm off. Cath's going to look after you now.'

'For how long?' said Kira, verbally grabbing for a lifeline. Something to tie herself to. Something she could work with – break down into days, hours, minutes – until she could go back home.

But Zoe had no lifelines to throw. 'I don't know, hon, but only as long as it's needed.'

A younger child might have cried, but Kira kept her tears firmly inside. I shouldn't have been, but I was grateful. None of us enjoy these moments – when children are passed from one stranger to another – these pinpricks of pain along the way.

Zoe handed me a folder. 'All the details about the school and everything are in here,' she said, 'and I'll email a second copy when I get back to the office just in case.'

'No problem,' I said. 'I'll get in touch if I need to.'

'Okay, well you two have fun, then,' she said. She aimed a final, positive smile at Kira.

Kira hugged her arms over her chest, digging her fingernails into her triceps. She didn't say goodbye but watched through the doorway until Zoe had driven away. It was only when I closed the door that she turned to look at me, and we each took a couple of seconds to size each other up.

She was thin and about average height for a twelve year old. Her hair was dark and straight, and her eyes were a rich shade of brown – the shadows underneath visible emotional bruises in the paleness of her face. Her fingers, still pinching her own skin, were surprisingly long and slender, and her body showed the clues that puberty was readying itself for ambush.

I don't know what it was she saw, but given I was fifty-two and happily grey, she probably thought I was ready for the grave.

'So,' I started us off on some neutral territory, 'I don't

suppose you could think of a name for the magpie, could you?'

Her gaze travelled to the cage and the bird inside. 'It looks like it's dying.'

'Mm.' I eyed the bird as well. His head was sagging sideways on his neck. That and the fact he was scrawny, and his feathers were still grey with youth, made him look old and frail to anyone not well acquainted with magpies. 'It does look like that, but it's only because he's been sedated. We can't see it because he's sitting on it, but apparently he has a broken leg. He's just come from the vet, who's put it in a splint.'

'Why's he here, then?'

'He needs someone to look after him while it heals.'

'Why didn't he stay at the vet?'

The questions were safe. The bird wasn't her.

'The facilities aren't right and it's too expensive,' I said. 'I do it for free.'

'Will he be here as long as me?' she fished, checking whether I'd been told more than she had about her length of stay.

'I don't know,' I said truthfully, and her mouth sagged. 'It'll take about three or four weeks for his leg to mend. But he'll have to learn to forage and fly, so at some point, he'll go into an aviary. A bigger cage.'

'I know what an aviary is.' She turned to her suitcase and grasped the handle. 'Where will I be sleeping?'

We were still standing in my front entry. There was an open door leading off it, which led to what I called my office, although there wasn't much in it except for the desk and chair, and a hallway that stretched towards the rest of the house. I picked up the cage to bring the bird with us.

'That's my bedroom.' I waved at doors as we passed. 'That's the bathroom, the toilet's in there, that way's the kitchen and the lounge, and here——' I stopped at another door '——is your room.'

I put the birdcage down while she preceded me in with her suitcase. The room was nice in a soft and tidy way. There was a king-sized single bed against one wall, a colourful checked quilt on it, a white chest of drawers, some shelves with knick-knacks and a built-in wardrobe. Given its purpose, the furnishings were intended to be gender neutral and acceptable to an occupant within the primary school to late-teen age range.

Kira's head moved slowly as she took it all in and, when her shoulders slumped, I sighed silently, seeing what she saw. Nothing more than the fact it wasn't her room at home.

'How about I let you unpack while I sort out this bird, and when you're ready, come and find me in the kitchen,' I said. 'We can have a drink and something to eat.'

'Okay,' Kira said.

Unpacking was another reminder that she wasn't here just overnight, and I gave her some privacy while she sorted her things into the drawers and the wardrobe.

I carried the bird with me back to the kitchen, which took up the rear half of an open lounge and dining space. I lived in the hills on the far outskirts of the city and my block dropped down at the back, giving a view out over the sloping bushland from every window. Another person may have landscaped in a lawn and garden beds, but aside from the fact I didn't have the time and energy to maintain anything like that, I much preferred the native bush. And so did the various animals that passed through.

I put the magpie's cage down near the window and saw he was now awake. He wasn't trying to get up yet, but his eyes were open and when our gazes met, he opened his beak and let out a plaintive cry. At his age, it was a cry that would have brought his parents had they been around.

'I'm sorry,' I told him, 'It's only me for the time being, I'm afraid.'

He squawked again.

'Okay, I'll get you a snack too,' I said. I went to the fridge and retrieved some chopped lean steak I'd had ready for his arrival. Using tweezers, I picked up a tiny piece, dipped it in protein powder made from ground insects, and held it out to him. The magpie looked at it but when he didn't open his beak to be fed, I left both the tweezers and food in the bottom of the cage. I wasn't worried. He'd eat when he'd had a chance to settle and was hungry enough.

A little while later, Kira came out and I made her cinnamon toast. It was old-fashioned and she looked dubious, but she gave it a try, and it made me happy when she ate three pieces. The afternoon tea also gave us time to run through her routine, which was basically just going to school. She was in her first year at high school and she'd been given the day off today, but she'd be back in class from tomorrow. I checked about dance classes, or swimming lessons, or sport, but she only shook her head.

'I don't like dancing or sport stuff,' she said. 'And I finished swimming lessons in like, grade two.'

'Okay,' I said, 'so there's nothing else you do?'

'You mean, besides being forced to go see the counsellor two times a week?' she asked, her voice tinged with heat. 'No, I don't do anything else.'

There were very few questions I ever asked the young people who came through my house – their journeys were often too fraught to share. It was always just the basics; just the information I needed. But there was one I always asked, just in case.

'Do you have any brothers or sisters?'

Kira's face clouded and she looked out at the bush beyond the window. 'I have an older sister. She's nineteen but she can't look after me. She's on drugs and she doesn't talk to me and my mum anymore.'

From that snippet, I figured that her father was also out of the picture – it was likely just her and her mother.

While I tidied up the few dishes, Kira took a wander around the lounge. There was a wood burner in the corner that would soon be in use in the evenings, as autumn trudged towards winter. A pair of comfortable pale green sofas were placed at right angles to each other – only one offering a good view of the TV – and some built-in shelving took up a whole wall. The shelves mostly held books but some of my favourite photos were also there, and Kira went to take a closer look.

'Are these your kids?' she asked, peering at an old photo showing my son and daughter at the beach when they were very young.

I smiled. 'Yes.'

'What are their names?'

'Eliza and Timothy.'

She went further along the shelves, looking at the others. She stopped at a larger one showing my much older, grinning daughter all gowned up at her university graduation. My ex-husband and I were also in that one, standing behind her, each with a hand on her shoulder.

Kira glanced back along the other photos. 'How come there're so many of Eliza and hardly any of Timothy?'

'He died,' I said. Said like saying it was easy. Seventeen years should have made it easy. But they hadn't — only easier to pretend.

Kira stared at me, and in her eyes, I saw her dreading having to deal with my pain. She had enough of her own.

'It's okay,' I said in reassurance. 'It happened a long time ago. He had leukaemia.'

'Where does Eliza live?'

'Not too far away. She's a teacher now.'

'What about him?' She pointed to my ex-husband in the photo, and I heard an undercurrent of trepidation that made me wonder about the other men in her life. Thankfully, she didn't need to be concerned about Eliza's father.

'We split up,' I said. 'I'm not actually sure where he lives these days. He moved to Queensland, but I don't know if he's still there.'

'Did you split because Timothy died?'

Astute. 'Yes.' It was a simple answer that didn't describe the despair, the anger, the *incredulity* of how our love — our bond — had shattered under the load of that pain. The shrapnel had wounded Eliza deeply — for many years, her father had left her, too.

The magpie squawked and tried to get to his feet. He wobbled and sat down again, but not before we had the chance to see the blue tape wrapped around his left leg. He opened his beak in a pant.

'He really needs a name,' I said.

Kira went to squat down next to the cage and rested her hand on the wire. The bird cocked his head, wary of human fingers.

'He looks sad,' she said.

'He does a bit,' I agreed. 'But he'll be okay. His head's probably still fuzzy from the anaesthetic when the vet put the splint on. As soon as he's had some rest, he'll pick up.'

I wanted to reassure her – to remove any looming pressure that the bird was in real danger. I'd had them die on me before, but usually that was when they were in significantly worse shape than this one appeared to be.

'Will you fix him?' said Kira.

'Well, not exactly,' I said. 'It's only my job to care for him. Make sure he's safe and secure so he has the chance to fix himself. It's all he needs – his body's quite capable.' It was the same for humans. Mostly. Painfully, not for Timmy. Helping the wildlife kept me from sinking into the quicksand of *why him?* The animals were my key to knowing that survival and healing were an inbuilt part of nature; they reminded me it was only sometimes that nothing could be done.

Kira wiggled her fingers, keeping the bird's attention, then her hand drooped. Her gaze drifted out the window and slowly went vacant as her thoughts claimed her focus. It was then that her face revealed where she was really at. Sadness weighed down the corners of her eyes, and anxiety compressed her mouth, but what looked overwhelming was her fatigue. Not the physical kind, although that was there too; the other kind that came from being on guard for too long.

It wasn't a requirement of the foster carer role that I ached for the kids who came to my house, but inevitably with each of them, there were clear moments where I did. But I never showed it. They might need shelter and food and transport and regular adult intervention, but the one thing they did not need was pity. That was salt water to their iron cores – a potent corrosive agent.

'You know what magpies like?' I said, and Kira's focus came back into the room, her attention finding me. 'It's watching TV. Do you want to bring him over?' It was an excuse to shift her out of her own thoughts, and I was grateful it worked when she picked up the cage and followed me into the lounge.

I located the remote and showed her how to use it. 'I have Netflix, Binge and Stan so hopefully you can find something that you both like.'

I loitered in the kitchen until she'd flicked through multiple options and landed on *The Baby-Sitters Club*. When I left the room to go to my office, the bird was watching the screen attentively, and Kira had taken her shoes off, and was sitting on the couch with her knees tucked under her chin.

My job was freelance copywriting, primarily working with real estate agencies to write descriptions of the properties they were trying to sell, and the flexible hours working from home suited my other commitments. Today, I had more emails than I expected, and I took my laptop with me back to the kitchen table so I could keep an eye on things. The magpie was still engrossed with the babysitters, but Kira was curled on her side, fast asleep with her head on a cushion. In sleep, her face was smooth and uncluttered – an aspiration of what it should look like when she was awake.

I worked for the next hour and a half. After that, I packed up and started preparing dinner. The bustle of the fridge and pantry doors opening and closing, the chopping and the sizzling – it was enough to eventually rouse Kira from her nap and, as soon as that happened, she was alert and standing.

'What time is it?' she said, anxiety in her voice.

'About six o'clock,' I said, but she already had her phone out and could see.

'My mum didn't ring. She said she would try at five-thirty.'

'I'm sure she will as soon as she can,' I said.

Kira's face caved with resignation. 'No. She won't. I told her they'd take her phone away as soon as she got there. They always do.'

Without knowing *where* there was, the logic confused me. I didn't understand why she'd been expecting a call if she believed her mother wouldn't have the means. Kira misread the confusion on my face.

'She's not in jail or anything,' she defended. 'She's in hospital. She's sick. She gets sick sometimes and she has to go. She can't stay at home.' The words rained on me like hail pellets – cold and with sting.

'Right,' I nodded, carefully avoiding showing emotion. 'That makes sense.' And it did. Patients in a regular hospital would be allowed to keep their phones and I guessed Kira's mother was in a different kind of place, that her illness was likely psychiatric. It also explained why Kira had hoped for a call. Her mother being allowed to ring was Kira's last hope that the hospital might not have admitted her, deeming her healthy enough to not require it. A phone call would have meant Kira knowing when she could go home.

'Is she allowed to have visitors?' I asked.

Kira shook her head, and her voice went carefully flat. 'It upsets her. She tries to . . . to hurt herself.'

Her words opened a window, one that allowed me a sudden glimpse into what had caught the attention of child protection services. I nodded. 'Okay. I understand.'

Aroused by the smell of cooking, the magpie let out a squawk and Kira picked up his cage and brought him into the kitchen with her. As soon as she put the cage on the ground, the bird stood up. He wavered for a moment, his rigid leg pushing him off balance, but then righted himself and squawked again.

'He's mad he's here and stuck in a cage,' Kira said.

Her voice told me she felt the same way.

'He might just be hungry.' I deflected. 'Do you want to try to feed him?'

She pointed at the meat in the bottom of the cage. 'He's already got food.'

'I know, but he's too young to have learned to feed himself. He'll be used to his parents giving it to him, so we'll have to do it.'

'You mean, like I should pick it up and hand it to him?'

'You'll need to use the tweezers, and when he opens his beak, you just drop it in.'

'Dumb bird,' she muttered. But she squatted down and unlatched the tiny door of the cage and put her hand in. When the bird hopped towards her, she quickly pulled it back out. The bird cocked his head and gaped, asking to be fed. Warily, Kira put her hand back in and picked up the tweezers. She picked up some of the meat and tentatively dropped it in the magpie's mouth. He swallowed it in a gulp, before cocking his head and gaping again, asking for more.

Kira looked over at me, her face aglow with a grin. 'He ate it!'

I smiled back. 'He must feel safe with you.'

Her smile stayed on her face as she fed the magpie some more, repeating the process until the meat had all gone and our own dinner was ready.

'It'll only be a week or so of that, and he'll look a lot healthier,' I said, putting two bowls of pasta on the table.

Kira left the magpie and came to sit down. She looked at her food. 'It's normally chicken nuggets,' she said. 'Or party sausage rolls. It's like there's a manual or something that you're all supposed to follow.'

'There kind of is, but I don't like chicken nuggets. Sorry.'

'It's okay. I'm sick of them anyway.'

I'd kept it simple, and we were having spaghetti carbonara. Even if they hadn't eaten it before, the kids were usually okay with the egg, bacon and cream sauce, and I used regular tasty cheese instead of parmesan. As a contingency, tonight we also had garlic bread.

The bird squawked, but when we looked at him in his cage on the floor, he was gazing out the window at the eucalyptus trees that made up my fence line. He called out again as some birds tracked across the sky, heading home in the dusk.

'Do you think he's feeling lonely?' Kira asked.

'He might be,' I said.

'What if he's missing his brothers and sisters and parents and like, whole magpie family?' She didn't wait for an answer before going on. 'What if he never sees them again? They'll just think he left them, or that he's dead, or—'

'No,' I cut in before she imagined a whole ruined picture of the bird's life. 'The wildlife rescue team are very careful about things like that. When he's better, they'll take him back to the same place he was found and release him there. Magpies tend to stick to their territories, so his family should still be around.'

'But four weeks is so long. Will they all recognise each other?'

'Well, he's sort of a bird teenager, so when he goes back he'll probably look a bit different than when they last saw him, but I'm pretty sure they'll all know each other.'

Kira still watched the magpie, the concern on her face morphing dangerously towards distress. 'What if they don't?'

'I guess that could happen, but even if it does, he'll still be okay. He'll be healthy and nearly an adult, and he'll be able to fend for himself and fly away to find a mate, and then one day have his own family. These weeks here are just a glitch. In the scale of his life, you and I will be just a moment in time for him.'

She stared for a few seconds longer, thinking about that. Then her gaze returned to her bowl, and she wound some pasta around her fork.

'Jam it,' she said, suddenly.

My eyebrows shot towards the ceiling. 'Pardon?'

She looked up and saw my confusion. 'Jam it,' she said again. 'J-A-M-I-T. The first letters of *just a moment in time*. That should be his name.'

'Oh, Jamit!' I understood.

'And when he's free again, this moment in time will have finished and he can go back to being called whatever magpie name he already has.' Kira smiled.

This moment in time will have finished. She sat easily with the concept that time was a constant, whether measured in moments, minutes or months, and I couldn't warn her of memory's power to warp it – the power to shrink long periods of routine to minutes or stretch out grief to eternity.

Instead, I smiled as well, and vowed to treat these memories with care so I'd get this period in time right for us both. The three of us, counting Jamit. 'That sounds wonderful.'

About the author

Bronwyn is from Melbourne, Australia. She usually writes thrillers, but having worked in mental health for many years, the theme and intent of The Hope Prize struck a deep chord, inspiring her to write 'Jam It'.

Mother's Milk

Kane Heng

Shortlisted

W ar stories formed the backdrop of my childhood like stark wallpaper. My mum repeatedly recounted apocalyptic scenes along with the daily meals she cooked for us. One victim left an indelible scar: a limbless man, sitting on his torso like a lopped tree stump. 'Do you have a cigarette?' he uttered his final wish, casually.

Last week mum took her last breath. I am left to grapple with the gulf between us. But all I have is clunky non-compostable memories.

We are sitting in the lounge room. I am staring at the gawky ceramics with painted Chinese blossoms, matching the polyester flowers collecting dust on the windowsill. Mum is exercising to make a point. On the wall behind her is a second-rate painting depicting a homestead fringed by rocky mountains. The irony of such a tranquil scene in this home.

She is swinging her arms in frantic motions while I silently judge her. She is oblivious to how ridiculous she looks, flailing awkwardly in a futile attempt to get me off the couch. 'You have to move or you'll get fat,' she warns me. Less than a year after arriving in Australia my Mum had doubled in size. The purplish black bruises on her belly matched the colour of rotting plum on her feet. A result of daily insulin injections. She is determined I do not make the same mistakes.

I start to say how exhausted I am, but I can see she's already got a smirk on her face. No hardship was ever going to measure up to the trauma of living under the Khmer Rouge. You see, I have a 'good life'. My Australian existence has made me soft.

I am never allowed to forget what it took for her to get me here. More than once she risked her life for food. She hunted down and butchered a deer. Stealing from the regime even when you're on the brink of starvation was punishable by death. There's a Cambodian saying, if three innocent people go into the bush with the Khmer Rouge only one will come out. I guess she was the one. I would not be here if she didn't. That fact does not elude me.

How do you make sense of the senseless? Inside my mother's womb the emptiness circulated, forming a vacuum in my psyche. My therapist was the first to tell me about epigenetics.

I imagine I was carried past landmines to collect drinking water in a cauldron of floating bodies. I was a foetus, drinking that bloodied, desecrated water.

Working all day on a communal farm, mum had to squat in a huge pit to shit. She was forced to carry the faeces with her hands to use as manure on the cotton farms. Stories like these were common in my youth. I don't need my therapist to tell me this is the genesis for my poo phobia.

It took a lot for my mum to flinch. She was fierce. No amount of blood and guts would make her recoil. She reigned the kitchen at Chinese New Year when our house was a smorgasbord of delicious gourmet dishes. I felt sorry for the live mud crabs foaming from the mouth from the stress of being packed so tightly in boxes. She would stick a chopstick into them and throw them without a thought into scalding hot water. She broke the chicken's neck and casually plucked it, like she was pulling petals off a flower. For me, any form of excrement would propel me to dry retch.

I wanted to know who taught her to cook like a Michelin chef? Was everything she knew self-taught?

'Wash the bean sprouts. Here you pluck the end like this.' She would impatiently shove me aside. 'Move away, you too slow! Talking too much.'

I always fell short. 'You never survive World War Three,' she would say. 'You be dead quickly.' She scoffs at me, 'You got three degrees but you only stay at home and look after kid?' She is illiterate and I have a HECS debt that one lifetime cannot repay. 'If you listen to me you would study pharmacy and open up a shop!' Chemistry made no sense to me. Writing made even less sense to her. We navigated such different worlds. The irony is that her sacrifice made my privileges possible. It brought me further away from her.

My mum decided I should go to an all-girls Catholic school on the outskirts of Fairfield, to escape the burgeoning heroin plague infecting Cabramatta's teenagers. As a child, my home town Cabramatta was littered with long-haired Vietnamese gangsters squatting by the side of the tracks. They spat insouciantly on the pavement like drug kings marking their territories. I pretended not to notice their gawping sluggish eyes. I walked past with curious trepidation while they did deals in dirty side alleys. I knew drug addicts on the nod were omens not to go down that path. One moment of non-productivity, hell if I slept in till eight am, my mum would curse in hostile tones, 'You wanna join a gang eh?'

*

Every morning the school bus drove past all the McMansions and I would stare at the nouveau rich houses. Originality was not at the forefront when designing these houses. Clearly size mattered more than taste. Each garish Greek column symbolised the long tedious hours endured by its owners.

I excelled at school; my English teacher called to congratulate me on topping the grade in English. 'What you want to study at university? What is journalism? You want to make money by writing stories? You know your cousin buy a car for her mum? She study accounting!'

'You have to work hard,' was the ongoing mantra thrust upon me by my mum.

I don't have many memories of my mum on weekends and holidays. Our Rooty Hill deli was open seven days a week, 365 days a year. It was the lamest place a teenager could be. It was a neighbourhood of rundown weatherboard houses with peeling paint and broken couches slumped on broken verandas. Number plate collections with 'Murray River' and 'Red Centre' were laid out in disjointed puzzles on the facade. The Australian flag hung limply on neglected lawns.

Seven am on a Saturday I would be curled in the foetal position in the back seat of our Toyota Corolla, desperately trying to get a few more minutes' sleep. Christmas,

Boxing Day and Easter were our busiest days. Everyone else was shut. I resented mum for that.

In my teenage superiority bubble, I would sit behind the counter and serve customers so unsophisticated it was beneath me to get up. I hated being interrupted from my reading. The only salvation the deli offered was literature – celebrity gossip and the latest fashion trends. Stumbling into the shop, the first thing I did was hoard all the magazines. *Dolly*, *Cleo*, *Vogue* and *Cosmo* were not just my survival stash but a way to vicariously live a glamorous life. I would pore over images of beautiful blonde girls with perfect complexions and doll-like blue eyes.

My daydreams were invariably interrupted by a customer in baggy trackies and an '80s t-shirt with 'Living the Dream' written on it. 'G'day love. A dollar of devon please.' I'd be rudely transported back to the banality of the shop. I'd move sluggishly to the deli window and take out the cheapest meat in our display. My mum hated devon. She scoffed about how it came from the fatty scraps the butcher swept up off the floor. 'Don't eat this or it'll make you fat!' she'd warn me.

The other annoying customers were the Rooty Hill kids. 'How much is that?' they'd ask pointing to the gobstoppers. 'And how much is that?' pointing to something else. Hours later and I'd be desperate to finish my *Dolly* quiz on which TV It Girl I was or how to look exotic with ethnic dressing. Finally, they would settle on mixed lollies. Twenty cents worth! I'd look down on these kids and their damn poverty.

Customers couldn't pronounce my name. Kheng Heng. I cringed while they came up with multiple variations. Our traditional Chinese names were as foreign to them as their mullet hairdos were to us. Even my Aussie friend at school, Barbara, would sing a chorus with my name. I wasn't the only one in my family whose name rhymed! *Kheng Heng, Seak Cheng, Meng Beng Seng.* She strung together our woefully rhyming names into a tasteless cadence that rung in my ears. I wished fervently that my mum had given me a better name. So we made up Aussie names. I was Kelly, my sisters were Jennifer, Cathy and Veronica. I became a stranger inhabiting a fake identity. Better than a name that rhymed.

I remember massaging her arms as she lay motionless on her bed. Her sloppy skin as I kneaded the dough, hoping touch could reconcile what words could not.

All those years I resented her working tirelessly.

I live in an inner city, renovated house in a leafy suburb because that's what working 365 days can do. That's what her sacrifice allowed me to have. The guilt sticks to me like glue, viscous and translucent but permanently binding.

My mum never complained about standing on her feet twelve hours a day 24/7. What could possibly ruffle you after what she had been through? What needs would not seem frivolous?

Even after death I still have mixed feelings about this matriarch who stood like an oak tree. She remains unfathomable to me.

Mum had learned broken English from her customers. Though illiterate, she obtained her driving license by memorising the road signs. Mum was an entrepreneur, recognised a thriving business when she saw it and could charm anyone. But she was never afraid to offend. She had a meanness in her that might have been born in the labour camps. When she saw a very overweight customer she would nudge me ruthlessly. She'd snicker at their muffin tops protruding and say candidly, 'Look at her belly hanging out.' She'd unashamedly ask the chubby little boy with man boobs, 'Exjuice me, are you a girl?'

'Are you happy?' I once asked, fiddling next to her in the kitchen while she cooked. 'Don't ask silly questions!' was the response. I can now see how dwelling on those philosophical questions was so frivolous. Happiness was a foreign and unnecessary concept. Or maybe it was dangerous to her. Maybe she danced on a fine ledge, where one slip and she would fall hopelessly into the abyss. Suppressing her feelings was not only necessary for her but also the only way she could function in a world that made little sense. She needed a daughter that was practical and I needed a mum who was emotionally attuned. We were tied to each other yet walking blindly in opposite directions.

I remember when I had my first baby, the intense feelings of love and navigating long nights like a zombie. The piles of nappies. She announced that she would come over every day and help me. The journey was far by train, she had to limp on knees damaged by too much weight and standing for long days.

I wanted to tell her that my cracked nipples were so sore that I flinched at any touch. I want to talk about my sleep deprivation and my lonely days listening to existential windchimes. I don't. We can't.

I quietly watch her go through my kitchen pantry. Every ridiculous item I buy is under her scrutiny. All my choices are questioned. All those years she shut down my questions.

*

My mum never spoke about her time in the Khmer Rouge labour camps. There's an image of a tree in Cambodia on the internet, with thousands of colourful bracelets tied to the trunk. There's so many it overflows and hangs like silent reminders. Soldiers bashed babies against it, to prevent them growing up and seeking revenge. They called it the killing tree. Did mum ever have to witness infants being flung against a tree and bludgeoned to death? I know it haunted her. I carry the nightmares as proof.

Raising a child in the comfort of my middle-class home was a world away from the killing fields where she had to raise my brothers and sisters. She had to worry about her kids being brainwashed by Angka and turned into communist weapons that could turn on her for stealing a pea. While I complained that my baby didn't sleep through the night to my mother's group, she worried that hers might be slaughtered against a killing tree.

Her visits lasted a week.

I long to retrieve those moments and rewrite them.

Only now can I sob for the child who instead of going to school had to spend her days in the scorching Cambodian sun selling sweets. I see her peering through the classroom window at the hieroglyphs on the black-board. The schoolteacher cruelly dismissing her.

I imagine what it was like for her to watch her brother go to school and become a doctor and what it felt like when the Khmer Rouge killed him for being one.

What was it like to be married at sixteen and have nine kids by the time she was 37.

How did she navigate a new country?

I think about how I can never leave her home empty-handed because she was programmed to give. I think about my mum working tirelessly in the shop as her labour of love for us.

When I was old enough, I left home to live in Paddington. My mum wailed as I left our driveway. She thought I was punishing her. Why couldn't I be like the other Cambodian daughters who stayed by their mums' side until they married? I couldn't explain why I loved the Victorian balustrade that promised bourgeois living and sophistication. Or why I felt a camaraderie with the boldness of gay culture.

On Oxford Street I went into delis and delighted in the smell of mouldy cheese and golden, crisp chocolate croissants. Customers ate baguettes smeared with duck liver pate, and salami hung to dry like skin turned to leather in the sun. There was no sign of devon. No cheap fluoro-pink finger buns or Aussie meat pies. On the streets there are labels everywhere. I like the designer ones not the ones that stigmatise.

I avoided going back to Cabramatta. There was always an excuse to miss family gatherings.

The last time all nine kids and sixteen grandkids were together, we had invited the Buddhist monks to chant for her soul to leave this world peacefully. We were huddled together in that small room as close as we would ever be for her.

She was the glue.

There is no longer the delicious smell of fried garlic wafting through the air as my mum manoeuvres with alacrity around her frying woks. The kids can no longer rapaciously rip open red envelopes from her on Chinese New Year. There is no one to urge me to move.

When memory assails me with regret, I am able to claw open her fingers and look her in the eye. I tell her gently like she's a child, 'It's okay.'

The essence of our relationship was and always will be love.

About the author

Kane Heng is a high school English teacher and mum of four kids who lives in Sydney's inner west with her husband. She has a passion for learning the Spanish language, travelling all corners of the world, diving into oceans and doing yoga to keep sane in the storm of modern life with kids.

Tinged with Gold

Rebecca Higgie

Shortlisted

Henry opened the fridge and there they were, eye-level, in two lines from oldest to newest: six bottles. Her breastmilk. The bottles were labelled with heart-shaped post-it notes, secured in place with rubber bands they'd collected from bunches of asparagus. *Saturday arvo. Sunday morning/midday.* Loose timestamps in her messy handwriting.

'We'll never have to bother with proper times,' she'd said. 'We won't keep them that long.'

There were varying amounts of milk, ranging from 50 ml to 160 ml. Some were from a single pumping session. Others were two or three, pooled together. They had separated into layers. On the bottom it looked like water that had been poured into a milky glass, murky and thin. It got whiter towards the top, where the fat, a thick layer of yellowed cream, floated.

Seventy-two hours. That's how long they could last in the fridge, according to the chart that she'd stuck on the door.

It had been eighteen hours since her death.

Ollie, their baby, was screaming. At the hospital, he'd had formula, but they were home now. Henry stared at those bottles. This was the last breastmilk their son would ever have. Henry closed the fridge, sat on the floor and cried. For a while, he couldn't hear Ollie. He ignored everything but the sharp, consuming agony of losing her. But Ollie's cries came back to him, the pitch higher, desperate.

He thought of all she'd done to make that milk. He opened the fridge, quickly calculating the times. The oldest was fine, just within that 72-hour window. He reached for it.

Feed 1, bottle 1: Saturday morning/midday, 110 ml

Her voice in his head: *Click the kettle on. Find the box of teats. Fit one to the bottle. Turn the kettle off before the water starts to roll. Never let it boil.*

He poured the hot water into a mug and swirled the bottle in it, watching the fat dissolve and the layers mix together. He tested the milk on his hand twice before the temperature was right. The droplets ran down his fingers as he went to Ollie.

Henry picked up his crying son, took him to the couch and fed him. Ollie gulped it down, making a mockery of the slow-flow teat. Henry then raised him up onto his shoulder, and waited for the burp. Ollie spat up a stream of milk. Henry swallowed his resentment as it ran down his shoulder.

Your mother laboured so much.

Late in the pregnancy, she'd found a new love for herself. She stared in the mirror often, naked, rubbing her belly that moved with the energy of their son. Whenever she was sad, Henry would take her to that mirror. She'd nod and smile at her new shape. The scars that other men had once carved into her seemed forgotten.

Ollie let out a happy squeal, bringing Henry back. The baby chose cooing, and then crying, over sleep. It was another hour of bouncing and crying together until Ollie's eyelids drooped.

Half an hour passed and then, a text message.

I'm at the door.

Dad. Aeroplane blindfold up in his hair. He said nothing, only embracing Henry.

Ollie started up his little waking cries.

'I can't take it,' Henry muttered.

'Go sit down,' his father said, leaving his suitcase by the door and following the cries to the bedroom. Henry sat on the couch and stared at the empty bottle speckled with flecks of her milk, as his father rocked Ollie back to sleep.

Feed 2, bottles 2 + 3: Saturday arvo + Saturday evening, 50 ml + 50 ml

Henry showered on his father's insistence. The bathroom was awash with the scent of her conditioners and creams, floral and sweet. Her brush was full of her hair. He spotted strands everywhere on the way back to the bedroom: on the backs of chairs, on his clothes, on Ollie's elephant blankie. Ollie was asleep in the middle of their bed. As Henry got dressed slowly, quietly, he noticed her clothes hanging off the chair by her dresser. He picked up a white singlet. It smelled like soured sweet milk.

It had been two hours and fifteen minutes since the last feed. Ollie stirred. Henry went to the fridge and got a bottle with only 50 ml, then topped it up to 100 ml with milk from the next bottle. He swirled it in hot water.

'I can feed him, give it here,' his father said.

Henry paused. His father looked at the bottle. It wasn't the pure white of the formula. It was something else, something tinged with gold.

His father knew. He smiled sadly and led Henry to the couch, handed him Ollie, and sat by his side. Tears rolled down Henry's cheeks as he offered Ollie the bottle. The baby gulped away.

'Please don't leave, Dad,' Henry whispered.

'I'm not going anywhere, son.'

His father managed to get Ollie in his cot. Henry lay on the double bed next to it, the pillow wall she'd constructed when she started co-sleeping now at his back. His dear dad, in his late sixties now, sat beside him, stroking his hair. Like Mum did, when he was little.

'How did you cope? When . . . how do you cope?'

Henry saw the answer in his father's eyes: *I didn't. I couldn't. I don't.*

But instead, the old man said, 'I asked for help.'

Henry finally slept.

Feed 3, remainder of bottle 3: Saturday evening, 110 ml

Her milk didn't come in for five days. She sobbed as Ollie's lips cracked, as his screams became more desperate. The formula was brought by a nurse who held her shaking hands on the bottle and said, 'You're still feeding your baby, hun.'

Every three hours, she sat at the breast pump for twenty minutes, the bottles turned up so the tiny drops of colostrum wouldn't get lost in the filter between the flanges that suctioned to her breasts and the bottles that collected the liquid. At first, the amount couldn't be measured. It was a drop only, fed to their gasping son on her pinkie finger. Then one day she made two millilitres, then five, then ten. The nurses fed them to Ollie with a syringe. She got an infection in her c-section wound, yet she still sat at the pump, her body shaking, antibiotics and painkillers surging through her veins. Before they left the hospital, after nine long days, a nurse told her, 'Dear, you can turn the bottles the right way round now. You're making enough.' That day, she collected twenty millilitres.

Ollie screamed at the breast. But every feed, she took him there, singing and cooing and crying as she tried to get him to latch. There was less agony at the birth, less agony than the whole pregnancy, than there was at a single feed. Her nipples cracked and bled. Ollie clicked constantly, breaking the seal, rarely latching properly. She did everything she could to get him on. Henry came home to find her standing up and swaying with Ollie on her breast. That day, it was the only thing that worked.

Now, Henry dreamed of her swaying, Ollie in her arms. They were laughing. Ollie's giggle was piercing. The laugh became a cry. Henry woke up. His father was already there, picking up Ollie.

'Just rest, it's only been half an hour. He can't be hungry yet.'

Henry went back to sleep, but soon his father woke him, convinced the unsettled cries were of hunger.

The large bottle Henry took from earlier had about 100 ml or so left. When he swirled it in the hot water, the fat that clung to the sides melted and revealed 110 ml. Ollie drank 80 ml and then refused. Henry kept trying. Ollie pushed the teat out with his tongue.

'Don't force him,' his dad said gently.

Henry persisted, remembering the chart on the fridge. *After infant has begun feeding, any leftover milk MUST be discarded.*

'How could you tell me he was hungry? He won't even take one hundred mil.'

'It's been two and a half hours.'

'How could you? I can't throw this out!'

Henry pushed the teat back into Ollie's mouth. The baby spat, pushing out his tongue.

'I can't believe you did this!'

Henry cried, letting out terrible howls that came from his belly. Ollie started crying too.

His father said nothing. Gently, he tried to take the bottle. Henry snatched it away. The old man then gestured for Ollie.

'Bet it's just a wet nappy.'

He changed Ollie. He sung to him, nursery rhymes filtering through from the bedroom. After ten minutes, he brought Ollie back. Henry was still on the couch, staring at that last 30 ml he knew he should throw away.

'It's only been a few minutes, son.'

Henry offered the rest to Ollie. He drank.

His father took Ollie again. Sang him a song about five little ducks and a mama duck that went *quack quack quack*.

'I'm sorry,' Henry said when Ollie was asleep.

'Nothing to be sorry for, son.'

Feed 4, bottle 4: Sunday 2 am early morning, 120 ml

She had a system. Boil the water and measure it into 120 ml amounts. Allow to cool and then chill in the fridge, waiting for the two levelled scoops of formula. Then, come a feed, offer the breast, then top up with expressed milk, then top up with formula. Then to the breast pump to express milk for the next feed and drain her breast so it got the signal to produce more. Ollie, his latch poor, wasn't stimulating it enough.

In the first month, the expressed milk was so small, so readily drunk by Ollie, that it never made it to the fridge. *Expressed milk may be stored in a room of 27°C for up to seven hours*, her chart said, but most of it never went past two hours of leaving her breast. Slowly, she produced more. One session she got 40 ml, and then 50 ml. One morning, a rare 90 ml, when formula wasn't needed for one feed. Then twenty millilitres, all day, every session.

Two am. Four am. Six am. Always there, her head bowed, her eyes closed. The breast pump whirling.

The next bottle, Henry could tell, took her at least two early morning sessions at the pump. She'd crossed out the initial time on her post-it note heart, replacing it with a vague 'early morning'. How she'd sat on the couch with the pump: resolute, still, like something carved from stone. His love, she couldn't be moved. God, how she'd persisted.

He heard her voice as he swirled that 120 ml in the hot water. *Persist*. He couldn't bear it. He fed Ollie on auto-pilot. The baby giggled, not knowing what they'd lost.

Persist.

Feed 5, bottle 5: Sunday morning/midday, 90 ml

At night, she left pre-made bottles of formula in the fridge. The breastmilk was left on the kitchen counter, or in the fridge if it was past seven hours, with a rubber band to differentiate it from the formula. Even as the expressed milk started to overtake the formula, even on those days when there was no formula, she still put those rubber bands on the bottles.

Expressing got her supply up. But it was co-sleeping that got Ollie on the breast. She and Henry initially took turns at night, taking shifts with Ollie while the other slept. But one night, she fell asleep while feeding Ollie on the bed. Henry woke up after an eight-hour sleep to find her curled around their son, both of them sleeping,

Ollie still suckling at her breast. She only needed one bottle that whole night. After that, Henry moved to the spare bed. Ollie never went back in the cot.

More bottles ended up in the fridge. They supplemented with formula three times again, and then no more. Only expressed milk, all the bottles with those rubber bands proudly declaring them of the breast. After two weeks of this, she stopped storing pre-boiled water. After three, she started with her post-it note labels to ensure they fed Ollie the oldest expressed milk first. After six weeks, they went from expressed milk at every feed to only needing two or three bottles a day. Still, she expressed every few hours, even creeping out of bed at night once Ollie fell asleep. She pumped in the chair that held her milk-sodden clothes.

As Henry reached for the fifth bottle, he remembered the moment she'd started to accept that things were working.

'Ollie really does like breastmilk,' she'd said.

'Of course.'

Her eyes darted away but she smiled. 'I tasted it. Just a few drops when I tested if it was warm enough. I know that's weird . . .'

'It's not weird for you. It's *from* you.'

'It's sweet,' she said.

Her voice, back then, was so full of awe, marvelling at what her body could produce. He swirled that 90 ml, watching the fat dissolve. As he tested the milk on his hand, he considered it: to taste a part of her, a part of her still living. But he couldn't do it. That part of her was never meant for him.

He took the bottle to Ollie. After gulping it down, Ollie burped. His breath smelled sweet.

Henry's father came out of the kitchen with a plate of scrambled eggs. It tasted like nothing.

Feed 6, bottle 6: Monday morning, 120 ml

That final bottle. One hundred and twenty millilitres. Expressed a few hours before she died. Ollie would want it in two hours or so. That last part of her, full of her anti-bodies, enzymes and stem cells. It wasn't like her hair or her smell, the dead parts of her that lingered. It wasn't like the many photos, with her smile beaming out from cheap metal frames. It was alive.

Henry couldn't bear to lose this last living part of her. The chart on the fridge: *Expressed milk can last in the freezer for up to three months.* He opened the freezer, emptied an inner drawer, and placed the bottle inside. Each month, on the twelfth, he checked on it. She'd died on the twelfth, and as each month passed, he felt himself getting closer to another loss.

Ollie was almost six months old now. Henry was a pro at making formula. He and his father followed her system, the fridge full of bottles of pre-boiled water. Henry threw all the asparagus rubber bands away.

Three months was almost up. He couldn't wait any longer.

He took the bottle out of the freezer. It had frozen solid, with milk crystals up the side. Its *Monday morning* post-it note was damp, the words bleeding. He put it in the fridge to thaw, hiding it behind a tub of yoghurt. Ollie took the next three feeds with formula. Henry waited, checking on the bottle occasionally, giving it a swirl to see if the milk had melted.

It was time.

Click the kettle on. Stop it before it boils. Cry. His father touched his shoulder, noticing the gold in his hand.

'It's alright, son.'

God, how she laboured for this.

Henry swirled the bottle in hot water. That last living part of her.

Ollie smiled when he saw the bottle. He reached up, trying to snatch it. When Henry let him have it, they held it together. He stared into Ollie's brown eyes. *Her* eyes. Like she was looking at him.

That last living part of her, the true one, was still there. The little person she made and sustained.

There were so many times in those first six weeks that Henry wanted her to give up. He couldn't stand what the fight was doing to her, all the expressing, all the battling with Ollie, the constant doubt. But when it worked, when Ollie turned his body towards her breast and smiled, it gave her something back, something that was taken when her proud body didn't do what it should, when it was monitored, injected, broken, and finally cut open.

The night before she died, Henry peeked into the bedroom. She was smiling as Ollie nestled into her. Their little boy was feeding, his tiny hand on her breast. His swallows were deep, sustained.

She had wanted to give birth without a soul interfering, for her body to have agency beyond what others would do to it. She had wanted to feed her baby exclusively on the breast, no formula, no pump. She had wanted to be perfect. When things didn't work, it hurt her. She needed to be the one who decided what to do. That night before she died, she accepted that her body was truly hers, that she had power. That night, finally . . .

'This is enough,' she whispered, stroking Ollie's head. 'This is enough.'

She didn't express that night. She waited till the morning. One last session. She waved the bottle at Henry, triumphant.

'This is enough.'

About the author

Rebecca Higgie is a writer from Boorloo (Perth, Western Australia). Her novel *The History of Mischief* won the inaugural Fogarty Literary Award for an unpublished manuscript and was published by Fremantle Press in 2020.

If God is the Red Gum

Emmylou Hocking

Shortlisted

I watch the late afternoon sunlight drip through the Moreton Bay figs in Carlton Gardens as we glide down Nicholson Street. It's that slow, syrupy sunlight you only really see in Melbourne's summer months. Groups of people pepper the grounds, pouring warm orange wine into cheap plastic cups and feeding each other expensive cheese. Mum used to pick the little apricots that grew in the orchard around this time of year. Just as they were beginning to ripen, Dad would cover the trees in white plastic netting to protect the fruit from the birds. Mum would promptly remove it every year, explaining that she didn't want the trees to ever feel trapped. She'd feed me small apricot halves each morning like other mums do with soft pears. Holding the fruit firmly in one hand, she'd meticulously cut out the brown parts with the other, pressing the small, red-handled knife through the delicate flesh until the blade arrived at her thumb.

Now I sometimes buy them at the market, expecting them to be soft and sweet. Their tartness always surprises me.

My body lurches forward, seatbelt tightening across my chest. A curt apology from our Uber driver after a screech of tyres on bitumen. We sit in silence for a while, waiting for our seatbelts to slacken and the lights to turn green. The soft whirring of the car's air conditioning melts into the sounds of the 96 tram as it slows down beside us. Cool air circulates the pine-scented air freshener through the car but does nothing to stop my bare legs from clinging to the vinyl beneath them. I look over at you, sitting just out of reach and clutching an old canvas shopping bag between your legs. You've filled it with my favourite chocolate, the noise-cancelling headphones Mum bought for me a month prior, and salads from the Lebanese cafe on the corner, crammed between two plastic containers.

'What salads did you get?' I ask.

'What?'

'What salads did you get? From the cafe.'

'I got the roast vegetable one with the pomegranate seeds and some kinda potato one. I can't remember the third. It has chicken in it. You hungry?'

'Nah.'

'You need to eat,' you say. A small declaration of love.

Nick Cave's rendition of 'Cosmic Dancer' starts playing on the radio. I notice your fingers slowly tapping along to it as the traffic lights turn green and the car slowly edges forward. You're all green eyes and sharp cheekbones. Skin pockmarked with freckles, an unruly, red beard. I've always loved the small creases by the corners of your eyes and how they deepen when you smile or concentrate hard. I love how you look to the sky when searching for the right words to a story, as if everything you're looking for sits above eye level. Bruised looking half-moons weigh your eyes down now. I've never seen you look so tired. When was the last time you slept?

When you came home and saw the flecks of broken ceramics scattered through the backyard, you silently reached for me. You pressed my heaving body against your chest and slowly breathed in the stirred-up earth I had feverishly emptied into the garden. A few weeks later, when you came home and found me shivering in the bathtub, your eyes swelled with a sadness I couldn't reach. Plants were never meant to live secluded, potted lives, I desperately cried at you. The fiddle leaf was lonely, and we mistook its hopefulness for health. The ceramic pots needed to be broken; the plants were begging for freedom. And bathtubs are the safest place to be when the earth cracks open and threatens to devour you or when the wind uproots everything solid and tries to suck you into space; bathtubs will protect you. I'm sure I learned that somewhere, maybe at school, maybe from Mum. But maybe I hadn't. Maybe I made it up.

A few days after you found me in the bathtub, you took me to see the doctor. He asked me whether I ever felt like books were speaking directly to me. I said, 'Only ever the good ones.' You smiled so deeply that I thought I had fixed it. He said I was 'deteriorating' as if I were sewn together with a delicate fabric. Maybe we all are — a mess of fibres expanding and contracting, desperately trying to adapt to an ever-changing environment. Maybe we're all just waiting for the right conditions to unravel. He said I was getting progressively worse, that I hadn't yet processed the trauma, as though this process were a grocery item I hadn't yet ticked off. I told him I didn't want to process it. He replied, 'You need to take some responsibility for your health and recovery.' I nodded. He shook his head. I thought about his wife and their marriage while he refused to make eye contact with me and spoke of what he described as my fragile and brittle temperament. He ended the appointment and turned his chair to face me, placed his hand on my right thigh and said, 'You should never have gone on that date alone.' I fantasised about breaking his hot, clammy fingers, one by one.

'Beautiful weather,' our driver says, breaking through the music on the radio.

He meets your eyes in the rearview mirror. You let out a soft murmur that implies you agree. 'I've missed the warmth,' I add.

You smile, but it's a smile that doesn't show your teeth or the creases by the side of your eyes. You've never been very good at lying. Your body always betrays you. I look down at the gold ring you gifted me years ago, wrapped snugly around my right index finger. A thick band with small indentations and grooves, speckled with small precious stones. You pulled it out of your pocket one afternoon while we were out on one of our regular walks along Merri Creek – just you, me and our wet, muddy dog. I'm not sure how you can be so bad at lying yet so good at keeping secrets.

I look back at you and notice the sunlight as it coats your face, your shoulders and the very tops of your arms, and I imagine the sun's warmth as it spreads through your body. Some days I'm capable of magical, unexplainable things and while I told you I wasn't 'experiencing feelings of grandeur' when you last asked, I'd be lying if I said I had nothing to do with today's forecast. I thought you might notice the sunlight, feel the warmth on your skin and with it, feel some form of hope or belief that things would be okay.

'I swear Melbourne's winters get longer every year,' the Uber driver continues.

He peels his eyes from the rearview mirror, shifts his attention back to the road and sighs.

'Thank God it's finally summer.'

'Thank God,' I reply.

Thank God.

When I told you the red gum out the front was God, I watched the muscles by your jaw clench. When I told you it sometimes spoke to me, I felt the rest of your body stiffen. It's home to that white-plumed honeyeater that shat on your head the day we moved in. You said being shat on was a bad omen. I said it was good luck. I read that red gums usually grow along creeks, river-beds and waterways and can survive immersion in floodwater for months at a time. They rely on their extensive root system to collect and transport oxygen, allowing them to live when they would otherwise drown. I think that's why, when my body felt like it was about to burst out of its skin and I felt simultaneously connected and disconnected from everything all at once, when I thought I might be dragged under and drowned in darkness and total despair, the red gum out the front spoke to me and reminded me to breathe. It held the whole world in its gaze yet somehow found the time to sit with just me. If God is love, then God is the red gum.

Our family dining table was built from red gum. Mum and Dad bought it from an antique store in Ballarat when they married. They bought it for cheap because the legs were slightly different lengths, and as a result, it used to tilt gently towards me whenever I pressed down on one of the corners too hard. Dad would sigh deeply and roll his eyes every time. Mum eventually placed a meticulously folded piece of cardboard underneath the shortest leg in an attempt to stabilise it. I watched the cardboard slowly compress, surrendering to the red gum's persistent calls to soften, and the table returned to its slightly wonky state. The morning sun used to coat the table in a golden warmth. It would seep into the grain and all its small indentations, lighting up the faint stains I had made over the years with sticky hands and colourful markers. I would lay my head against the table as a child, letting the red gum hold me as I breathed in its scent — an earthiness muddled with polishing oil and dried porridge. My eyes would follow Mum as she floated around the room, brushing her fingers across my back and the tabletop as though we were one and the same.

The driver makes a sharp turn as we abruptly pull to the curb. I feel him watching us as we clumsily exit the car, briefly checking for cyclists, cars and distracted pedestrians. We begin walking down Princes Street. You clutch the canvas bag with one hand and hold my hand with the other, and as we walk, I watch the sun sink closer and closer to the horizon, turning the sky and everything the light touches a soft grapefruit pink. We follow the last of the sunlight to a small car park and walk towards the entrance of a large building. A sign above the sliding doors reads 'EMERGENCY'.

It's cold in the hospital waiting area. Aggressive fluorescent lights bear down on discoloured plastic chairs that are securely bolted to the ground. I find myself feeling a sense of sorrow for those chairs. You walk towards a small desk on the far side of the room and begin speaking to a nurse sitting behind a piece of reinforced plastic that separates her from the rest of the world. She introduces herself as triage and promptly starts flooding you with questions. I hear dribs and drabs of the conversation, something about bathtubs and lonely plants, talking books and the weather, red gums and drowning. As I listen, my body begins surging with homesickness, a rolling heat that starts at the base of my stomach and rises through my chest before finally resting in the middle of my throat. I want to go home. Back to our bed, our muddy dog, and the bathtub that keeps us safe. I'm worried I'll be permanently disfigured by this. I don't want to be left behind, and I want you to stay with me. I think I might entirely fall apart if you're not here holding me together.

Before I have time to speak, the nurse is confirming my name and date of birth and wrapping a thin paper bracelet around my wrist. A door opens to the right and we walk through a maze of corridors lined with beds, filled with people in varying levels of distress. Antiseptic and sweat cling to the air and the white fluorescent lights force out all that is soft and warm. There's nowhere for the grapefruit-coloured sunlight to seep in. We're taken to a small private room where a doctor appears, clipboard in hand. He's tall and gangly looking with pockmarked skin and an aversion to eye contact. He asks me about my childhood and my relationship with Mum and Dad and how often I shower and my quality of sleep and if I'm having 'feelings of grandeur' or maybe 'thoughts of self-harm' and why I am agitated and why I deny being agitated and why I think the red gum has the time to speak to me. I can't settle on answers for most of his questions because I'm too busy desperately trying to squirm myself out of the small box he's already preparing a ribbon for. He says a nurse will check on me shortly, smiles matter-of-factly, closes the door and suddenly everything is quiet.

I'm not sure how to fill the silence he's left us with. In some kind of desperate and feeble attempt to fix everything I'm breaking, I bury my hand into the bag you've brought and pull out the quickly softening block of chocolate. I split the block in two, carefully ripping the foil and paper before offering you one of the halves.

'I thought you said you weren't hungry,' you smile, and it reaches your eyes and completely undoes me. I feel my body heave with tears and something too big for me to contain any longer. I surrender control and let everything fall away. I loosen my grip, unclench my jaw and I do it all because I think we'll be okay. The world goes on. The citrus-coloured sunset continues to exist beyond these walls. I'm sure of this because, while the bathtub kept me safe and the red gum kept me breathing, you're the one who's loved me through it all.

About the author
Emmylou Hocking is currently studying a Masters in Writing and Literature at Deakin University and lives in Naarm/Melbourne, Australia. This is her first literary publication.

Beasts of Burden

Isaac Hogarth

Shortlisted

There are wild horses running in the hills; see them on a clear day moving across the ridge, equine ghosts haunting the wrinkles of the Earth, long-haired memories of time gone by. When I was a kid I'd go up into those hills to look for them, but I never found so much as a trace. No hoof marks. No piles of shit. No neighing or whinnying. They only ever existed at a distance; up close, they disappeared into the thin space not even a child can fit into, the dark behind the eyes, you know – the place where lost things go to stay lost, where free dreams run unburdened by life and love.

I remember every couple of months a black helicopter would come buzzing overhead. Enormous metal wasp circling like a dark halo over the hills. Part of a government initiative to restore some kind of equilibrium to the forever tilted world. The horse population was always running amok, they were trampling all the native grasses, they were killing off the kangaroos. Remember hearing gunshots beat through the valley, louder than anything I'd ever heard before, or ever heard since. And me and Jess, sitting on the wraparound porch, the sound still echoing somewhere down in the valley's sunken belly. She would say:

> they're beautiful
> but they gotta go

We played a game one evening, who knows what it was or what the rules were or how any of it worked, but Jess was chasing me around the house. I tripped over, fell towards the corner of the coffee table. It cracked me in the cheek, knocked the saliva out of my mouth along with a loose molar. The shock of it, I started bawling. Jess tapped me on the shoulder though, coaxed me into removing my head from my hands. She held my fallen tooth in-between her pointer and thumb. There were thin trails of torn gum dangling from the root of it. It looked like a tiny white octopus with blood-red tentacles. She scratched me on the head, mussed up my hair, pink spit bubbling out of my mouth and running down my chin as I sobbed.

it hurts

> it's okay,
> it's okay

*

Yes, Mum and Dad had left by then. Not at the same time; one after the other, a few years apart. Yes, I will never remember either of them solidly; I see them in the primordial haze of infancy, like glowing blobs floating in a lava lamp. I had glossy fresh eyes, I only had room in my head for a few new words and a few new foods; every silhouette was unbounded, every face was featureless. By the time I was old enough to remember anything tangible they were both long gone. Jess wouldn't ever say much about them, neither.

And Jess didn't care much about the horses either. We would be sitting on the porch and a herd of them would come over the horizon as if born from blue sky, galloping through the already-trodden grass, small as insects at a distance but somehow still bigger than anything within arm's reach. Jess wouldn't look up from her book, wouldn't be distracted from her cigarette.

look
look at them

                                        busy

just for a second

                                    i'm busy

She was 21 or 22, I never really knew, in any case quite a bit older than me, and most of those years had been grim. We had Grandpa nearby who took care of us, was our official guardian until Jess turned eighteen. We still saw him pretty often, he was a positive person, not at all like Jess; she had a very low opinion of the world and of people. There's only one thing she'd admit about Mum and Dad if I asked where they went, why they went, who made them go.

> believe me
> you're better off

why?

> they couldn't bear the weight

the weight of what?

> you know,
> of loving their children
> of loving anyone, anything, even each other,
> couldn't bear the weight of it

If I pressed Jess any further, I'd get nothing; that's where the conversation started and ended. It was all I knew about Mum and Dad: they couldn't bear the weight of it.

Jess picked me up from school one time, maybe I was about eight. On the way home from town we found a donkey walking by itself on the side of the road. It had a wooden sign tied around its neck that said, 'FREE TO A GOOD HOME'. He was tough on the eyes, fly-bitten all over, ears ragged and torn, top lip always flapping and showing big human-like teeth.

we're a good home

                        not happening

We argued till I cried. Had driven far ahead of the donkey by then, it was lost to the watery mirage which danced on every summer horizon. I unlocked the car door, opened it just a bit, stuck my foot out threateningly.

i'll jump out this car
if we don't go back and get that donkey

                      go on
               you can limp home

i'll stop eating and drinking water
till i die,
i mean it

                      go for it

We drove the rest of the way home, calling each other pretty terrible things. Pretty much as soon as we parked I ran back up the road, found the donkey again about twenty minutes from the house. I led him home by the reins. Jess was sitting on the porch, bent over with her head in her hands, groaning muffled into her palms.

you're such a fucking pain in my arse

i'll take care of him,
you won't even notice

you're such a fucking pain in my arse

He lived outside the house, free to leave if he wanted, seeing as there wasn't much in the way of gates or fences except for the one at the mouth of the driveway, which had come loose from its hinges anyway. I loved him, loved how bad he smelled and how hideous he was. So I called him Ugly.

I was still little, so I would ride the donkey around; Grandpa showed me how. He was my dad's dad and an incredibly old man, by my standards anyway. Big grey beard, tired eyes, broken blood vessels webbed across his cheeks. He taught me how to look after Ugly, keep him clean and happy.

he'll want a friend, though

i'll be his friend

a donkey friend

jess will kill me if i bring home another one

Grandpa lived a few properties over and kept something like a thousand head of cattle, a real farm full of workers and bordered by electric fences, but he always had time for me when I came around, would make lunch or put the TV on or whatever, and sometimes he'd even come around to our place to drop off groceries, little knick-knacks or surplus appliances. One time he gave us a toaster, that was cool, it had six different settings. For Ugly, he gave me a brush and some other implements, said he'd drop off whatever else I'd need later.

how's your sister?

she's always mean to me

nah, she loves you,
she's just had a rough go of things

she doesn't like the donkey
i don't think she even likes me

don't say that,
she loves you

she hates me

maybe sometimes,
but that's okay

It was summer then, me and Grandpa and Ugly moved through a viscous, hypnotising heat, like pushing through warm honey. I looked at the fields of sickly yellow grass, the bone-thin cattle with their tails swinging like pendulums counting down to I-dunno-what, crying crows perched on powerlines, trees billowing in the hot wind, their thin limbs dancing a futile rain dance. Grandpa was shaking his head at me, though I hadn't said anything; maybe he was disagreeing with some idea he knew I had in my head.

> loving somebody,
> really loving them,
> it's like carrying around an extra soul.
> it can be a real burden

what's a burden?

> you know, something heavy.
> something you've gotta carry round everywhere.
> loving someone can be a real burden.
> but, you know, the idea is
> that they carry a bit of your burden too.
> then the both of you are a little lighter

i really hate jess sometimes though

> that's okay,
> sometimes

*

I got older, a bit taller, and a lot more difficult. Me and Jess argued too much, sometimes would go days without talking to each other. I said horrible things to her, she said horrible things to me right back. Why is it that we feel safe being so mean to people who care for us, who we care for too? Jess practically raised me and somehow that gave me license to upset her. She felt the same, just the other way around.

Once, after a particularly bad argument, I left the house and took the car. Didn't have anything close to a license but Jess had let me get behind the wheel a couple times, so I knew enough to get into town. I did a shitty park out the front of the library, where they had computers. I was gonna find out something about Mum and Dad, but I wasn't sure what, wasn't even sure what to look up. Started with their names. I'd never heard Jess call them by their names, but I'd found things around the house: old letters, old electricity bills, etcetera. A lot of results turned up on the internet, I wasn't sure which were Mum or Dad. There was something like twelve people with Dad's name in the country, all doing different things; he might've been a carpenter, he might've been doing IT, or something else that wouldn't even show up on Google – a McDonalds fry cook, or a contract killer, or a department store guy, or something like that. Searching for Mum yielded about the same results. I guess some of them looked like they could've been related to me, but you can convince yourself of similarities to just about anyone, just like you can convince yourself of being the complete opposite.

After that I loitered around town feeling sorry for myself. Tried and failed to get into the pub. Didn't drive home till after midnight; Ugly was awake and staring towards me, Jess was smoking a cigarette on the verandah, waiting.

> i don't get paid to look after you,
> i don't even get a thank you.
> so you don't get to pull this shit

you don't have to worry

> i do have to worry,
> forever, i'm going to have to worry

She blew out a lumpish pillar of smoke, snuffed the cigarette out against the chair leg. Despite the hooting of the night birds and the bugs buzzing and the drone of the highway a little ways over, there was a strange quiet, a silence like something enveloping me and Jess, a grey slime. I tried to push through it, but Jess pushed through first.

> you probably think that
> your life will be a work of art.

something that you chisel out of marble,

whatever shape you like.

but it won't be.

life is an open wound

and it's your job to stitch it back together

it's not my fault

yeah, well,

it's certainly not mine.

so

I went inside, went to sleep, she stayed up smoking on the verandah for who knows how long. In the morning I made coffee and ate toast and waited for Jess to wake up and come into the kitchen to eat, but she didn't. It was a weekend, maybe she was sleeping in. But by noon she still hadn't shown. I noticed the car was gone too. I waited for it to return, she was never out for longer than an hour or so at a time. Something like three hours went by. She didn't come back.

I decided she was gone for good. Must've decided I wasn't worth the trouble, that she could have an easier life without me in it, and she'd be right, too. I opened a pack of her cigarettes and sat smoking on the verandah as the day dragged on. I took one of the little white pills in her nightstand and got drowsy, got calm, like I didn't care about anything at all. But I did.

About midnight she came home in the car. She was drunk as shit and lucky not to have crashed the car and be dead in a ditch somewhere. She was staring at me with half-closed eyes, swaying in place. I stubbed a cigarette out, stood up. She waited for me to say something, waited, so she could say something back. But I just went inside to sleep.

In the morning I took Ugly over to Grandpa's. It was autumn and an invisible drizzle was coming down, only noticeable by the slickness of my arms and the coldness in my hair and the sparkling beads woven through Ugly's dreadlocked mane. Grandpa and I went out to feed the cows, a bag of carrots thrown over each of our shoulders.

The cattle were standing out in the paddock, a hulking mass of them. Pale limbs of sunshine tore through the cloud cover and stretched narrowly across the field, burning yellow stripes into the beasts' trembling backs, golden circlets which faded as the rain thickened and began to fall hard. Grandpa was talking.

> i like cows.
> they got hearts bigger than your head,
> and brains smaller than your prick

We fed them. They had thick, heavy tongues that looked like entirely separate animals. Headless red eels spotted with yellow and pink and black, wriggling out from the deep deep dark and stealing the carrots from my palm, leaving a slippery mucous sheen. I looked over at Grandpa. He rarely answered questions about Mum and Dad, but I thought I'd give it a go.

couldn't find either of them
on the internet

        i dunno how anyone finds anything
            on the internet

all this time and not even a fucking
phone call

        shame's stronger than most
            other things

we're just not worth the trouble

I remember him frowning at that, shaking his head. Then I could see a memory had resurfaced; I think his eyes lit up a little, or maybe they dimmed like he was recalling something he'd rather just forget.

        before they had either of you two
         they kept around this beautiful
           retired racehorse.
        everytime i passed by, though,
       the horse just looked more skinny

and more sad,

till one day he disappeared completely

what happened?

they said they sold him off,

but in hindsight, i dunno.

i guess they really didn't have it in them

A blue haze had formed around the cows, their hot breath mixing with the pale light and the rain. The smell of shit and mulch. Groaning their laments, the strange speech of livestock. We had run out of carrots. Ugly brayed, shook his head back and forth, stood by a nearby fencepost. He was soaking wet; he would stink all week. Grandpa spoke again.

but, you know, they're the ones losing out.

one day, they're gonna feel so heavy

with a lifetime's worth of living,

and they're not gonna have you two.

you and jess, though,

you'll be alright

Not long after that, maybe the next morning, I took a rusted shovel from the shed and went digging out the back of the house. Don't know how I knew, I just knew.

Wasn't shovelling for five minutes before the autumn storm kicked up again, thunder like the sound of the sky splitting open, releasing this cold grey rain which cascaded off the gutters and threaded glimmering pearls through Ugly's hair. He stared at me from his partial shelter, like an apparition come to watch, sequined in dreamlike glow, his black eyes blinking slow and sad.

I dug up nearly the whole yard; Jess was going to throw a fit. The holes varied in depth, and the piles of dirt beside them varied in height, a city of mud with a grave on every corner. Was maybe the thirteenth or fourteenth hole when the shovel struck something brittle and cracked straight through it. Frenzied, I dug faster, though I was hurting, though my whole body was one long ache. Wasn't long before I exhumed the thing; Mum and Dad hadn't buried him deep. Bones jutted out of the wet dirt like the Earth had sprouted baby teeth. The spinal cord wound through the soil, ashen tree root, pale snake in waiting. Femurs nearly as tall as my entire body. And the skull, webbed in grime, eyeholes spacious and sad with a watery blackness flowing out of them, lower jaw detached and laying elsewhere, misplaced, abandoned in a deeper grave.

The car pulled in. The wipers were going fast but to no use. The headlights like two bright eyes unblinking, then switching off, eyes closed. Jess watched me from behind the heavy flow of water coming down the glass.

I saw her mouth making the shape of various expletives but I couldn't hear them. Then she stepped out of the car and into the rain.

what the fuck?

it's mum and dad's horse

i don't give a shit

it died and they buried it

i don't care

i'll fix the yard

you're such a fuck up

My body was filled with this poisonous heat, like a green flame. It poured out my eyes in a flow of warm tears. Dripped across my lower back as a cold sweat. Ugly brayed, shook his head, threw needles of water in a clockwise arc around him. Jess's face softened a bit, then.

are you crying?

why don't you just leave?
you never wanted to do this

do what?

all of this

The grave was filling up with rainwater. The bones were floating now, an inch high, another inch, drifting circularly around this tiny mud sea, broken white islands in motion and never touching except to throw one another off course. Lightning drew fluorescent blood from the sky in a glowing tree-like vein. Thunder shook the world and Ugly brayed and I couldn't stop crying. Jess stepped forward, I thought she might slap me. She didn't, though. She wrapped me in a hug, squeezed the air out of me. We hadn't hugged since I was little. The grave had overflowed, the horse bones now floating around our feet. But it didn't matter. I sobbed into her shoulder with my full weight. She could bear it.

no, i never wanted to do this.

but i'm not going anywhere

Later on the rain let up, the sky cleared a bit. At dusk I saw the wild horses as jet black silhouettes, like dozens of pupils drifting across the enormous yellow eye of the setting sun. We were on the verandah, Jess smoking a cigarette beside me, we weren't talking, but it was nice. Somewhere in the gathering dark of the paddock Ugly was chewing grass or looking dumb. As the sun sank over the hills like something deflating, something draining away, the silhouettes of the horses merged into the windblown black sky like drops of rain absorbed by a flowing river. Jess sighed. I looked at her; she was tearing up.

now *you're* crying

                                                          yeah

                                                      shut up

                                                  i dunno why

it'll be alright

                                                        yeah?

yeah.
you carry my burden,
i'll carry yours, too

About the author

Isaac Hogarth is a student from Sydney, Australia, completing a Bachelor of Arts at The University of Sydney. He is currently in Pamplona, Spain on a study exchange, and hoping to complete a collection of short stories in this time.

WWRGD?

Eleanor Kirk

Shortlisted

The shirt my mother lent me itches around the collar, and I wonder if it's the type of soap she used to wash it, or whether it's just because it's been hanging in the cupboard so long that dust mites have burrowed their way into the fabric and made beds for themselves there. I wouldn't have borrowed it except Mum said I couldn't very well wear a T-shirt on a first date, and she'd have more idea than me about what women like these days, even if she is almost 60. All I know about women is what I've learnt from her or from movies, and I'm never sure how much truth I should take from the latter. The only DVD I had for ages was *The Notebook*, so I watched that over and over because I thought Rachel McAdams was beautiful and liked the way she and Ryan Gosling fought and then kissed in the rain. When they moved me to the second place and I started working, I could finally save up for some others – mostly romantic comedies set in the '80s or '90s in New York – but I always ended up going back to *The Notebook*, because it was just so classic. The other blokes made fun of me relentlessly, but I didn't care. It was my education. I'd heard guys talk about their girl-friends, but that was mostly about sex or child support, nothing that ever sounded like love the way it seemed in those films. Mum and I talked about them often, over the phone or whenever she came to visit. She reckoned Ryan Gosling was a real spunk.

My shirt is still itchy and it's four minutes after twelve, which is when we agreed online that we'd meet. I'm sitting in the booth seat facing out at the cafe, so I feel like if she'd already walked in I would have seen her, but then again you can never be too sure because people don't always look the same in real life as they do in pictures, especially now there are all these filters and artificially generated images and so on. I'm pretty sure I look like mine – Mum only took my picture the other day, against the white concrete wall in front of her flat because she said it was always good to have a neutral backdrop. Most of the profile pictures I've seen don't have neutral back-drops, they're all girls sitting at bars or standing in groups on balconies or something, but by the time I realised that I'd already posted mine, and it was either that or pictures of me from back at high school when I looked a lot differ-ent, that being fifteen years ago now.

James? someone says, and I look up to see a woman peering over at me from the entrance with her bag clutched in front of her chest. She looks nervous, and exactly like her photograph.

Yumi, I say.

Her whole face lifts in relief and she approaches the table and bends down to kiss my cheek. At the same time, I leap up to greet her, so our heads sort of collide and she reels backwards.

Sorry, I say, my whole body turning red, and she laughs. When she laughs, she looks exactly like one of the pictures on her profile, the one where she's sitting on the beach holding a smoothie, her face turned sideways into the sun. She shrugs out of her cardigan, which she drapes on the back of the chair, and then sits down across from me. I sit down again too and suddenly wonder what to do with my hands. I place them on the table, then on my lap, then slide them underneath my thighs and sit on them.

How are—we both go to say at once, then stop. She laughs again.

Sorry, she says. I get so nervous at these things.

Do you do them a lot? I ask.

Well – not *a lot* a lot, she says, frowning. Just, like, a normal amount?

I nod quickly and say that I've done them a normal amount too. My shirt is itchy and I reach up to scratch my neck just under the collar and then pick up a menu, even though I've already decided what I'm going to order because I looked the place up online a few days ago. Mum gave me $50 when I left this morning, which I told her was too much for the Reuben sandwich, but she shook her head and told me, You'll be paying for hers too, as if that much was supposed to be obvious. She took the money from the old sugo jar in the cupboard, where she puts all her spare change and whatever she gets paid in cash on odd jobs. Back when I was a kid, she was always counting it out at the table with this line down the middle of her brow, muttering about where it'd all gone (and to be fair, I used to steal from it a lot when she wasn't looking, so no wonder she was always so stressed).

Tell me about yourself, Yumi says now, pouring out water for both of us. I feel nerves creep up onto my skin from the inside. Like what? I ask.

Like – what do you do for work?

I decide it's best to just be honest. I, ah – don't have a job right now.

Oh, okay, she says. That's cool.

I'm looking, I go on quickly. Done heaps of applying and stuff. Just haven't heard back from any yet.

Cool, she says again. In what kind of field?

For the last five years, I was paid two dollars fifty an hour to work on a vegetable garden, planting and weeding and watering and fertilising and all that. Depending on who was supervising, sometimes I got to take some of

the herbs with me afterwards, or a carrot or something
if there was one that looked particularly stunted. The
meaner supervisors wouldn't let you, but there was this
one guy, Barry, who always turned a blind eye when he
saw me slip something in my pocket, and then winked
and smacked me on the arse as I was leaving. He liked me
because we could talk about films together, and because
I was a natural with the vegetables. The other blokes
called him a pervert, but he never tried anything on me
other than the arse smacking, and there were blokes at
the last place doing far worse than that.

Anything really, I say, and then I follow it up with,
What about you?, because that's another thing Mum said
to do, to always turn the question around and ask it back
of them. (Not enough men ask women things, she said.
All they do is tell you about their jobs and their crazy
exes and then try and get you into bed.)

I work in policy, Yumi tells me, and then she starts
talking about how she's on a climate change bill at the
moment but because of what's been going on in Indonesia some things have been put on hold. I nod and make a
mental note to find out what's been going on in Indonesia.

My shirt is still itchy, and when the waiter comes to
take our orders, Yumi asks for the couscous salad and a
bowl of wedges for the table. I'm good at maths from
all the calculations I used to do when I worked on the
garden, about how much money I was making and what

I could buy with it (more DVDs, a pack of cigarettes, a music player), so I quickly realise that with the wedges I won't be able to afford my Reuben sandwich. Do we need wedges? I ask, and both she and the waiter look at me like I've just said something very insulting. We don't have to, Yumi responds in a sharp sort of voice. It's the same kind of voice my mother used to use when she caught me taking money from the sugo jar, and it makes me feel just as on edge as it did back then, so I quickly change tack. Never mind, I say, and I flip the menu back open and find something cheaper at random, even though I have spent the last three days salivating at the thought of pastrami. I'll have the toast with preserves please, I say. The waiter asks what kind of preserves I want, but I don't know what's on offer and don't want to look stupid by asking, so I just say butter is fine.

The flow of conversation changes after the wedges comment. Yumi starts looking at her fingernails and answering me in short, clipped sentences, and it reminds me of Mo, my roommate back at the first place, who would come back from phone calls with his girlfriend and not want to speak about it because they'd had a fight or broken up again. I want to ask her more about her job, but don't know what there is to say about climate policy, so instead I ask what she does for fun and she says she likes dressing up as video game characters and going to conventions where lots of other people dress up too.

It gets a bad rap for being this gross fetishised thing, she tells me, but it's actually a really supportive community. I've made friends online that I love more than family.

I don't know what to say to that, so I just go, Hmm, and keep eating my toast. Eventually she runs out of steam from talking about it and then checks the time on her phone and says she should probably go.

Okay, I say. There are still five wedges left in the bowl. I stand up to kiss her cheek, hoping to get it right this time, but she doesn't see because she's turned the other way to get her cardigan, and by the time she's turned back around I've sat down again, so I just wave and say, Bye. She gives me a weird look, and then she goes.

When I get home, Maggie, the wiry neighbour who used to look after me whenever Mum was off on a job, is out on the shared verandah inspecting her tomato plant, which she's got growing out of a mop bucket. She lights up with her whole body when she sees me. James, she says, just the person I was hoping to see. Here, what am I doing wrong?

I inspect the plant's yellow leaves and tell her it's probably overwatered. People think you should water a plant more when it's drooping, but the secret is sometimes just to leave it. Better to under water than over, Barry always used to say. You can always come back from under. Maggie squeezes my shoulder and says, Wish my Rob learnt half the useful things you did when he was in there. He just came back with a stick-and-poke and a Panadol addiction.

When I get inside, I take off my shirt and wash it in the sink with warm water and hand soap. Mum scolds me and says there's a laundry downstairs, but I'm used to washing my things this way and say I don't mind. She asks about lunch with Yumi and I tell her it was okay. She gets a hanger out of the cupboard for the shirt and then puts it on the doorknob so that the water runs down the sleeves and leaves puddles on the carpet. Do you think you'll see her again? she asks.

Don't know.

Well, make sure you follow up, she says. Women like that.

How? I ask.

Send her a message. Say you had a nice time.

I pinch the back of my own hand. But what if she didn't?

Mum just tilts her head at me and says, What would Ryan Gosling do?

I remember how Ryan Gosling followed Rachel McAdams onto that Ferris wheel to ask her on a date in *The Notebook*, and how he wouldn't take no for an answer. I ask Mum if I can borrow her phone, and we sit on the couch together to draft a message.

It was nice to meet you, we write. *Let me know if you'd like to do that again sometime.*

Mum tells me I should leave it at that, but when she's not looking, I have a sudden stroke of inspiration and add: *Sorry about the wedges.* I press send and then lock the phone, and we sit there in silence for a few minutes.

What if she never replies? I ask.

Ah well. Mum pats my hand. You'll always have me.

We turn on the telly, which is in the middle of showing a film about Christmas in England. They play a lot of Christmas films in December, I've found. This one has an ensemble cast of different kinds of people falling in love and being tormented by it, interrupted by ads for a hardware store with prices that are low and staying low. Towards the end of the film, each of the men does some sort of grand romantic gesture to win over the women, and like fate, Mum's phone dings.

Hey! the message says. *Yes, that was nice. I would love to see you again :)*

Mum gives a little squeal and then rubs my shoulders. See, she says. I'll bet it was the shirt.

I'm pink all over. The phone dings again: *Not sure what you mean about the wedges haha*

Mum looks at me confused, and I tell her, Don't ask.

*

233

The next date goes much more smoothly. I've come straight from a job interview so my hair is combed, and even though I'm just in a T-shirt, it's a clean white one that I bought on sale at Lowes, and I feel confident in how I look. We get ramen and then walk along the water into the Botanic Gardens. I ask Yumi more about the video game conventions she goes to, and she tells me about one coming up in January, and what character she's planning to dress as. When she shows me pictures of her costume, I'm speechless. It's amazing and intricate, all blue body paint and white gemstones and prosthetics. I open my mouth, but can't find the right words.

I know it's lame, she says shyly, putting the phone away. I just – it makes me feel more confident, you know?

Why? I ask.

She shrugs, not looking at me. Maybe because I can pretend I'm someone else for a while.

Her chin is tucked right into her chest when she says that and I want to touch it, to lift up her face so that she will look at me and I can tell her how amazing I think she is, but I'm paralysed. I think about how Ryan Gosling walked Rachel McAdams home after they went to the cinema and then danced with her in the middle of the street. He wouldn't hesitate, I think. He would just take the girl and kiss her.

Do you want to dance? I ask.

Yumi snorts and covers her mouth. What, here?

I nod, and put both hands on her waist just like Ryan Gosling did. We sway, even though there's no music. You're so beautiful, I tell her. I can feel her squirming in the dark.

You can hardly see me.

Still, I say – but she cuts me off by kissing me. I can feel her moving towards me, but even then it's a surprise when her lips touch mine. I haven't kissed anyone since I was fifteen behind the toilet block at school, where I used to go with some of the others to smoke, or, in the later years, shoot up. It feels the same now, except even better somehow, and I'm sober, or maybe that's why. It's wet and clumsy and raw and magical. I stand still as a statue and she wraps her arms around me and I feel like I'm floating.

We kiss for I don't know how long and then hold hands and walk back to the trains together, both of us giddy like school kids. She has lipstick on her nose and says she'd like to see me again. I basically fly home. There are buds on Maggie's tomato plant, little beads of fruit promising to grow. Inside the flat, Mum has fallen asleep on the couch in front of the telly. She always says it's an accident when that happens, but I know she just does it so that I'll take the bed for a change.

Yumi and I go on three more dates before she invites me to meet her friends. We go to a popular bar just outside the city. Outside, there's a wooden table with an umbrella for shade, where two of them are already waiting. They introduce themselves as Avanthi and Gretel, and both smile at me and wiggle their eyebrows at Yumi. Clyde's inside getting drinks, Avanthi tells us. You both good with beer?

Oh, Yumi says, um – James doesn't drink.

Why not? Gretel asks, and Avanthi nudges her and says, You can't ask people that. Yumi squeezes my hand and tells me I can get my own drink from the bar. I'll have one too, she says.

Of what? I ask.

Whatever you're having.

I'll have what she's having, I say in a garbled American accent, which is a line from one of the movies I used to watch at the last place. Avanthi laughs loudly and says, Classic, which makes me feel chuffed.

At the bar, I see who I think is Clyde, juggling a frothy jug and a stack of glasses. He's more clean-shaven than in the pictures Yumi showed me, and wears a button-up shirt with the sleeves pushed back. Yumi told me they used to see each other for a bit back at uni, but it was nothing serious. I didn't mind when she first told me, but now seeing him makes me feel funny in my stomach, like it's turning itself over, and I think of how Rachel McAdams dates that other man for a bit in the middle of *The Notebook* before going back to her first love, and wonder which one I am. I'm so in my head about it that I forget to order Yumi anything, so when I get back to the table I give her the cola I bought and say I already finished mine.

The group is discussing some couple that recently broke up. Gretel and Clyde are on opposing sides of an argument about whose fault it was. But what about the bit where he dropped her hand on the way to the dinner party? Clyde is saying. Gretel shakes her head and says, That's what I'd do too if it was the first time I was finding out my partner had a kid. I mean, legally you should have to disclose that stuff straightaway, don't you think?

They're talking about some reality show, Yumi tells me with an eye roll. I nod, wetting my lips, and watch her drink my cola.

Do you watch much TV? Avanthi asks me.

Sometimes, I say.

What kind of things?

I look back at Yumi, who smiles and pats my knee encouragingly under the table. Um, I say, well – recently I've been watching a lot of Christmas films with Mum.

You live with your mum?

This gets the rest of the table's attention. I nod, feeling my cheeks grow warm.

Is it a short-term thing? Clyde asks. He's sitting so near Yumi that sometimes their elbows brush, and the sight of it makes me squirm.

Yeah, I say.

Where were you before?

My stomach flips and then plummets. Yumi lets go of my knee to take another sip of her cola and bumps elbows with Clyde again. I feel sick and thirsty and petrified.

I was — somewhere regional, I say. My voice sounds like there's a hand around my throat.

Oh really? Gretel says. Regional where?

I look at Yumi, who is watching me curiously, probably because this is the first she's hearing of it. Perhaps because it just hasn't come up, or perhaps I've been avoiding it on purpose. I haven't lied, I know, just omitted, but still — I think about what Gretel just said about the person on the reality show who didn't tell them she had a kid, and feel suddenly faint with shame. It's now or never. My mouth is dry and my armpits are wet.

Goulburn Correctional Centre, I say.

The pause that follows lasts a whole eternity. I watch glances bounce between the others like a ping pong ball, Clyde to Gretel, Gretel to Avanthi, Avanthi to Yumi, Yumi to Clyde. The silence feels heavy, like it might crush my chest. Yumi puts down her glass and says quietly, You didn't tell me that.

There is a roaring growing in my ears and I can't look at her, can't look at anyone. I am too hot all over. Clyde asks another question but I don't hear him. There is a vibration now across my skin and the sinking sensation of realising this is over, like waking up from a dream to find out you're in your cell again. I stand up and mumble that I should go.

James, Yumi says. I don't meet her eyes – can't bring myself to see the disgust that must be there. Bye, I say, and I turn and leave. Nobody calls out; nobody follows.

Maggie is out the front again when I get home, palms upturned, holding tiny, shrivelled tomatoes, like hard brown beads. What happened? she cries. Why did they stop growing?

Because, I snap, you killed them. She looks up at me in surprise. You killed them, I say again, and I am shouting now – You killed them, you killed them! I don't know what to do with all that I am feeling, so I turn around and swing my fist into the wall. There's a crunch and my head is pounding and now the white paint has red on it, and so do I. I keep punching, keep screaming, You killed them, as the world clouds over. James, Maggie shouts, stop – but it is coming over me, the white-hot rage, the chemical imbalance in my brain, and there is no stopping once it's started. I throw punch after punch, shouting until my voice grows hoarse. Somewhere on the other side of the fog, Mum's apartment door bursts open and then she is grabbing me, wrapping both hands around my wrist and pulling me backwards, even though she is smaller than me, even though I could spin around and fling her off this balcony easily if I wanted. Come on, urges her voice in my ear, let's get you inside, come with me, let's go. I scream and wrestle but Mum is strong, she has dealt with worse before, and she pulls me with her.

Inside, I drink three handfuls of water from the tap in thick, fast gulps, and then strip down to my underwear and curl up in a ball on the couch. Mum wets a tea towel and rolls it up to dab my forehead. She killed them, I whimper, but I am losing steam now, shaking like a leaf. Somewhere far off, a phone rings. I shake for a long time before I finally fall asleep.

When I wake up, there are two missed calls from Yumi. I don't listen to the messages – I already know what she wants to say, can feel the sting of her disdain through the phone screen. I delete them both, and then her number. She doesn't call again.

Online, I update my profile. Beneath my name and age, I write: Six weeks out of Goulburn Correctional. I don't get any new matches for three days, and then stop looking because I probably never will.

My parole officer helps me get a job at the hardware store where prices are low and staying low. The assistant manager shows me around on my first day and tells me how everything works. There's a plant section up the back, with rows of saplings, and I spend ages walking through them, fingering all the different coloured leaves. I stop in front of a tomato plant at one end, tall and green and dotted with plump red fruits entwined around the wooden stake.

Oh yeah, says the assistant manager. She's a beauty, isn't she?

I touch the leaves, which feel thick and full of life. I had one at home, I tell him. But it's dead now.

Hmm, he says. You water her enough?

You have to be careful not to overwater them, I say.

Well sure, he agrees. But you still need to give them *something*.

I keep looking at the plant and say: It's too late now anyway.

Oh well, he says. You never know.

The tomatoes stare back at me, taunting, and I wonder: What would Ryan Gosling do?

The video game convention is at an enormous warehouse in the outer suburbs. I am wearing the shirt I borrowed from Mum again, which is still itchy, but I force myself not to scratch, thrusting my hands deep in my pockets as I follow the crowds through the doors. Inside is a maze of tents, people walking around in full costumes and posing with one another for pictures. Mounted television screens play animated reels and techno music, and flash signs for things like 10AM VIRTUAL REALITY TOUR. I weave through the crowd, peering above people's heads, until I catch a flash of blue.

Even with her hair woven in braids, her face dotted with gemstones, I know at once that it's her – like seeing her in the cafe all over again. Yumi floats through the room like she's weightless, a goodie bag hooked over one wrist and the other hand clutching a stack of pamphlets. I move towards her, my heartbeat quickening so much I can feel it in my ears. My shirt itches and my palms are clammy with sweat. I wipe them on my jeans.

Just as I'm getting near, someone moves into the path between us to greet her. They are large and painted green, draped in a long black robe and clutching a staff with prosthetic gnarled fingers. She smiles up at them – that same smile from the pictures, from our first date, our first kiss – and they take the goodie bag from her and then her hand. Together, the two of them head towards the virtual reality tour, and I feel an emptiness where my heart just was. Perhaps if I were Ryan Gosling I would follow – but my feet are too heavy and my shirt is so itchy it's like my skin is on fire. I stand completely still and I watch them disappear.

*

Someone has cleaned the wall outside our apartment from where I hit it and left blood. I arrive home late after my shift at the hardware store and go inside. Mum is half asleep on the couch but perks up when she hears me come in.

How did it go?

I shake my head and can't find the words. She shuffles over and pats the space next to her, and I fall into the cushions and say nothing, just stare at my own knees, and the beds of my fingernails, which are now black with soil. Mum takes one of my hands and holds it. Never mind, she tells me. You'll always have me.

Mum falls asleep on the couch again, so I take the bed. When I wake up, the front door is open and I can hear her out on the verandah, talking excitedly with Maggie. When she comes back inside, her face is shining.

James, she says, come and look.

I get up and follow her. On the verandah, Maggie is fussing over the mop bucket, circling her plant, which is tall and green and heaving with bright red fruits. She looks up beaming when she sees me. I don't know what happened, she says. I just woke up and it was like this.

Wow, I say. There are stars in her eyes that make me feel like crying.

I thought it was dead, she laughs, and I laugh with her. She comes over to hug me, and I hide the dirt in my nails as I hug her back.

Oh well, I say into the top of her head. You never know.

About the author

Eleanor Kirk is a fiction, non-fiction and television writer living and working on Gadigal land in Sydney, Australia. Her writing has appeared in publications such as *New Australian Fiction 2023*, online literary journal *adda*, and *The Sydney Morning Herald*, as well as on television networks such as the ABC and Stan.

Ultramarine

Tessa Lunney

Shortlisted

Abram met Ruth in a refugee camp in the winter of 1946. February and the snow was so pure it looked blue, the same blue as the sky when the sun shone. Abram could see the veins in Ruth's arms, her skin was so pale, almost translucent. The veins in her temple. Her blue eyes.

Her name was Ruth Blau. He took it as a sign.

It took weeks of work to show her he was not like the tall German soldiers, the wide Polish guards. Just him, small and spry. He smiled gently, he joked kindly, none of the gallows humour of the last decade, none of the deep irony. He brought her flowers, he grew the flowers himself in any little pot-like object he could find – parts of bombed pipes, abandoned tin cups – wildflowers and the prettiest weeds. He brought her delicacies: American chocolate, French cakes with sugared forget-me-nots. He found the money to buy these treats by running errands

247

almost too rough for his frame, but he did it with a good cheer he never had in the camps. She rewarded him with a smile, with deep blue looks. All winter, all spring, the sun shone in her smile, the sky in her eyes, he said. He named the colours for her: sapphire, duck egg, ultramarine.

They wanted to emigrate. A land with sky. Canada or Australia but Australia gave them passage first. So much sky: royal, violet, Abram struggled to name the almost-purple of the noon Sydney sky. They were in a land of giants but each had some kind of smile in their eyes, sun in their voices, even when the words were snide or shouted.

They had as many children as Ruth's body could manage. Four children, three miscarriages, then they stopped. Still, so many, it gave them so much.

Ruth's family, the Blaus, had a kind of secret. They made cyanide. They enjoyed irony, however bitter.

Ruth's father told a story. Heracles poisoned his arrows, he said. The Spartans threw smoke bombs at the Athenians. Ancient Chinese sects used arsenic smoke in their wars. Henry III had his navy throw quicklime at the French. The Qing dynasty used stinkpots.

Ruth nodded, she smiled at her father's smile. Then his smile deepened. He enjoyed the irony more than he should.

The British thought about using chlorine gas in Crimea in the 1850s but decided against it, he said. The French may have used gas first in 1914, but the Germans used gases most effectively in that first year of the Great War. They got around the Hague Convention by letting the wind pick up the chlorine gas and carry it to the French. German soldiers watched gas float over fields and fell not only the French soldiers but the French horses, the field rabbits, even the tiny spring robins, even the poppies, all keeling over frothing, unbreathing.

The creators called it blue acid, *Blausäure*, but everyone else called it Prussic acid, the killer from Prussia. Ruth smiled back at his smile.

The Blaus worked for IG Farben. They knew Fritz Haber and Max Born, whose Born–Haber cycle created fertiliser and explosives, life and death. The Blaus started making Zyklon A, then moved to the more commercially successful Zyklon B. Zyklon B might have been sold as a pesticide but always held a military interest – the Versailles treaty had even banned it for use as a chemical weapon.

Ruth was a Blau and her father was a chemist. He was in love with blue acid, the blue killer. Or was it the killer of blue? He handled it perfectly safely; the irony tickled him. Even when the laws came in, he was given special dispensation. See? he said, perfectly safe. Ruth tried very hard to return his smile, but no one else was smiling, even her father was not really smiling, not by then.

Ruth wanted a degree in chemistry too; tradition called to her. But she wanted to work with colour or with medicine. Not pesticides: with art, with life. She wanted.

The ghettoes happened not long after.

When Ruth met Abram in the deportees' camp, all she had were her dead. Like so many of them, like Abram himself, she had no family. She had her dead, that's how she thought of it, she had the memories of how her father was taken into a hut to work and she never saw him again, how her mother was sent into the other line and off for a shower, how her sister stood beside her and worked until she caught a cold that made her shrink and shrink until her skull burst from her skin like a sunrise into her own death. What was the chemical composition of that death? Ruth spent her time wondering. Even when the Americans came – or was it the British? – it wasn't the Russians, that she knew – was it the Americans with their bowl helmets or the British with their plate helmets? – she couldn't remember and eventually it didn't matter. They were living and she was living only with her dead. The memory of her father's backward glance, so full of fear. What was the chemical composition of fear? There must be one, she could feel fear course through her like a drug, it must be squirted into her bloodstream, but what was the chemical composition of that hormone? Where could she find medical textbooks in German to find out? This was Holland, they hated anything German, they would cut her tongue out of her head if she spoke. She wandered into a university to listen silently to a lecture but every man in the lecture hall stared at her; she felt fear course through her like a drug. She found the library and found a medical textbook but could only understand some of the words. Would she need to learn Dutch? Surely not, she couldn't bear to, she had to leave this godforsaken continent of snow-covered rubble.

It felt good, if with a faintly bitter ironic taste, to think about chemistry.

When she met Abram and he spoke about tomorrow, like it existed, like they could live there, she was shocked. What tomorrow? Where? There is only yesterday. Surely? He gentled her, the blue of the sky in her eyes, the blue of her eyes in the sky, he said, they could live there. Ruth could feel the excitement of his smile course through her like a drug. What was it, that flooded her when he smiled? She wanted to know, she had to know, she could hardly bear to be borne along on his smile, on all this excitement, her memories slipping from her, her intimate knowledge of fear slipping from her, she couldn't bear it.

Abram turned up one day with a fat book. It was frayed at the edges, it was grey in the pages. He held it out to her with a smile. A medical textbook.

But you don't speak German, Ruth said. They spoke Yiddish to each other, their shared language; the German he'd learnt in the camps didn't count. He shrugged, with a smile.

You don't read Dutch, or Polish, or English, or any other language I could help you with, Abram said, just this one.

Just this one. She could smell the irony in his words, she could taste it.

I'm going to learn English, she said, chin up. There, she had said it. She ignored the memories for the moment.

Abram nodded. Good; we'll need it.

She was too afraid to ask what he meant by that. She delved into the textbook to read about hormones.

Abram's father had sold jewels and gems. Not gold and diamonds, no, they weren't that fancy, but turquoise and amber, garnet and amethyst, malachite and lapis lazuli. He even sold bakelite, that jewel-bright plastic, rows of bangles in the windows for the flappers.

Abram's uncle had sold colour. Paints and crayons, pencils and dyes. He even made his own colours with their own names: tiger-eye, a warm yellow; lilithine, a deep red purple; Grunhilda, a browny-green like a forest floor. But his favourite was not his at all. It had been passed down through the family and at the end of the day it was the thing that really made them money: ultramarine.

Abram's uncle ground the lapis himself. He had been taught by his uncle and his uncle before him. Not father to son, no; this recipe was too precious for such a simple lineage. Someone had to present themselves as the keeper of ultramarine. For Abram, this wasn't even conscious. His uncle recognised him as the keeper straightaway; stroking the lapis stones, holding them in his palm until they were warm, holding them on his tongue, his uncle knew what he was seeing in young Abram.

Abram mixed the paints through his childhood. Through the Depression and the ghettoes too. His father lost the jewellery shop but his uncle kept his paint shop, it was needed. A quirk of fate and Uncle Gold was in no position to argue.

There wasn't much demand for ultramarine. This was a good thing, as there wasn't much lapis about – Prussian blue, easy-peasy, but not ultramarine. Abram wanted to take it all for himself. It preserved perfectly in ideal conditions, but that wasn't life, certainly not his life. Of course, in the end, he could take nothing.

In the colourless place, he dreamed of ultramarine. The ultimate blue, the original, the pinnacle, the irreplaceable. Only perfect in perfect conditions, otherwise mutably alive. He dreamed of blue cloaks on chapel ceilings, blue stones on fat fingers, blue eyes that saw him in full colour. All mutable, alive.

When he met Ruth, met her full blue gaze, he knew straightaway. That she was called Blue was merely confirmation.

Zyklon B came from chlorine gas, from cyanide. Blue acid, the blue killer, or perhaps the killer of blue. Boxes of it in the camps, *gift gas*, branded with skulls and *Achtung*. The irony was bitter as the Blaus toiled. Ruth was just old enough to be useful. The line to the right. Her cousins, too young, line to the left. Ruth didn't see anyone in that camp, no one, only an ever-expanding absence. A place without colour, even in the height of summer there were no green leaves, there was no blue sky. It was a monochrome place, but that too was a trick, as the red blood of each camp inmate beat fierce and wild. Ruth felt it, beneath the heavy blanket of exhaustion that covered them hour to hour, that smothered colour. She felt the wildness like it was its own gas, unstable, lighter than air, light enough to float into any nose and colour it red.

But Zyklon B didn't make her hate chemistry. Chemistry was still the building blocks of life, of everything that mattered in the world; it was family. She just hated that vicious use of a chemical that was meant to bring such wealth to humanity. But Abram became afraid of chemicals that were meant to be ingested, injected, or inhaled. He had to be tricked into swallowing antibiotics. He had to be gasping hard before he would use his asthma inhaler. And vaccines? Ruth had to sedate him and then give him a tetanus jab herself. He gave her a lapis pendant shaped like a heart, as thank you, as sorry. She forgave him everything.

Abram had been a boy of crushes. His first crush at age seven was sweet Sarah across the hall. Sarah had blonde hair in braids, a blank gaze, who did exactly what her mother asked, including refusing to speak to Abram. He thought of it later as a training-wheel crush.

At nine he graduated to Leah. Leah had one lazy eye but a very quick mind and a sharp tongue to go with it. So funny! She could argue anyone into a corner and she insulted Abram in ways that were inventive and playful and hurtful. He wanted to join in but he couldn't quite manage; another lesson.

His crushes continued to include every girl of his acquaintance. As long as he could; soon they started leaving, for relatives in North America, for anonymity in South America. Then they started disappearing, into workhouses, into hospitals, into camps, into the grave. It was hard to daydream, though he managed – encountering a feast of pancakes and feeding them to the bright-eyed girl next to him – finding a soft hiding spot where they could watch the snow fall in winter, watch the sun set late in summer, his bright-eyed girl and him. This bright-eyed girl was every girl because she was no girl, as there was no one in particular to love. Then the boys disappeared, then he disappeared into a camp.

Dreams were suspended. His body was a trap, a mine-field, he was numb, he was overwhelmed. He sometimes wondered, a face as it came off the train, a glimpse he glimpsed as she went to the left, how her lips might feel on his collarbone, how her hipbones might feel in his palm. Then he looked at his palms, calloused and cut; when he looked up, she was always gone. Then he stopped noticing, his dreams suspended in the abyss of his body.

But then, the Americans! With their chocolate so rich it made him vomit, but even his vomit tasted good, after all this time – chocolate vomit! The soldiers sneezed whipped cream, it was said, they pissed champagne. These well-fed boys with their horrified stares, never mind, they'd get used to it, everyone always did, and anyway, it would change soon. And it did, with American nurses! Abram started to wake up. He started to learn English, a word here or there, he threw it out with as much flair as he could manage and oh, he gained a smile, some-times even a laugh, but always recognition. Abram was hungry now, his whole youth had returned to him in one gulp. He was patched up, he was handed over to the British nurses who gave him to the British army who put him in a refugee camp. They called it a camp, but it wasn't a real camp, no, it was more like a holiday resort, with his own bed and a proper pillow and soft cotton sheets and three meals a day, yes, it was a holiday!

And then Ruth came. Her sad blue eyes, he knew just what to do. His whole youth returned to him in one gulp, followed quickly by his future. Was it the lingering stare she gave him, like she saw him and everyone he lost, all in one look? Was it her tiny size, just perfect for him? Was it the click of her wrist as she turned it, such a delicate bone, cracking the joint like she was about to fight? Where had she got that habit, or her habit of staring into the middle distance, or her snaggle-tooth or her frown? He wanted answers to all these questions. He called her back from the middle distance once and she laughed in surprise. He became addicted to that laugh. Once he admitted that to himself, he knew what came next.

Ruth loved it when Abram told her about ultramarine. Rare and precious and worth the effort. She listened to Abram's tales of his family creating colour from nothing but rocks. She shared her family's history of conjuring death from the air and bottling it. The rubble in Arnhem, everyone so thin, the Dutch with their haunted preoccupied post-occupied expressions. Ruth knew she should look like them, but Abram showered her with his words of precious blue, he held her hand and her waist, he kissed her, breathed blue into her. She looked at her reflection and saw ultramarine.

They sat in the dusty cold hall. Abram traced the blue veins in her inner arm. Ultramarine is permanent in perfect preservation conditions. But perfect and permanent: that's not life. Everything fades and changes, comes unglued, returns to its original form or morphs into something new. Ruth nodded. There is a synthetic blue – Prussian blue – popular in Berlin. But, Abram traced that vein, it wasn't as rich and rare as true ultramarine.

Synthetic ultramarine didn't exist until almost the twenty-first century. It was flat and pure and lifeless. Only the artist's skill could make it vibrant, unlike the original ultramarine, so potent that even a child could pick up a paintbrush and speak of God. Abram often thought this was a metaphor for love.

Ruth and Abram had already left the Dutch camp before they were together like a married couple. They were not married. They had not applied for a civil ceremony, they didn't know how to, they couldn't speak any Dutch, despite its teasing similarity to Yiddish and to German.

They certainly hadn't married in a religious ceremony, they no longer knew anyone who could do such a thing and in any case who would they invite they had no one to invite it would be so quiet and desperate and anyway who would – Abram grabbed Ruth's hand and kissed it hard to stop her head from spinning. They had left the Dutch camp for London and were living in the East End, a place with herring and blintzes and a dizzying combination of pitying, garrulous, enthusiastic, devastated, overjoyed looks – really, they hadn't encountered so much public emotion for a long time. The British were supposed to be buttoned-up, stiff-upper-lip, no-nonsense types, but compared to the flat despair of the camps, the patina of hatred from the guards, the wide-eyed American soldiers and hyper-focused nurses, the preoccupied post-occupied indifference of the Dutch, the variety of looks from these Londoners who actually saw them, who saw them as two individuals, Abram and Ruth, unique and wondrous for having survived hell – well, it was a shock. In every shop, in every bus, on every corner, someone saw them and emotion flitted over their face, unbidden and unhidden. London showed itself for what it really was – not grey, foggy, bombed and hungry, but a place full of people with a tenacious grip on life and the humour to joke about it, the confidence to whinge about it. Because, Abram told Ruth, whingeing means you expect things to be better, you expect things to change, it's a hopeful activity.

So we should be whingers? Ruth raised her eyebrow. Yes, he jumped up, yes, let's whinge for life!

Because life was what they were after. It was what Abram had, it had all rushed back to him in one gulp, and it rattled Ruth, then it made her laugh. It was in London, with the doorman whingeing about 'bloody rationing', that they found a bed near an unsmashed bagel bakery. After spending the day in shops with women serving them, they managed a spread of bread, pickles and sardines. They ate these delicacies in their pyjamas, a gift from the shop women, who whinged to them in-between gossip and laughter and whistles and clucks. Duck, Ruth was called, pet, love, poppet. They called Abram 'big man' but it wasn't unkind, they sighed and they smiled when he kissed Ruth's hand. They could hear Big Ben chime the hour, six, it was dark, it was cold, they didn't care. They fed each other while Big Ben chimed seven. The big clock chimed eight, a soft warm sound, Ruth thought, a solid sound, Abram thought. They undressed each other slowly, Abram reverent, Ruth careful, Abram nervous, Ruth determined, Abram delighted and so Ruth delighted and so they fell into bed. A real mattress with springs, a real down quilt, real down pillows, was this heaven? The big clock chimed nine, perhaps it was, perhaps Ruth's sighs were really the sighs of angels, perhaps Abram's encouragements were divinely inspired. The big old clock chimed with their heartbeat, they were together, they were here here here.

In the long night afterwards, wrapped in each other, dozing but not sleeping, hands free at last to seek and to know, Abram told the story of ultramarine.

First, said Abram, hundreds of years ago, the Trader — let's call him David (Ruth giggled, yes, let's call him David, Abram laughed, alright, let's call them all David) David went east. He set out from Lvov, which was the centre of the world then, and headed to the Caucasus.

His thumb ran over Ruth's nipple and an angel sighed.

Then David, said Abram, travelled across the Caucasus on horseback with the Tartars. It was lucky he wasn't murdered! But then, David was lucky.

Ruth's hand found a soft place and stroked.

David went across the great plains until he came to the mountains. There were mosques there, blue and green and gold, people danced to symbols and sang in great wails, you couldn't find a bagel but there were dates and honey galore.

The line of her neck, the hard slope of his shoulder.

Abram continued. David had a mission. He had to find blue. His family had scarlet and ochre, pine green and mustard, but they didn't have blue, a true blue, a proper deep blue. David walked behind herders, he hitched rides with caravans, he gossiped with traders. He knew, from what people said, that he needed to go deep into the mountains to find it.

It took years. David travelled and travelled, he sweated and shivered, he went round in circles and loops and hairpins, following the trail of blue. He fell in love and despair and joy and fear, he was spoken to by the angels, told that love is the only truth, that to give is more holy than to receive. He followed blue.

He remembered his family, his wife, his children. He remembered his father, his mother, his grandmother. He had to return to them with blue, with something in his hands for all his searching.

He came to the mountains. They sang his name, David David, he followed the herder who followed the path up the mountain and down into the valley. The trees sang his name, David David, he followed them to a cave, the herder left him at the cave entrance as he went inside. The walls of the cave were dark, but when he struck a light, they sparkled. They glowed blue.

David had been taken to a cave of lapis lazuli. He filled a bag with the stone. An old woman of the village demanded payment and he gave her the last of his treasures from home: gunpowder. The old woman was delighted at the bang it made, she laughed with no teeth, her eyes glinted. They shook hands, they nodded, David could return anytime.

Another two years and David was home with this stone. His parents were wary of him, his children nervous, his wife unsure. He walked to his wife, he kneeled down at her feet and kissed them. Noise erupted, they covered David with kisses, his long absence forgiven.

They worked together on the stone. How to get the sparkling blue onto canvas? David's wife (let's call her Esther, Ruth said between sighs, let's call them all Esther. Not all, said Abram into her neck, some must be called Ruth) David's wife Esther worked out the mixture in their kitchen. Grind the stone, add wax, resin, oil (his skin, her skin, sighs turned to moans) Knead the mixture and soak it in lye. Do this three times (like a spell? Ruth's voice was breathy. Like a prayer, Abram spoke directly to her clavicle) The ash at the bottom, the detritus, the leftover, this is blue, this is ultramarine. This is worth more than gold (blue is worth more than gold? Ruth gasped. Always, Abram said to her navel and lower, blue is always worth more than gold, blue is everything) this is the colour of gods and kings, of holy virgins and the sky of paradise. Blue is everything.

Ultramarine became highly prized during the Renaissance. David gave it to his son, David, who gave it to his daughter, Esther, who gave it to her niece, Ruth. Ruth kept the ultramarine down and down and down through the generations, until it came to my grandfather, until it came to my uncle, until it came to me.

This is a fairytale, Ruth bit her lip. It is the highest truth, Abram said and then showed her how so.

The big old clock chimed here here here. Angels sighed. The world had a future.

The fairytale was told over and over. They told it on the boat to Sydney, with David's journey invaded by waves. They told it in the Nissen huts at the refugee camp, the air thick with cicada song. They told it in their first home, blue and gold decorating the architraves, David's tale growing to go through the tropics, on planes that flew high above rivers, always ending in Abram and Ruth and their babies safe in bed. Blue is the highest truth, Abram would whisper, and Ruth never tired of hearing it.

In Australia, Abram continued to mix colour. How precious is tradition. His workmates called him Big Man ironically, they didn't understand the literal meaning of growing up on nothing. Abram took it with good grace but he grew taller when he had his own shop, when his teenage helpers called him Sir and Mr Gold.

Ruth was Mrs Gold, but Abram insisted on her being Blue Gold. Their children were all Blue Gold: David Blue Gold, Esther Blue Gold, Joel and Rachel Blue Gold. Abram changed his name as soon as he had citizenship. The shop was called Blue Gold Colours. Like true ultramarine, he whispered in bed, holding her, his nails stained blue with paint, like all that is precious.

They had no family but themselves. They found other survivors in Sydney for blini on the holidays. So much colour in the gold blue green white place with its pink and grey birds, its rainbow birds, with its huge and peaceful sea. They even spoke Yiddish; so precious.

And then there were the dark days. Memories rose unbidden and unwelcome, summoned by a smell, a sound, by nothing at all but blood thickening in veins, by a too-shaky breath on the stairs.

A pomegranate broken open and bleeding over the kitchen bench. Ruth screamed and wept, seeing real blood from a real broken skull in the ghetto.

A cold gloomy grey wet day, midwinter, Sydney's usual sun in exile, Abram happy at first, the weather so Polish, then nervous, then tense, why did he feel tense he wondered, then his limbs felt heavy, then his feet, then his head. The cold gloomy grey wet over the KZ, Abram as numb as he had been in the camps.

Ruth kneeling by the rubbish bin in the dark, eating the rotten bread scraps and potato peelings directly from the bin.

Abram unable to throw anything away that belonged to his children, not a note from school, not a scribbled painting, not a singlet stained with food. Everything kept, in boxes, with inventories on the outside of each box, in a garden shed, then another garden shed, then a third. Everything kept, Abram sitting in the sheds in the dense heat and remembering remembering remembering remembering.

Glassware was smashed. Ruth and Abram screamed at each other, a white rage taking hold of them as they yelled in different languages, then they broke down sobbing mumbling in Yiddish or in gibberish or just moaning. Clutching each other. Not noticing their frightened children, not noticing anything. Eventually the children worked out the early signs and blocked out the chaos by making a cubby house around the radio, then the television, until their parents had weathered the storm.

Days of silence. Abram shuffling. Ruth stumbling. The children learned how to boil their own potatoes, how to make their own sandwiches, it was that or go hungry and if they'd gone hungry then they would have got in trouble. Going hungry was unforgivable.

Some years the dark days were frequent. The year before Abram got his own shop was a year of storms. The year their youngest left for university was another turbulent year, Abram and Ruth shocked by the emptiness of their house, shaken by it, unravelled and untethered. But then Ruth got a better job, a daughter-in-law came, then a baby, then a son-in-law, and so on and so on. Their house concertinaed – too empty too full too empty too full – but it felt right and Abram and Ruth could breathe again.

Ruth took a long time to become a chemist. At first she couldn't even be a chemistry teacher, her accent was too foreign for all the freckled kids. She did gain a reputation as an excellent after-school tutor; the first hour free, to get used to her accent, then high prices. She had no degree, only great results. Only an innate understanding of irony.

Ruth did get her degree, about the same time as her youngest child. She worked at a lab that created synthetic ultramarine. When the blue was finally made, stable and too pure, Ruth gave Abram a lapis lazuli paperweight, their initials carved in gold in the lapis. The lapis was the biggest she could find, bigger than a fist, bigger than a baby's head. Abram wiped a tear when he unwrapped it. His wife, his Ruth, did the amazing thing and then gave him a gift. The lapis was not the gift of love, whatever it symbolised. Their life was.

Gift, he said, we changed it from a poison to a present. Ruth smiled.

When is blue gold? – a favourite joke, she smiled as she snuggled into his arms. But he couldn't give the punchline, *when it's ultramarine*, he was too full, the moment felt too precious.

'You,' he said, unplanned, 'you are ultramarine.'

About the author

Tessa Lunney lives on Bedigal land in Sydney, Australia and has published two thrillers set in 1920s Paris, *April in Paris, 1921* and *Autumn Leaves, 1922*. Her short fiction won the Josephine Ulrick Prize for Literature in 2016 and her short fiction, poetry, and reviews have been published in *Southerly, Cordite, Griffith Review,* and *Mascara* among others.

The Shadows Cast
by the Moon

John Merkel

First Place

P ushing down hard on her rage over her daughter having gone and lost her mind – again! – and this time properly, Ethelwyn Macken spent the month of May and half of June swatting away hearsay on the steps of the church and at the yacht club ladies lunch, and replacing it with a story about a virus from a grass tick that had gotten into Molly's brain, but now she was doing just fine, thank you very much.

Picking Molly up from the hospital, Ethelwyn took her straight to the flat above the shop in Carrickmines she had recently added to her property portfolio. It was just far enough from her home on the bay to ensure she wouldn't have to deal with fevered visits out of the blue that might alert friends and neighbours to Molly's true condition, but not so far that she couldn't keep an eye on things.

As they drove through Sandyford, Molly rubbed her temples and cricked her aching jaw side-to-side as she struggled to remember the events that had landed her in hospital. Her treatment had left gaps in her recent memory – more gap than memory.

'Where are Patrick and the children?' she asked her mother.

'They've gone.'

'Gone where?'

'To the country.'

'Are they—'

'That's all I know! I don't know where to, or for how long, and I don't wish to discuss it any further.' All of her pushing down was pushing back up. 'You'll have to sort that out for yourself. You accused him of trying to poison you, do you remember that?'

Molly didn't remember.

Hurrying her up the stairs at the rear of the flat with her suitcase and a box of groceries, Ethelwyn issued a set of keys and instructions about security and housekeeping. She looked at her daughter – her face sunken and ghostly from a month and a half indoors, muck food, and the electrical charges of terror and its remedy – and told her she would return soon, but that she was not, under any circumstances, to come to her.

Molly sat in a square of sunlight by the back door, and looked down at the upturned pots spilling cylinders of dry dirt onto the concrete slab that was her new yard. She tried to identify the plants from their dead and dying forms: buddleia; a Japanese maple maybe; an ornamental olive in a blue-glazed pot lying on its side, two wiry arms thrust out begging for a drink.

She tried to think. Had she really thought that Patrick was trying to poison her? Her mother had reminded her of the one thing that she, and her doctors too, would have liked to remain forgotten. She tried to focus on other things – or on nothing at all. Thinking about nothing at all was the most difficult thing, but had been made easier by her treatment. She looked down at the yard again. Dogwood. Apple. Starry magnolia?

She had seethed at her psychiatrist, her fear a thick paste in her mouth, when she'd first been admitted. A keen student of history and the holy bible, she had insisted to him that in times past she would have been made a saint like Christina the Astonishing who had witnessed heaven and hell, who had been conducted by angels to places of glory and others of gloom, filled with souls enduring torments that were impossible to describe. Like Christina, Molly had instructions for a righteous life for anyone who would listen, but in the industrial age it seemed that the destiny of the seer was the asylum, and the obliteration, by chemical and electrical means, of all that had been seen. Rejected by family and friends, she had been left with no choice but the choice of the state, which was to flatten the landscape of her memory and emotion, and to make of it a desert in which troubled thoughts and strange ideas could not take root and grow into even stranger and more troubling things.

Molly didn't remember any of it: the blowouts with Patrick and her doctors, the physical restraint, the turn of the dial. But now that she was on the other side of her treatment she agreed that, on the whole, erasure had been helpful. She felt dull and stilled, and it was a relief. The desert was her oasis. But she did want to know certain things – like where were her children?

The two youngest were in a wheelbarrow, Molly pushing them along as they bounced and laughed their way down to the bottom of the garden where daffodils and pink rock lilies splashed their colours between rows of vegetables and kitchen herbs. Parsley, leeks and lettuce, for soups and salads. Rosemary, carrots and tarragon for Sunday roasts. They were going to plant strawberries, she remembered that. She had challenged her children to reach some agreement about what they would choose if there was only enough room for one more thing – talk to each other, no hitting or yelling – and strawberries had won out. But when was that?

Lost in time, Molly uncrumpled the leaflet she was clutching in her fist:

Find Support Amongst Friends.

A woman had come to her that morning, while she was being discharged, to tell her about the self-help groups she ran, but Molly had been groggy, and had struggled to understand what use it would be to sit with others with the same kinds of problems, to talk about the strange fabulations of their minds, all together and at the same time. Surely it would only heap confusion on confusion. And where would she begin, even if she wanted to? By telling them that sometimes and unexpectedly she devoutly believed that she was Eve, or the Virgin Mary, returned to rid the world of sin, or to pay her penance for her part in it?

But the woman had also said something about needing help in the office. Simple filing and mailing, nothing at all demanding – things Molly was familiar with from running a household and the boat hire business she and Patrick had bought when they'd run away to the coast. And the woman had been kind. Molly turned the leaflet over and saw the name Annabel and a phone number written in a scribbly hand.

For the rest of June and most of July, Molly slept most of the day and not much at night. She sat in the sun by the back door when there was some to be sat in, trying to think – but not too much – about how she had ended up where she was, and what might be next for her. When she thought about her children – where they were, and what they might be doing – she had the vague notion that she should perhaps be feeling more for them, but was thankful not to be overwhelmed by feelings of shame or longing; feelings of any kind at all. The day after her birthday, Ethelwyn turned up, ill-tempered and empty-handed, to take Molly for her 'scheduled maintenance' – a short sharp shock – then delivered her back to the flat with renewed confidence that she wouldn't be causing any trouble or embarrassment any time soon.

Annabel held Molly's hands, and praised her fortitude in making the short bus trip to the city like she was welcoming her home from a great odyssey. She showed her the cramped office they would both have to squeeze into if Molly felt like staying to help, even for an hour or so.

'It'll be cosy with two,' she chirped. 'I told Doctor Monaghan you might be dropping in, and he said if you felt like making tea down in the meeting room, you could just listen in on this morning's group. Then, if you want to, you could join in. But only if you want to.'

When she arrived at the room where the doctor sat in a circle of six, Molly heard a slurred and raucous voice.

'It was a sunny day! I remember that. Bright and sunny! If your life is suddenly going to come unstuck, it might as well be on a nice sunny day!'

The man was bellowing and throwing his hands about as the others sat still. Molly wondered why they had let a drinker into a meeting that was supposed to make people feel comfortable to sit and talk. She went quietly in and put her tea tray on the table beside a steel urn.

'I was good at school,' the man was saying now, swaying on his seat, gripping his knee to steady himself. 'Especially maths and drama. I liked reading plays!'

Molly looked at him again. He was about her age, maybe younger, closer to thirty-five. He was tall, and neatly dressed in navy trousers, a blue linen shirt under a tan jacket, and a paisley cravat. As Molly was wondering if the cravat was really a good match with his jacket, he glanced over at her, and she dropped a saucer clattering onto the table.

'Ah, and this must be Molly,' Doctor Monaghan announced cheerfully.

'Hello Molly!' the man called out.

'She might come and join us at some point,' the doctor said. 'Would you like to join us now, Molly?'

'No thank you, I'm busy.' If she was going to join in at all, she would wait for another session that wasn't being hijacked by a noisy drunk.

'Thank you Molly, I love cups of tea!' the man called out to her.

'It's good medicine,' the doctor agreed. 'Would you like to go on, Joseph? Tell us a bit more?'

'I was twelve years old, on my pushbike, on my way to a rehearsal of the school play, when I decided to take a shortcut down a side street – and bang!' He clapped his hands together. 'I was hit by a bus!' His account was so loud and abrupt, it was as though that same bus had just slammed into the timid circle, making the others startle, as Joseph laughed. Why was he laughing, Molly wondered as she laid cups out on the table.

'And that was that. All over, red rover. I was in a coma for five weeks, and when I woke up, I had a tube in my neck for breathing.' He hooked a finger into his cravat and tugged it down to reveal the craterous scar of a tracheostomy. 'And I lost a lot of my hearing, so I'm a bit deaf. Am I talking too loudly? My da says I have to watch out for that. Shouting!' No one seemed to want to say that he was perhaps a little loud, so he went on undiminished. 'And there's a metal plate in my skull.' He rapped his knuckles on his head. 'Hear that!'

Molly could see that beneath his blonde curls his forehead was slightly indented, and that his handsome face drooped a little on the left.

'And that day left you with some other problems too, didn't it? Some psychological ones,' the doctor prompted. 'Would you be able to tell us about some of those?'

'Yes! Like I might just be sitting with my parents, listening to the radio or watching TV, and suddenly the walls rush away and I feel like I'm shrinking. It's very frightening, so my mother gets the little mirror from her dressing table to show me I'm still the same size, but it's hard to tell because *nothing* really seems the right size when I'm feeling that way . . . It's hard to explain . . .'

'And, how do you feel when—'

'Or sometimes I feel like someone else is living inside me. Once I woke up thinking I was Horatio Hornblower from the movies, and my parents had to come and find me at the beach. But other times it's someone I don't even know or like, and man oh man, that really spoils my day.'

Molly tuned her ear. She knew just what he meant.

'Oh well,' he said, quietly now, sensing that he might have overdone it. 'Never mind, you can't help bad luck. That's what my ma says.'

Back in the office, Annabel gave Molly some flyers to fold for a Family Day aimed at getting loved ones more involved at the centre. She knew her sister would come if she was around, but she was on the other side of the country, a farmer now, well away from the society their mother had imagined for them, with no plan ever to return.

Joseph appeared at the door – excited.

'You're both invited to my party! I'm getting my own flat, just down from my parents' place, just for a couple of months to see how it goes. And thank you Molly for the tea. It's not easy to get a good cup of tea these days – especially from someone who is actually beautiful!'

Molly laughed and made precise and unnecessary adjustments to her stack of flyers.

'Alright Joseph, that's quite enough,' Joseph said. 'But I do drink tea all day long because my medication makes me so thirsty. The perpetual cup of tea we call it. Do you like parties, Molly?'

'Sometimes, if they're not too big and noisy.'

'I'll be the biggest and noisiest thing there.'

'A house-warming party sounds lovely,' Annabel said.

'But don't say house-warming.' His tone was suddenly urgent.

'Why not?'

'It feels too hot, like the flat's getting too hot inside, and we'll all have to get out quick.'

'Alright then, let's just call it Joseph's house party.'

Molly felt an urge to say something encouraging before he left. 'You look a good size today . . . I mean you look the right size. Not too small, or too big either.'

'Just right, then?'

'Yes.'

'Thank you, Molly, that's good for me to know,' Joseph said, quietly now, the storm inside him momentarily stilled.

When Joseph left, Annabel asked Molly if she'd like to take a break and sit in the anteroom with Michelle, a young mother who'd been anxiously rocking her sleeping baby in the talking circle. The baby was awake and crying now, and as soon as Molly sat beside her and touched her hand, Michelle began to cry too, saying over and over again that she didn't know what to do. Molly took the baby and waltzed him softly around the room, inhaling his sweet milk breath, cooing him back to calmness – and his mother too. She took him close to the window where his hand could reach for a blood-red velvet curtain shimmering in the sunshine: a dazzling novelty to silence the last of his sobbing. She told Michelle she had found being a mother hard at first, too, but that it got easier as she went along.

Molly spent the afternoon helping Annabel in the office, and making more tea while she eavesdropped on Doctor Monaghan's next session with another group who weren't nearly as forthcoming as Admiral Hornblower. They were nervous and circumspect in their responses to his gentle probing, and the entire effort seemed to grind to a stop before it even got underway.

'You should put Joseph on the payroll,' she said to Annabel when she returned to the office.

'Really? Why's that?'

'He talks so easily about his most terrible problems, and laughs about it, like he's telling a joke, and maybe it's not quite so bad as it seems once it's said out loud.'

'Ah.'

'But I don't know if it's for everyone . . . telling every-thing about yourself like that.'

Molly arrived at the end of her first day at the centre with a feeling she hadn't had for a long time. Though only faint, it was a feeling of steadiness and fulfilment through useful work, and of belonging to a clan of kindred spirits. Even Eve, the first woman – always lumping her writhing sack of sinners as big as a hill along behind her – seemed too tired, too smudged out by electric convulsion, to argue or even whisper against faint hope as they lay down to sleep that night.

Joseph's house party was a hit at first, and not too hot. Soren, his father, played The Temptations and Gil Scott-Heron on his portable record player, and dispensed cigarettes and rations of rum and cola, while his mother, Natasha, shimmering in sequined silk and handmade jewellery, went out of her way to make Molly feel at home. As the party reached its second hour, Annabel arrived with chocolates and flowers to find Joseph taking the floor, urged on by his parents and cousins to do impersonations of movie stars and people he had met.

'I think we're all very grateful to Molly for coming today,' he said, wringing his hands and nodding earnestly, 'to sit with us and tell us a little bit about how she's getting along.'

'Doctor Monaghan!' Natasha cackled, chugging on her rum.

He did some others — Al Pacino and Barbra Streisand — but then was overcome by the shrinking feeling as the walls rushed away. He wanted to abandon the party and the new flat altogether, and go back home. While Natasha calmly saw off the guests, except for Molly who she asked to stay for tea, Soren sat with Joseph in his bedroom, talking him down to steadier ground, easing the walls back in, and propping them in place with slender sticks of gentle reassurance.

'I heard talk of pie and peas,' Soren said after a while. 'Will we go and see if that's still on?'

Trying to hide a smile, Joseph followed his father back out to the lounge room where Natasha and Molly were shelling peas, drinking wine, and talking about the Romans in England.

'It really ran away on me that time,' Joseph said to Molly. 'I got too excited. I'm sorry if it was all a bit stupid.'

'I thought you were funny — everyone did.'

'Oh man. That's good to know, Molly,' he said, slapping his forehead as he collapsed into an armchair.

Natasha was shocked at the state of Molly's flat when she drove her home that night. Fatigue and dejection had caused her to neglect herself and her usual commitment to keeping house. Clothes were strewn all around, dirty plates and pots stacked high in the sink. Food cans, open and half-eaten, littered the table, and the air had a rancid whiff of giving up about it.

The next morning Natasha told Annabel what she had seen, and said that she was thinking of offering Molly the spare room in Joseph's flat.

'Don't you think it would be a lot for them both to manage?' Annabel asked. 'Maybe too much?'

'I think they could help each other. We're taking care of a lot of the cooking and cleaning, so . . .'

'How do you think Joseph might cope if Molly had some kind of episode when it's just the two of them?'

Natasha looked right through her, into the long-forgotten dream of having a daughter she'd had when she was still only a girl. Since her son's accident, she had become so overwhelmed by the complexities of the human psyche that she had, over many years, boiled it all down to a simple personal philosophy about love and kindness.

'Joseph's no stranger to strangeness,' she said at last. 'None of us are. I think he'll cope . . . We'll all cope together, and we'll see if we can't bring some love into her life. That's what it's supposed to be about, isn't it?'

Annabel wanted to agree that it was, indeed, all about love, but her daily work told her another story about how love alone was not enough in the lives of people like Molly and Joseph. She had seen and felt the heavy air

that could descend upon a clear blue day to smother deli-
cately held feelings of safety and self worth, making the
people in her care lash out, ferocious and afraid, against
imagined threats that often took the physical form of
husbands and wives, parents and children, and were as
real as the shadows cast by the moon. Or, if not lashing
out, retreating deep inside, only to find their demons
chasing them all the way into the smallest recesses from
which escape was impossible as they curled up in their
beds, the corners of hospital wards, or beneath cardboard boxes on city streets.

It was midsummer, and Joseph had invited Molly to go
to the beach with him and his parents, but now a new
medication was making his skin splotchy and red with an
itchy rage whenever he went out in the sun.

'I don't think my da even likes the beach,' Joseph said
to Molly as he pushed a chair into a narrow strip of shade
along the edge of her concrete yard. 'I think he just does
it for me.' He mimicked Soren behind the wheel of the
car, dragging hard on a cigarette stub: 'Man, oh man, why
does everyone on the freaking planet want to go to the
beach at exactly the same time!' He flicked the butt out
the window.

Poor old Hornblower, Molly thought, having to stay
out of the sun and away from the sea. 'Why don't we go

to the river at Shackleton Mill,' she suggested. 'They've got canoes for hire – and it's shady.'

'Let's go! I'll phone my da.'

'You know, we could go by ourselves if you like. Just the two of us. We can get the bus, and your da can have a day off.'

'What about lunch?'

'I'll make sandwiches – and a flask of tea. Or we can get fish and chips at the kiosk.'

At the end of their day out, as the sun dropped below the trees above the picnic ground, they packed up their things and headed back to the bus stop.

'There's something I do with my parents sometimes,' Joseph said as they walked along the river path. 'We take it in turns to say things that happened in the day. It can be good things or bad things, it doesn't matter. It can be something that was funny or annoying or sad . . . Do you want to try it?'

'Okay.'

'Good. I'll go first. We paddled a canoe. That was good.'

'We fell asleep on the grass,' Molly said. 'That was good.'

'But we *didn't* slide down the weir, and *that* was a bit sad,' Joseph said.

'Why sad?'

'Because my head would spin right off if I tried it, but watching everyone else do it made me think of all the things I miss out on – but not for too long. Your turn.'

'We had fish and chips,' Molly said. 'You know, I could teach you to cook some things.'

'My ma always cooks.'

'I know. But now that you've got your own place . . . Imagine if your ma came over and you'd made her a plate of pancakes, or a fried egg on toast.'

'And a dry martini.'

As a couple on a bicycle went racing by, Joseph side-stepped and grabbed Molly's arm to stop himself from falling. 'Oops, that was close,' he said, swaying back to centre. 'People think I've been drinking, the way I wobble around.'

'Let them think what they like. They don't know anything,' Molly said, holding him until he was steady again.

Come, live with me, and you will know me.

Molly remembered these words from somewhere, but had only ever reflected on them in the shadowy light of her life with her war-ravaged husband, Patrick, who drank heavily and shouted at the sky. Patrick had indeed come to live with her, had married her and had children with her, and now was gone. But Joseph was not complicated like Patrick — or not in the same way. She liked spending time with her man-child friend who could dispatch his demons with confetti and a kazoo on his better days, and whose affectionate nature relieved some of her shyness and anxiety. So, when Natasha put it to her that she should come and live in Joseph's spare room, it took all of Molly's still scattered powers to say no. She understood now that his mania was an after-effect of his accident, and an often volatile influence on his natural talkativeness, one impelling the other until he blew a fuse or wore himself out and fell asleep where he sat. Molly knew she wouldn't be able to cope with all of that at close quarters, between the same four shifting walls. She had children of her own somewhere out there, and knew their demands as well as their affections. She would not risk her new friendship on the promise of clean sheets and cooked meals.

To assuage Joseph's disappointment, she made up a story about needing space for her children when they come to stay.

'We can get more beds,' Joseph pleaded, 'and they can live with us, too.' But he saw from her faraway look that her mind would not be changed.

Joseph and Natasha spent the afternoon with Molly in her flat, sweeping and cleaning, and throwing the doors and windows open to the fresh air. After they'd hung the washing out in the sun, Molly stood the olive up in its pot, rubbed its dry soil through her fingers, and searched the edges of the yard for a tap, only to find one without a handle. Back inside she settled Joseph into an easier tempo, showing him how to make origami cranes from sheets of gift-wrapping paper that had lined the wardrobe shelves; folding and pressing in meditative repetition until they'd made a small flock of them to decorate the kitchen wall.

Saying many goodbyes as they were making to leave – in the hall, at the top of the stairs, and again at the bottom – Joseph reminded Molly that they'd be happy to pick her up on Saturday morning if she wanted to come with them to the Family Day.

'I'll think about it,' she said. 'I'll see how I feel.'

Sitting at the kitchen table, Molly watched the streetlights blink on along the street as she sorted and folded her clothes, still warm from the sun and smelling of soap flakes. In the deep silence that now replaced the clatter of cooking and the chatter of children gathering for a meal, her mother's words came creeping back in. Had she really driven Patrick from his home like a criminal? A poisoner? Had she frightened him away? Poor Patrick. They had tried to love each other – to save each other – and now exile and an empty kitchen were their rewards for all they'd done and made.

She had to stop thinking about it. The hours and minutes of Molly's days had become an exercise in resolve: in finding even the smallest of reasons to get out of bed in the morning and to not get back in again until night-time. Or to find no reason at all, yet to still eject herself from that place of torpor beneath her sheets by force of will. In the last of the light, she went down into the yard and carried the olive back up to soak its roots under the tap in the bath. As happens with those who are true gardeners, in thumb and blood, she felt it quenching her too, doing her good. Heavy from its drenching, she wrapped her arms tightly around it and lifted it up. Imagining its new green shoots and the dark roundness of its fruit, she danced it along the hall and placed it down by the kitchen window where it would catch the first rays of the morning sun.

About the author

John Merkel is an Irish Australian who also writes under the pen name Ryan Delaney. Originally from Gumbaynggirr country on the east coast of Australia, he currently lives in Edinburgh. In 2024 his first novel-in-progress *The Gospel Under the Southern Sky* was chosen for development at the Irish Writers Centre. 'Franky Unbound', a story about being the youngest in a big family, was shortlisted for the All Ireland Scholarship, and 'Once Upon an Algorithm', about a writer getting into a psychological struggle with a chatbot, was shortlisted in the RTÉ Radio 1 short story competition.

The Best Pieces not from Me

An Ngo Lang

Shortlisted

Yours was the first name I uttered, or so I was told. Just two simple letters to make a word, with a descending accent mark and a falling tone: Bà. How comforting it was to let it plummet from my lips each time you were near. In our tongue, it means grandmother, but for me, it meant a smile of black lacquered teeth like piano keys, lips stained ruby red from the betel nut you loved to chew, broad shoulders that blocked the sun above, and a barrel-sized waist perfect for my little arms to hug.

That day, our steps were in unison on the dusty ground, mine clad in pink clogs – the ones I wore because I thought they made me a princess – and yours bare. I couldn't help but stare at your big toes. Instead of lining up with the rest like soldiers, they curved and jutted out like thumbs. Mom said it was because you were a true Vietnamese woman, descended from the original people who came to our land, your bloodline pure. I wasn't sure what that meant, so I said it was because your big toes must have tried to run away but couldn't escape.

With one hand, you held mine, and in the other, a bowl of leftover braised pork, and together, we passed your vegetable garden of stripy luffa and red chili with your dogs at our heels, their tongues long and lolling, hoping for a morsel. I stroked the leaves with my free hand as you did when you watered and tended them, willing them to grow tall and abundant. The branches of the giant mango tree arched over our heads, and when I looked up, oblong green fruit hung like the dainty jade earrings Mom wore when she went to elegant dinner parties with Dad and left me with you.

And under that tree, we reached the pond with lily pads on top and fish underneath. Dragonflies did what they did best – shimmer and flit up and down over the water's surface, their wings a blur. It was next to your house, which I learned years later you had built with your two hands and made into a home from mud, straw, bamboo and dirt after you fled from the North to the South from those people you called the communists. And in this home, surrounded by rice fields and banana trees, the laughter of loved ones echoed, rice cooked, babies cried, chopsticks clacked and incense burned.

You told me to sit on the bench by the pond with the long wooden table at my back. This was where our clan, your six children and their families, gathered every Sunday over lunch. It was my favorite time of the week. My legs swung back and forth, and I admired how fast they could go while you pierced a small piece of meat with a silvery fishhook, sauce – amber and sticky – sliding down your fingers. Your movements were slow, your voice gentle and warm next to my ear like summer air as you showed me how to hold the rod with both hands, and together we cast the thin line out to the middle. Bubbles rose and popped on the lime green water. I looked at you, and your eyes shone like twin moon slivers. I'll never forget this.

But then the morning came when the people who made you flee from the North rumbled with their tanks and guns to the South, surrounding our city. We trembled and cowered inside the house. Mom prayed, and I followed, but I didn't know what to ask. I tried to think of the big words Mom and Dad always said but only remembered one: Help! And so, I covered my ears and whispered it over and over even while the walls shook, and rockets whistled and boomed outside.

Dad said, 'We must escape, or else we die.'

My thoughts were like seashells tossed and tumbled by crashing waves. I said, 'But what about Bà? Isn't she coming too? We must go to her home.'

Dad's eyes got wet as he shook his head. 'She wants to stay. She's tired of fleeing.'

I shook my head and thought, No, it can't be true; we should not leave you.

Then I remembered. I had been your shadow, watching you when you weren't aware. All those times you used to sigh long, drawn-out full-chested breaths, and said, 'Family is everything.' Or when you bowed with a lit joss stick between your palms and prayed at the altar to the ancestors to keep watch over everyone. It wasn't just for us, your children and grandchildren; it was for the brothers, sisters, and parents you left all those years ago in the North. One day, you would be reunited; this was the hope you guarded in your heart.

But now, this family, the one you made, was splitting apart.

Dad said, 'Hurry!' So we all ran to the car, leaving everything behind: our home with the black and white tiled floor, the pretty dolls with round open eyes in the glass case, and you in your home, alone. And inside of me, it rained, but I didn't let it show. Surely, Mom and Dad would be proud that I could hold it all in, just like them.

Clogging the streets outside, scooters weaved, women cried, holding babies and bags, and men carried televisions on their backs while helicopters roared overhead. Along the way to the airport every grandmother I saw I thought was you. But they clutched other children's hands while mine were empty.

After we came to America, I trusted you would join us. Your hope grew in me that we would one day be together again. As you sat by the pond, did you believe it, too?

When the weather turned cold, I imagined you shivering, just like me, in thick, woolly coats and matching mittens, your breath melting the snow on top of my head. Here, signs displayed *No hat, No shoes, No service* so your feet could no longer be bare, and those toes would be wrapped warmly in socks.

I knew you would take care of me while Mom and Dad worked hard, and I wouldn't have to go to a place Mom called day care. Because I remembered how it used to be: you, me and stories before bedtime, but the days became weeks, and the weeks became months. I had so many firsts in this strange new land that I wanted to share with you – like the time Mom went shopping for food. Instead of an outdoor market with raw meat and fish and flies abuzz, Mom and I walked into a store with rows of fragrant fruit, fresh meat wrapped tight in plastic, and soothing music. Or that here bathrooms were places for showers *and* toilets and located in a house, not like the shed at the back of your home where you bathed me from a bucket of water teeming with mosquito larvae, and your toilet was merely a hole in some planks on the bridge that spanned the pond. Or that televisions were in color, that people walked their dogs to exercise them, that cars obeyed traffic rules and stopped at red lights, and grandmothers baked cookies, and their lips were red only from lipstick, not betel nut.

I often thought to myself, if only the rest of you had taken heed of your toes and fled with our family, my todays would be like my yesterdays.

A woman from church – with short, white, curly hair, a tall nose, and eyes the color of the birds I later learned were named blue jays – told me I should call her Grandma. I didn't mind calling her that as long as I didn't have to utter the word that meant you. Instead of brown, callused hands and short fingernails rimmed with dirt, hers were blue-veined, soft, and fragile pink. Her teeth were white, and she took them out at night. When I told her you had to dye yours black when you were a girl to look less beautiful to the Chinese invaders, she looked at me, and her eyes became pools. We played cards and the piano, colored in pictures of castles and puppies, and read books with words that had rhythm and rhyme written by a man whose first name was Doctor and whose last name was Seuss. I took naps in her big, soft, pink, patchwork-quilted bed, and I felt like a princess again, but without my clogs and always without you.

Then there was the day the news arrived, many months after the fact. Mom was in the kitchen preparing dinner while I watched. She answered the phone, her face turned white. Her other hand gripped long chopsticks as if they were weapons to ward off something bad.

You were no more.

A bed. Your lifeless body. The still, humid air — drenched with the pungent scent of moist earth, stagnant pond water, and notes of sweet jasmine blossoms. Outside in the rice field near your home, a water buffalo lowered his head, huffed, and silence descended. This was how I imagined it must have been, but I will never know the truth.

Mom said she missed you so. She knelt to my height and held me close, making circles with her palms on my back. I said nothing, only nodded; my fingers coiled around her bouncy hair, my throat tight. I thought about the last time when there was a you and me, back to the pond, the fish, the dogs, the dragonflies, and the mango tree. And I remembered.

I never said goodbye.

There was no rain in me this time, only pieces that splintered and scattered like the fallen autumn leaves outside.

The years passed, as did the festive times like birthdays, Christmas and New Year. For me, at home, it was just Mom, Dad and two big brothers. School friends talked about their treasured moments, get-togethers punctuated with the laughter of grandparents, aunts, uncles and cousins too. I recollected when our family knew the same, a blurry vision, and my loss loomed large. I wondered whether these children knew how lucky they were to have memories with family, enough to fill closets, while I had so few. I longed for more, especially everything that had to do with you: your lined cheek like the bark of a tree next to mine, the way you never called me by name but *mụn đàn bà* or little woman, long before I understood what it meant to be one; and those times, as long as you were near, even in our quiet, there were tethers that wrapped me to you.

And then the strangest thing occurred as time went on. When I thought of you, no matter how hard I tried, I couldn't remember you as a whole, only parts: your legs clad in loose, black pants; the smell of sweat and fish sauce that lingered in my nose when you took me in your arms; the way you shuffled rather than walked; your inky hair rolled into a black cloth that looked like a halo on your head. You, like me, had fractured and could never be complete again.

Until the day I was a teenager, and my body changed. Dad winked and said, 'You look like Bà.' *Were you once like me before you married and gave away your innocence, and the war etched lines of worry onto your face?*

I snatched your black and white photo from the altar and held it close to my chest. To the full-length mirror I ran, my body twisted this way and that, desperate to glimpse what he could see, and I could not. Sparse black eyebrows led down to a roundish nose. Long black hair fell onto broad shoulders and hips that curved out.

My skin was tawny but could turn just as dark as yours when under the sun. Short, ridged fingernails that looked familiar. Same body. Same skin. Same hands. In the mirror, I saw my lips curve; my eyes became thin crescents. And in that moment, I understood. Fragments of you lived on in me. You are with me.

About the author

An Ngo Lang is a writer, actor, and model originally from Vietnam and now calls Sydney, Australia home. To explore more of her work, visit her online at anngolang.com.

Things my Dad Told Me

Madelyn Postman

Shortlisted

England, 2015

'Your mother loved gardenias,' my dad always told me. He didn't mean my stepmother, who was 'Mom' to me for as long as I could remember.

He meant Bonnie.

You could see her in my eyes, literally, her Cantonese genes pinching the outside corners into an almond shape. My skin was fair, the easy tanning of my youth left behind – and in any case, England didn't put it to the test.

In profile, I could recognize the outline of my father's nose. From the front, I was Chinese and from the side, Eastern European Jewish. Inside, I didn't feel much of either.

When I was in my early twenties, I bought a gardenia plant in an attempt to cultivate her. With a dull pain in the pit of my stomach, I watched the plant slowly die, its deep green leaves yellowing and dropping. Acidic soil and

305

daily misting were not enough; it required some other kind of nurturing to ensure its survival. I would never witness the blossoming of its guileless white flowers touched by pale yellow at their hearts.

'Mama, can you pass me the pancakes?' There was no lazy Susan at our table at the China Diner, meaning no dishes whirling around, no serving spoons to reposition away from tall water glasses. It meant I could relax.

I passed the floury, paper-thin pancakes to my eight-year-old son, then plum sauce in a small dish – taking care to keep the teaspoon balanced on the saucer's rim – then fine cucumber sticks. He reached over to help himself to more duck and barely wrapped up the pile before stuffing it into his mouth.

'Remember to chew, Arden,' I said, half-teasing.

Crispy duck, chicken noodle soup, rice, barbecued spare ribs. My grandmother, Poa-Poa Corri, loved ribs and peach pie. An image of her came to me, in her pink terrycloth robe, slowly counting out scoops of coffee into the machine, one, two, three; Californian sunlight fell onto the kitchen island through a pyramid-shaped skylight while unruly Pacific waves sprayed a salty film onto floor-to-ceiling windows.

Parker blew on the soup in her beveled ceramic spoon. Without warning, she dropped her spoon back into the bowl, splashing out some broth. She grabbed her chopsticks and brandished them at her brother, commanding, 'En garde!'

Does she act like that at kindergarten, or is she saving this for us? So much for relaxation. Arden kept eating intently. I glanced over at my husband and caught him smiling to himself.

'Parker.' My warning tone snapped her out of fencing mode.

As we settled into a few moments of silence, I scanned my children's faces. Arden had my eyes and nose; his full lips came from Christoph. Parker most resembled a cousin on my mother's side.

I said, 'My dad once told me that if I had kids with a Chinese guy, they'd be three-quarters Chinese.'

Arden and Parker both grinned at the impossible idea of their mother having children with someone besides Papa.

I thought of a half-Chinese, half-British girl they knew. 'Arden,' I said, 'if you had kids with Georgie, they'd be . . .' I found a pen in my purse and jotted on a napkin, *1/2 German, 1/4 Chinese, 1/8 Polish, 1/8 Lithuanian* and next to it, *1/2 Chinese, 1/2 British*. Then I wrote, *3/8 Chinese, 1/4 German, 1/4 British, 1/16 Polish, 1/16 Lithuanian*. I converted everything to sixteenths in my head to check that it added up. Arden and Parker peered at the paper and chanted out the fractions through their giggles.

When we ordered dessert – fried apples, fried bananas, ice cream – the waitress wrote Chinese characters on her grey notepad. She noticed me watching and asked, 'Can you read this? Do you speak Mandarin?'

'No. I'm half Chinese but I don't speak it. The Chinese side of my family went to America four or five generations ago, so we pretty much lost all the language and culture.' That was the level one explanation.

'Oh, you're American,' she acknowledged warmly. 'I'm from Malaysia. Never actually been to China.' She nodded to conclude our exchange, then headed towards the kitchen.

I was relieved that she didn't probe further; level one was simply saying that I was half Chinese and attributing the blame of my lost culture to America's great Shake 'N Bake, in which everyone mixes together and comes out as some new dish, an interesting one, but lacking clearly identifiable flavors.

Escalating to level two meant admitting that my mother died when I was young. When I got to level two, people usually shut up.

Maybe my kids thought their Grandma Pat was very pale and blonde for a Chinese woman, or more likely, they didn't reflect at all on her race. In any case, they hadn't realized yet that their biological grandmother was gone, and I dreaded telling them. There was no playbook for this truth – how much to reveal, and when. When

I became a mother, I started to understand my dad, who had said to my brother and me, early on, 'I vowed to myself that I'd only tell you good things about her. I didn't want to dwell on anything painful or negative.'

But the truth was both painful and negative.

Sharing the whole truth – how she died – was level three. I barricaded that knowledge inside of me; it rarely saw the light of day.

One bedtime, about a month later, Arden chose a magician, a cowboy, and a pink-mohawked punk as his friends, a kayak for transport, and a suit of armor to wear on his adventure. His fingers skipped around the colorful illustrations in *You Choose*.

A stack of more advanced books sat on the floor, but some evenings he preferred the comfort of pictures to words, a throwback to a younger version of himself.

I got up from the edge of his bed to close the blinds against the rosy sky. I turned back to find him looking up at the ceiling, eyebrows scrunched together.

'I'm blond from Papa and have green eyes from Papa. Why is my skin pale and Parker's is dark?' Indeed, Parker chose a brown crayon when she drew herself, while Arden used pink.

So this is how it will unfold, I thought. *Through genetics.*

He had never asked why he had a bunch of Chinese aunts. The seemingly endless options of his day-to-day life, like those in *You Choose*, were probably more at the forefront of his mind.

I didn't know how my mother would materialize for my kids: perhaps as a snow angel, ephemeral and light . . . or as a chalk outline, criminal and gruesome.

I sat back down next to him, my stomach churning. 'Grandma Pat isn't my biological mother,' I said slowly. 'My real mother died when I was young. She was Chinese and had darker skin like Parker, and my aunts – your great-aunts.'

'What was her name?'

'Bonnie.' *My Bonnie lies over the ocean, my Bonnie lies over the sea, my Bonnie lies over the ocean, oh bring back my Bonnie to me.*

'Does Papa know?' His question was so innocent, thinking that I would share this fact with him, yet keep it a secret from (or somehow forget to tell?) his dad.

'Yes, he knows.' There was a photo Christoph took of me during a trip to Prague. My eyes were red and puffy because we'd talked about her the evening before. Level three.

'I'm so sad I can't meet my grandma.'

That said it all, the same feeling I had about not meeting her properly, not knowing her.

Arden was silent for a beat. 'Let's talk about something else. I'll tell you a joke to make you happy.' Now he seemed older than his years, using the tried-and-true parental technique of distraction. And very sweet, wanting to change my mood.

A couple of tears slid down my cheeks.

The inevitable moment I had been dreading for years had simply passed. It came and went in a whisper, padding in and leaving on tiptoes.

He added, 'Maybe we'll forget about it by the morning. I don't want to not have a mama.' Heartbreaking. I felt awful for having introduced that possibility to him.

'It's okay, sweetie.' I hugged him and rubbed his back. 'I'll always be here.'

Christoph and I agreed to tell Parker soon. We didn't want to saddle Arden with a secret that could become a vulnerability as much as a weapon against his younger sibling.

A few days later, I found Parker tumbling around on our bed.

'Parker.'

She froze, waiting for a rebuke.

I took a deep breath and dived in, like a plunge into icy water. 'My mother died when I was little,' I stated quickly and evenly. *I was about your age. Actually, a year younger.*

At first she looked relieved at not being reprimanded, then her face morphed to confusion. 'Isn't Grandma Pat your mother?'

'No, she's my stepmother.' *The one I call Mom.*

'How did your mother die?'

My heart thumped. She wasn't ready for my biggest secret. 'I'll tell you when you're older.'

'Why when I'm older?' She started rolling across the mattress again.

'It's just better to know in a few years. It's too early now.' I couldn't bear the subject anymore, or the flitting frankness of a five-year-old's questions. I wondered how I had reacted to that horrible news so long ago, when I was even younger than her?

I pulled some vintage dresses from my closet, one by one. 'Have you ever seen these?'

Parker's eyes widened. 'Whoa! Those are so beautiful!'

'These belonged to your great-grandmother. My Poa-Poa Corri.'

'Paw paw?'

'Poa-Poa means grandma in Chinese, the grand-mother on your mother's side. My mother's mother. Her nephew was a fashion designer. She modeled for him, and he gave her these dresses. I used to wear them a lot at parties.' The smell transported me straight into my grandmother's walk-in closet: a straight-shot maternal line that could tighten and propel me through time and space like a thread gathering folds of fabric.

'Why don't you wear them now?'

'I don't go to that many parties these days.'

'You could wear one when you go out for dinner with Papa tonight.'

'Hmmm, sweetie, it might be a bit too fancy for that.'

Parker screwed up her face. 'Why too fancy?'

'Well, these are special dresses for special occasions. Look how they're made, all the hand stitching. Look at all the work put into them. Our clothes aren't made like this anymore.'

Parker glanced at the tiny stitches and then left the room, looking for somewhere she could bounce around without all this family history and confounding death. When I put my cousin's vintage pieces back, my finger-tips lingered on the feather-soft orange chiffon gown that I had worn as my wedding dress.

I wanted to protect my children from the bitter knowledge of the whole truth, but I knew that it had already begun to germinate – it was just a matter of time. I wondered how they would deal with it, what it would grow into.

I thought about choices and consequences, what we speak about and what we keep hidden. What we toss away, resigned, and what we nurture with hope. Births and deaths, tragedies and triumphs.

My friends who didn't know how my mother died may have assumed cancer or a car crash or, due to my reticence, perhaps they silently guessed suicide. But I rarely voiced that word; I didn't stare into the sun.

Speaking of her death goaded the ugly grief that lay in wait just below the surface. The handful of times I divulged the information (the usual verb was still 'committed,' as if it were a crime or sin), tears would stream hot on my cheeks before escalating to body-racking sobs. My eyes would stay puffy into the next day. The friend would be consoling, shocked, and I would feel angry and resentful that I had this vile fact to share, and they couldn't do anything about it. I hated level three. It left me empty, as if I had been eviscerated. I wondered when that beast would retreat.

Though I grew up knowing about my mother's suicide, I never understood how she could leave my brother and me behind; he'd just turned seven and I was four. There was never a formal diagnosis as far as I knew — it was the '70s, and whatever my mother was going through (depression? bipolar disorder?) was surely stigmatized.

What sort of relationship would we have had? How unstable would she have been? How often would I have had to rescue her? Was I better off without her?

I ordered a copy of her death certificate and kept it in a desk drawer. 'Oriental', 'Housewife' – such outdated terminology. Did that sum her up? I recorded both her birthday and the date of her death as recurring dates in my calendar.

With a touch of bureaucratic irony, I had to obtain my own birth certificate before I could request her death certificate. It was apt: in examining her death, I was trying to better understand my life. 'She was just like us,' my aunts told me. 'Like you, like me, like us.'

Scattered facts from my family that could fill in her outlines – her love of piano, painting, swimming – wouldn't make her come alive again. They wouldn't bring back a missing mother.

The memory I assigned to that day in 1977 is at our family friends' place, playing with a dollhouse on their porch. It would have been hot and dry in Reno on a June afternoon. I never asked my dad if I was really there. Would he even remember?

In my mind's eye, I would flick through my dozen or so memories of her, frozen like snapshots, which I created in our four years and two months together. Because they were seen through little Madelyn's eyes, I knew these moments weren't stolen from photographs. My mother lifts me to a kitchen cupboard; she takes me to a self-service car wash; I clamber up the impossibly tall steps of her painting studio.

The dead parent was rarely discussed. She stepped on nobody's toes, had no wrinkles and sprouted no grey hairs. She never screamed, never sobbed, never cared too little nor too much, never smiled, never slept. She drifted upward into sainthood like a pale pink balloon accidentally released from a small hand on a summer's day.

As a teenager, I was scared that my up-and-down emotions were the first signs of mental instability, that I was doomed to share her fate. Around that time, my dad told me, 'I've always thought that you had a guardian angel.' We both knew why I had been granted the angel: perhaps it was Bonnie herself who had donned gossamer wings.

Once I got past adolescence, I felt like I had stepped off the rollercoaster onto stable ground, sticking the landing, arms up in the triumphant 'Y' I practiced for gymnastics meets years earlier.

I was always waiting to heal. The grief could show up as an unexpected wall of water that would knock me off my feet and drag me under. Or the waves could lap against me; I could dig in my toes and barely notice.

I turned thirty-one: my mother's age when she truncated her life. Two years later, I became a mother. *I'm going to be his home base*, I realized when Arden was born. Whether for a hug or consoling words, he would seek refuge in me.

Bonnie's absence became painfully conspicuous. I conjured up the missing grandmother. What anecdotes and advice would she have offered? Would she have had a stiff back as she bent over Arden's stroller? Would she have caressed my son's fresh, plump cheeks with age-spotted hands? The emptiness put a lump in my throat.

Once I experienced the primal power of motherhood, I could understand even less how Bonnie tore herself away from her children. What did she think would happen to us? How could she drop us and leave us in shards on the floor? But that potent maternal love also showed me that her despair must have been so encompassing that it prevailed over everything.

Parker was born almost three years after Arden — the same age gap, nearly to the day, as my brother and me. Watching my kids, I would imagine Bonnie with my brother and me, the scenes taking on the look of a Super 8 movie. These visions bruised me.

When Parker and Arden got past the ages of four and seven, I stopped comparing dates and numbers. With my guardian angel at my side, I marched on.

One day, a package arrived from Dad. It was large enough to hold a length of rope which could be tied, hands shaking, into a noose. Or it could have contained ashes — but my mother was long-since buried. I visited her grave once, soon after I learned to drive and could choose my own destination.

I sliced open the cardboard and found Dad's note. *The pain never goes away. I love you more than words can express.*

Nestled inside a cloud of tissue paper was a cellophaned, white box in dimpled card with watercolor grey and oxblood zigzags chasing themselves around its circumference. Inside was a heavy glass bottle of lotion.

I rubbed the heady, flowery scent onto my hands and arms. The zigzag-decorated box was now empty, practically weightless.

It was then I realized that I had to open the door to the demon and let it live in my house. I would get to know it a little, glancing obliquely at the unwelcome creature, though I could never predict its machinations.

The memory of gardenias rose off my skin. I inhaled deeply.

About the author

Madelyn Postman's unpublished short story collection links memoir with her family's intergenerational tale: the tragedies and triumphs of Chinese and Eastern European Jewish immigrants who converged in California. 'Things my Dad Told Me' is the first story in the collection. She is American and lives near London, England with her husband and two teenage children.

A Veiled Courage

Zubia Sarfraz

Shortlisted

Chapter One

'Light the candle Rana,' her mother whispered into the dark.

Rana awoke in the darkness, pushed back the scratchy old blanket, and climbed quietly out of the warm cocoon, leaving behind her silent, sleeping siblings. Rana moved through the small mud hut in the pitch-black night, the air permeated with the buttery scent of last night's ghee infused rotis. Rana's stomach grumbled in protest – she had only eaten half a roti, the rest shared between her squabbling siblings. But now was not the time for hunger.

In the blackness, Rana silently counted the steps to the clay choolah. It would take her exactly seven big steps before she would feel the heat of the dying embers. Just before dawn, her mother would light the fire again under the clay earthen stove, but for now the faint flickering embers had finally curled up to rest.

Stretching her hand to the left, Rana soundlessly moved her hand over the few vessels they owned. *No, not this one.* Hurriedly, she moved onto the next vessel. Her fingers carefully traced the cold steel rim of a large bowl, and once satisfied, she pushed away the greasy rag covering the contents of the bowl. Her hands now familiar with this routine, she reached into the cold belly of the bowl, carefully retrieving the contents. A soft waxy candle, a long thin pencil and a piece of paper.

'Hurry, it will soon be dawn,' her mother urged from her charpai. In the darkness of the night, Rana measured the candle against her index finger, worry snaking to her chest. There was not much of the candle left. A few more nights, perhaps.

Through the eerie darkness, Gullerin felt her child's unspoken concern, as only a mother could. Although she could not see the little girl, her subdued despondency echoed through the stillness of the cold night.

'Do not worry Janam,' she whispered to the child. 'God will make a way.'

A few hours later, the call to prayer emanated from the small terracotta mosque next door, illuminating the dark hut. The melodic invitation, *Come to prayer, come to success* marked the end of the night and the approaching dawn. Rana, her dark brow furrowed in deep thought, looked up at her mother's face. Gullerin huddled in a cheap woollen blanket and peered down at her through tired eyes. The older woman's face was radiant in the warm honey-coloured light from the candle flame. 'Good girl,' Gullerin murmured. Rana's pale mouth curled into a shy smile, a tiny dimple dotting the curve of her cheek.

'Now prepare for the morning prayer and hide away your things,' Gullerin whispered, squinting nervously towards the wooden door. At the break of dawn, the men would roam the streets, looking for targets, for the rule breakers. Rana, glancing longingly towards the candle flame, puffed out her cheeks, and blew it out. Instantly, the hut was plunged back into darkness. Silently, Rana counted the steps from her mother's charpai back to the earthen stove, returning to the large bowl, whose belly swallowed her most precious belongings.

Chapter Two

'Whose daughter are you?' the shopkeeper barked. His eyes, black with rage, stared down at her, foamy spittle puddled at the corner of his dark lips. 'Answer me!' he roared.

Rana trembled, rooted to the spot. Her hand lay frozen on the book. She had been careful, as careful as she could, she had waited and waited until the shop-keeper had a line of customers. She had waited until he was so busy conversing with the customers that he had forgotten about the shawl-clad girl in the corner of the shop. Even then, she had waited with bated breath under the pretence of counting out a few coins, until the shop-keeper was engrossed in a heated discussion with a large, plump man over the rocketing price of bread. Then from under her black chador, her tiny hand had slipped out to touch the book.

She didn't know who had written the book, or where it had come from, or even what it contained. She didn't know if there were gardens of words blooming inside, or whether pristine, crisp sheets patiently awaited elegant penmanship. She didn't know if there had been vast worlds of stories captured within, or exciting adventures to be anticipated. All she knew was that it was the most beautiful book she had ever seen.

She had been restless since she first laid eyes on the book, a few days ago.

Her mother had pressed a few coins into her hand and shooed her out the door. 'Buy the cheapest bread,' she whispered through her veil, ducking nervously behind the door as a young man passed. The man frowned at the space where her mother had been standing, and then on seeing Rana, sneered. 'Go inside!' he commanded loudly. He was dressed in a starchy white thobe, a long black rifle sitting snugly against his thin shoulder. Rana disobediently placed her sandal clad foot further onto the muddy lane.

'Are there no men in your house?' the man asked angrily.

'Rana,' her mother had hissed, and grabbing her roughly by the shoulder, pulled her back inside. They waited until the man had gone, before Gullerin pushed her out into the lane again and ordered her to take her whiny brother along.

Ahmed, tired and listless from the dry heat and his mounting hunger, remained silent until they reached the shop. Then, eagerly observing a small group of boys playing with colourful glass marbles, he begged to wait outside the shop. The clink of the glass upon glass captivated him. Rana saw Ahmed's eyes on the beautiful marbles, his delight paining her chest as the tiny coins burned into her palms.

Yet there wasn't enough money to buy better quality bread or even cheap offcuts of meat, let alone glass marbles.

Leaving Ahmed entranced, Rana entered the shop, marvelling at the mountain of oranges the colour of full eastern suns, their syrupy scent beckoning her. She stood in awe underneath the orange mountain, her mouth watering at the thought of the sweet, juicy nectar. During the harsh winter nights, when nothing but cold silence and the threat of tyranny roamed the dark streets, her mother had often told Rana and her siblings stories of the shop. Huddled over tiny glasses of black tea or boiled water and cardamom when there was no tea, Gullerin would bring magic to her children's otherwise black nights. She would watch as they listened silently, mesmerised with her narrations on life before the rule of evil men.

'Many years ago,' Gullerin would tell them, 'the shop had been a hive of activity, full to the brim with luxury items, food and festivity.

'Citizens would travel far and wide to buy their goods and indulge in the luxuries the shop had to offer. Abundant with crunchy Iranian sugar-coated almonds, in the prettiest pastel shades, while fiery Indian spices fragranced the air with roasted cumin and zingy coriander. Mounds of toasted semolina adorned with turquoise green Afghani pistachios greeted the customers, and rose petal tea would be served in tiny, crystal glasses in the adjacent tea shop. Sticky, syrupy pastries dressed in shiny silver foil would await the customers, splendid on huge gold platters. That was before the evil men arrived,' their mother had told them, her face lined with sadness.

Now, there was only a mountain of local oranges, so expensive that no one could afford to enjoy them. The tea shop had been bombed so badly that all traces of it ever existing were gone. Rana had never seen or eaten many of the fruits, vegetables or mouth-watering pastries her mother had shared stories about, she thought sadly while walking through the shop.

Suddenly, someone shoved her out of the way, and she wandered sullenly down the almost empty aisles of the now barren shop. It was only when she turned the corner that her eye caught the book. It had glinted under the golden sunlight: enticing, opulent. A royal navy dust jacket adorned the book, the cover pressed with gold foil, depicting a sumptuous Persian garden. Golden deer lay idly within the confines of the garden, while silvery butterflies glided above their tawny heads. Delicate gold filigree encircled the garden. Rana was mesmerised. That night she dreamed of the book, and the secrets it contained, her mind awash with possibilities . . .

'Answer me!' the shopkeeper screeched, breaking Rana's trance. The tiny bell above the shop door tinkled, carrying along a soft breeze. Rana remained rooted, and then, intertwined in the soft breeze came her father's voice, comforting her, enveloping her. 'Courage is your veil my child,' the breeze whispered, embracing her desolate heart.

'Rana Sultan,' she whispered, her heart aching for her father.

The shopkeeper coughed loudly, peering down at her with his bulbous, raging eyes. 'Your father's name is Rana Sultan?' he queried. A few men loitered down the aisles, curiosity pulling them towards the shopkeeper and the cowering little girl. Crowding around the shopkeeper, they scrutinised the young girl. 'No, my name is Rana Sultan!' Rana replied as loudly as she could, although her heart thumped so hard she was afraid for a moment it would jump out from within her chest.

The shopkeeper shuddered. The men nearby visibly recoiled, taken aback at the sheer audacity of the young girl. 'You shameless creature!' the shopkeeper hissed, spittle flying everywhere. 'Womenfolk have no names!' he barked. Rana took a step back, anger uncoiling within her stomach.

'What did she do?' An old man with rheumy, grey eyes asked. 'Is she a thief?' he pressed. 'No,' the shopkeeper replied, narrowing his eyes. 'She touched a book.' The men glared at Rana, whose hand still lay languidly on the forbidden book.

'How dare you touch a book, books are not for women!' the shopkeeper insisted. The other men murmured their agreement.

Rana swallowed the lump forming in her chest, forcing out the words stuck like dry roti in her throat. 'Why not?'

The shopkeeper, now incandescent with rage, clenched his fists. 'You belong to a man and are known by a man's name only! What is your father's name, I ask again, I will go and tell him of your crimes!' he roared. Rana felt her bottom lip tremble as the men watched on. Her threadbare shawl hung limply at her sides, and balling her fists underneath it, she dug her heels into the dry ground.

Horrible, stupid man, she thought. Tears pricked her eyes, threatening to spill, but she pushed them back.

'My name is Rana Sultan!' she repeated as bravely as she could.

The men stood frozen. From the front of the shop, someone called out to the shopkeeper, momentarily distracting them all. The shopkeeper's upper lip curled in frustration and he adjusted his white turban and stepped forward, raising his hand. Rana closed her eyes, bracing herself for the slap. 'I'll teach you to touch books,' the man hissed, his breath putrid with smoky tobacco and betel nut. Yet the man's hand never touched Rana's face. She waited. *Silence.* But, nothing.

Rana waited some more.

Then, peeking through half-opened eyes, she glanced towards the men. To her surprise, they were no longer looking at Rana. Instead, their attention was on someone else. A young man stood in the middle of the men, his right hand holding the shopkeeper's bony wrist, his voice firm. 'I know where she lives, I will take her home.' His voice was deep, poised, and the men eyed him curiously.

The shopkeeper shrugged, but the young man held firmly on to his wrist. Finally, the shopkeeper stepped aside, defeated. 'Take her home and tell her father,' he growled. The young man nodded, stepping back. The other men slowly dispersed, satisfied a conclusion had been achieved, and the audacity of the young girl would be dealt with in the appropriate manner within the sanctity of her home.

Chapter Three

'Come on little one,' the young man spoke. Rana followed him sullenly out of the shop, now embarrassed at the commotion she had caused and fearful of what her mother would do. *What if her mother became so angry that she would no longer teach her at night?*

The thought broke her heart, made her want to weep. All she had wanted to do was touch the book, to trace her fingers slowly along the delicate, gold filigree. *Why was that a sin?*

'Hurry along,' the young man ushered. Rana followed him dourly, deliberately staying a few steps behind. *Who was he?* Ahmed was nowhere to be seen. The sun beat down relentlessly, burning her skin, making her want to sob.

The young man occasionally glanced back yet continued to stride ahead. He was tall, taller than her mother, with almond-coloured skin and a dark beard framing his narrow face. He greeted passers-by jovially as he made his way through the market. *Who was he?* Rana wondered. She had never seen him before. An old woman with snow-white hair and a large basket of apples stood up to greet the young man, handing him one with a soft rosy hue. Thanking the old woman, the young man kissed her wrinkled hand, and to Rana's surprise, offered her the fruit. Rana took it greedily, hiding it in her black chador, her mouth watering at the thought of biting into the sweet, crisp flesh.

Rana continued to follow the young man. Although she didn't know who he was, she didn't want to walk home alone either, in case the evil men were lurking. Soon they arrived at the mosque next to her home.

The peacock-green dome of the mosque glistened resplendently, jewel-like in the bright sunlight, dazzling her eyes. 'Are you one of the evil men?' she asked the young man, feeling braver now she was closer to home. She sighed deeply, her forehead beaded with sweat, her mouth dry.

The young man pondered the question then laughed softly. 'May God the Almighty take my soul before I ever become evil,' he replied. His teeth were white, like the tiny white pearls Rana had seen a long time ago in one of her father's books. The thought of her father caused a strange pain to rise within her chest, making her feel breathless.

'This way,' the young man said, stepping through large wrought-iron gates, into the courtyard of the mosque. Rana hesitated. One night, not long ago, the evil men had driven through the village, shouting through loud-speakers, frightening everyone in the neighbourhood. Rana's siblings had hidden under the woven charpais, their frightened, glassy eyes visible through the thread-bare rope. In their harsh, cold voices, the evil men had informed the locals that women and girls were no longer to go to mosques, markets or even outside, but to remain in their homes at all times.

Yet the evil men roamed free, in the markets, the fields, at the dirty teashops and Rana would bet her apple not one of them ever touched a book. *So why couldn't womenfolk touch the books? What were the men so fearful of? What was hidden in the books and what would happen if women read the books?* Rana wondered.

The foreigners were also evil men, Rana thought angrily as a khaki jeep pulled up close to her. The rowdy foreigners jumped out, making their way to the market as the local crowd parted slowly to let them through. Rana watched as one of her neighbours spat on the ground angrily as the foreigners waded past.

Although they didn't dress like the local evil men, the foreigners were just as evil with their straw-coloured hair and strange languages and the way they leered at women and girls. They had thrown bombs on the schools and wheat fields, destroying the crops and all hope, yet they roamed free, in their big leather boots and heavy artillery.

One day, from behind the veil, courage would be unveiled. She would fight them, all of them, and banish every evil man from her village, Rana thought to herself. *Then the women and girls would be free, and books would no longer be for menfolk only.*

'This way, child,' the young man urged, breaking her thoughts. Rana hesitated. *Should she go inside? What if the evil men were lurking inside? Was this a trap?* The punishment for rule breakers was very severe. Rana thought sadly of her teacher, Madam Afreen, who had been beaten by the evil men, leaving her with a broken wrist and scars on her once pretty face. Madam Afreen's sin had been to hold secret night classes for the local girls. Now, Madam Afreen never smiled nor spoke and Rana missed hearing her lyrical voice.

The young man had disappeared. With shaky hands, taking a deep breath, Rana went after him into the court-yard. Inside it was quiet and she stopped to admire the whitewashed walls of the small mosque. The sun peeked through the carved arabesque window frames, covering the carpeted hall in an enchanting, sparkly light. Rana hurriedly turned a corner and found the young man. He was in conversation with an older man. There was no one else around. *Perhaps the evil men were waiting in a room for her,* Rana thought worriedly.

The older man was dressed in a tan thobe, his right hand strumming wooden prayer beads while he nodded his head in agreement to something the young man said. To Rana's surprise, the young man beckoned her to come closer, while the older man smiled, welcoming her. Rana tried to smile back, confusion lining her face. She thought of her mother at home, hiding behind the veil, and Ahmed lost somewhere in the muddy lanes. *What if these men hurt her? Who would tell her mother?*

Sensing her discomfort, the young man raised his hand. 'Look over there, child,' he murmured, pointing towards a small corridor. Rana peered into the dimly lit corridor. Nestled inside the corridor were white shelves fitted snugly against the grey cemented walls. Rana blinked. *Surely not.*

'Take a closer look,' the older man encouraged, walking off to greet a young boy.

Rana gasped. The shelves were lined with books, in every colour she could have imagined. 'Go on, take a book,' the young man said. Rana stood still, momentarily stunned. 'I . . . I can't . . . the evil men said women cannot touch books,' she whispered, her voice strained with the longing, the desperation to hold a book, to read, to learn. The young man silently brought his hands together, and then looked away sadly.

'The evil men are wrong,' he said, clearing his throat. 'Allah Subhanahu Wa Ta'ala has created man and woman equal.'

'Really?' Rana asked him, incredulous. She felt faint, cottony light like one of her mother's summer veils.

The young man laughed, his teeth glistening in the soft light, his eyes a warm burnished amber, like her father's. 'Yes, and if a man can touch a book, read it and learn from it, then a woman or a girl can too.'

Rana was stunned into silence. 'But . . .' She whispered, juggling the apple from one hand to the other, unsure of what to do or say.

'We have all been created equal, a person is only better than another in good deeds, not by gender, wealth or position. Go on, take as many books as you like.' As Rana shuffled quietly towards the books, breathless with anticipation, the older man joined them in the dim corridor. His face was kind, like the young man's, his voice gentle, nurturing.

'Here child,' he offered. Rana stared at his outstretched palm. Nestled inside his large palm, were two large, white candles. 'So that you can read at night,' the older man smiled. Rana stared, astonished.

Her mother's words echoed in her mind, *God will make a way*.

'Come on, it's time,' the older man murmured to the young man. The two men politely bowed their goodbyes. The older man rested his hand on the younger man's shoulder and led him away.

Standing alone in the middle of the dim corridor, surrounded by books, candles clasped tightly in one palm, the apple in the other, Rana felt something stir within the deep chambers of her heart. A feeling she couldn't remember having before. *What is this feeling?* she wondered, *This tingly feeling running through her veins, bringing life back into her body?* Her father had told her stories of it, before the evil men had dragged him away and the foreigners had watched silently. *What is this feeling?*

Hope.

It was hope, and as the young man climbed the stairs to the tall minaret, preparing for the call to prayer, Rana remembered the words of her late, beloved father.

My darling Rana, from behind the veil courage and hope will be unveiled.

Glossary

Chador – shawl

Charpai – a traditional woven bed used in South Asia

Choolah – clay earthen stove

Janam – my darling

About the author

Zubia Sarfraz is an analyst from Yorkshire, England who enjoys reading in her spare time and is currently working on her first novel.

Creating Ripples

Jacqueline Warner

Second Place

The day is already hot. The man aims the hose at the wilting plants and sprays them, the water droplets sparkling and shimmering in the early morning light. He isn't really paying attention. Some water makes it to the plants while most pools on the patio bricks.

In these quiet early hours he imagines that she is in the kitchen, bustling around, making his breakfast. The radio playing in the background, tuned as always to the golden classics station, and she is singing along to some song or another. She always knew the words. It amazes him that she always knew the words.

He turns off the tap and throws the hose absent-mindedly to one side. He knows he should roll it up and put it away carefully, like he usually does, but today he can't be bothered.

The pools of water are already drying up.

Going to be another scorcher, he thinks as he ambles inside.

The kitchen seems dark at first but his eyes soon adjust. He moves to the sink and fills the kettle. Switching it on, he reaches for the mugs in the cupboard above.

'Ron?' he hears her quavering voice from the bedroom. 'Ron?' There is panic in her voice. He sighs.

'I'm here,' he says, walking into the room.

She is lying in the bed, the covers up to her chin.

Even smaller, he thinks. *Is she shrinking?*

'Where have you been?' It is almost a whine.

Querulous, he thinks. Querulous is the word she would have used. So clever with words. Loved them. Their definitions, their sounds. Brilliant at crosswords.

He shakes his head. *Not now.*

He helps her from the bed and to the bathroom. He washes and dresses her and leads her to the kitchen. He sits her at the table while he prepares her breakfast. She is childlike in her compliance. He places toast and a cup of tea in front of her and turns to make his own.

'So what are we doing today, Ron?' she asks between mouthfuls. She sounds perkier. More like her old self. He knows mornings are her best time. If he needs to take her out, he always picks a morning. Home by the afternoon. In the late afternoon he can see the change happening. As the shadows lengthen her confusion grows. Her eyes become cloudy and sometimes frightened when she tries to tell him something, telling him stories that were partly true, but jumbled; facts, ages, names – mixed up, forgotten, imagined. So mornings are the time to do things together. Outside. In the garden. Or away from home.

'Today,' he tells her, 'we are catching the train into town. You have a dentist's appointment, remember?' He doesn't know why he adds the last word, habit perhaps. She nods, smiling, as if she knew all along.

He sits next to her at the table, reaches over and squeezes her hand. 'Maybe we'll get a bit of lunch while we are there. You always like a cappuccino and cake when we go out.'

She smiles back at him. 'Hopefully my face won't be too numb.' She pops another piece of toast in her mouth. 'Have to give my teeth a good clean before we go.'

His heart leaps, as it always does. She sounds so normal. It's just like before. And he hopes, like yesterday and the day before and the day before that. Maybe this is over. Maybe it will all go back to normal. But he knows, deep down, that this is his new normal.

He feels guilty when he wishes he could go back. Go back to the days when the children were little, when he worked all day in his office, came home in the evening to a good meal, clean home and a smart, loving wife.

'But memory gilds the past, remember?' he can almost hear her saying.

And it is true. They had their moments like all married couples. Arguments, stupid arguments over nothing important. Slammed doors and frosty receptions when he came home. They never argued over money because, as she used to say, 'We never had any!' They argued over the children, over imagined slights and one memorable fight when he had bought her a frying pan for her birthday. He remembers her throwing it into the garden, the fury in her eyes. She was beautiful, tempestuous, changeable.

He could never understand why she had married him. A lonely sailor writing to his mate's girlfriend's sister. To his amazement she had replied, enclosing the photo he still carries in his wallet. And when they met, she had led him a merry dance. On again, off again. So much that on the back of the photo he had written: 'My dream girl. What a nightmare!'

Even after the diagnosis, when they could still laugh over a few forgotten names and items that would appear in unusual places – the milk in the laundry, the phone in the fridge, it had never seemed real. He never realised how hard it would be.

He watches her at the table. She is drinking her tea. She sees him watching and gives him a wink. He smiles, *If only*.

She holds his arm as they board the train. She is happy and smiling. He chooses their seats at the back of the carriage. She watches the scenery passing by. Watches as other passengers get on the train at the other stops, occasionally leaning towards him to make comments on their appearance. She is particularly scathing about the women.

Not everything changes, he smiles to himself. He remembers her mantra as a young woman.

'There are no ugly women,' she would say. 'Only lazy women.' She used to think it an insult to womanhood if they didn't wear makeup or wear nice clothes. A product of her generation, he surmises.

But he loves this time with her, when he can imagine that nothing had changed.

The train is half full when a young man gets on. He is scruffy and long-haired, wearing ripped jeans and a t-shirt. A washed-out portrait of the Beatles. Their Apple music phase, he notes. A faded Paul McCartney in full beard.

Probably doesn't even know who they are.

'Looks like he needs a good wash,' she leans over and whispers. He nods.

The young man is struggling under the weight of an impossibly large backpack and a guitar case.

She's not wrong, he thinks. *One of those backpackers. Another useless waste of space, a dole bludger, a free loader.*

The man smiles to himself ruefully. *She's not the only product of her generation,* he admits to himself.

She touches him on the arm and points out of the window. Together they watch the scenery flashing by. Soon the train begins to slow as it approaches the next station. It is their stop.

The platform is empty except for a young woman with a baby in a stroller, standing by the ticket dispenser, struggling with her bag. She obviously can't find what she's looking for. She takes her hand away from the stroller and delves deeper into her bag. The stroller begins to roll. Slowly at first, then picking up momentum.

He sits up straighter. Can no one see this? The stroller is heading towards the railway tracks. The train is slowing. The stroller approaches the edge of the platform. The mother looks up, then screams in horror. He cannot hear the scream but the look on her face tells him it is happening. The small stroller slips under the carriage and out of view as the train stops.

There is a collective gasp then silence. No one moves.

He is on his feet in seconds and rushing for the door. No time to think, just react. He punches the button to release the door and jumps onto the platform as it opens. He is aware that someone is following him.

He can hear his wife calling. He rushes to the side of the carriage and falls to his knees. He tries to see underneath but it's dark. He can't hear the baby crying. Not good. There is a young man at his side. The backpacker. They look at each other. The young man nods then slides down the side of the platform and under the train.

The man can hear people behind him starting to gather. The mother cries hysterically while someone tries to comfort her. No one else offers to help with retrieving the baby. The train driver hovers anxiously nearby.

The handles of the stroller appear from underneath the carriage. He reaches down and grabs them. He flinches, preparing himself for what he might see. The young man wriggles from beneath the train and helps to lift the stroller up, the man dragging it onto the platform. The baby is still strapped into the stroller, seemingly unharmed, though very quiet.

Stunned, is how he describes it later.

The mother rushes forward and pulls the baby into her arms, collapsing to the platform floor and rocking back and forth. A woman pushes forward.

'I'm a nurse,' she proclaims loudly and proceeds to help the mother up and lead her and the baby to a nearby bench. 'Someone, call an ambulance,' she orders. The crowd gathers around the women.

The man offers a hand, helping the backpacker back onto the platform.

'Well done,' he says to him.

The young man nods. 'You too.'

He pushes his way through the crowd, back to the train. He is relieved to see her still sitting in her seat. He takes her gently by the arm and helps her up.

'Come on,' he says, and they make their way off the train and away from the station.

The next day the papers are full of stories about the amazing rescue and heap praise upon the nurse, calling her a hero. She is beaming on the cover of the morning paper and gushing when interviewed on the evening news. She doesn't mention the two men. No one does.

He is a quiet man, a man who shies away from the spotlight, a man who guards his emotions, who is methodical and measured – never making a fuss.

He is extra quiet this morning. He's brought her a cup of tea. She is sitting in the garden; it is not so hot today. She is listening to the radio. It is talkback. She prefers the music but can't remember how to change the station. He went inside a while ago, she's sure of it. She starts to feel anxious. He doesn't seem himself. Something happened yesterday, but she can't quite recall what it was.

She hears the voices on the radio. They are talking about the train incident. She freezes. She hears her husband's voice. He is angry. He tells them about the young man, about how brave he was, he tells them he doesn't know his name but he is the real hero. His voice breaks, he cannot speak any more. The radio presenter is kind but smoothly finishes the call.

She remembers. She stands and makes her way slowly into the house. She searches for him.

She finds him sitting on the edge of their bed. He is sitting, head in his hands. He is quietly crying, his shoulders shaking.

She watches from the doorway. She watches this man, this strong, gentle, man. It is morning and her mind is clearer. She knows what he does. She knows how difficult it must be. Sometimes in the moments when she doesn't seem to be there, when her mind is thick and foggy and the thoughts and memories won't come, when fear ripples through her because she should know and she should remember, sometimes she surfaces like a drowning swimmer gasping for that lifesaving breath, and she sees him, really sees him and all that he does for her. She walks over and sits beside him. She wraps her arms around him and holds him close.

'You are *my* hero,' she says.

About the author

Jacqueline Warner is a writer from Perth, Western Australia. Her short stories have been published in various Australian anthologies. The Hope Prize is her first international award.